THE
DEAD SIDE
OF
THE MIKE

THE
DEAD SIDE
OF
THE MIKE

Simon Brett

Charles Scribner's Sons/New York

Copyright © 1980 Simon Brett

Library of Congress Cataloging in Publication Data

Brett, Simon.
The dead side of the mike.

I. Title.
PZ4.B846 De   1980   [PR6052.R4296]   823'.914   80-18269
ISBN 0-684-16729-8

Printed in the United States of America

TO DORIS
who will understand
that I'm only giving
the hand that fed me
an affectionate nibble
(and with thanks to John
for the title and to
David, Peter and Richard
for their help)

CHAPTER ONE

CHARLES PARIS PAUSED at the top of the steps leading down to the Ariel Bar, momentarily unable to see a path through its voluble mass of humanity to the source of alcohol. Mark Lear, with the assurance of a BBC native, plunged into the thicket of people, a rhetorical, 'What do you want?' thrown over his shoulder. Rhetorical, because he had known his guest long enough to supply the answer, 'A large Bell's.'

Charles managed to wedge himself against a high ledge just inside the door. It was hot; the weather had suddenly changed and, for the first time that year, in early July, offered the possibility of a summer. Above the babbling surface of heads, he could see the room's fine ceiling, which still boasted the building's ancestry, its luxurious past as the Langham Hotel, where elegance had occasionally reigned and Ouida occasionally entertained guardsmen. But now the petalled roses and coving of the ceiling had been painted in the institutional colours of a hospital or government office. Proper BBC austerity. By all means let the staff enjoy themselves, but let them not be seen to enjoy themselves. For a moment the drab paint over the fine curlicues of the ceiling seemed a symbol of the organisation, of flamboyant creativity restrained by proper Civil Service circumspection.

Still, it was comforting. Charles always felt on BBC Radio premises as he did on entering a church: not that he shared the faith of the celebrants, but that it was reassuring to know such faith still existed. He relaxed. He had found the afternoon a strain. It was always difficult to explain to fellow-actors who hadn't done radio why one should feel tension working with the permanent safety-net of a script, but total reliance on voice, without any of the rest of an actor's armoury, imposed new anxieties. Even when working with a producer as sympathetically cynical as Mark Lear.

Mark worked in Further Education (a department whose exact function and intended audience Charles could never grasp) and that afternoon they had been recording a programme on Swinburne. It was one of

5

a series called *Who Reads Them Now?*, in which various faded literary figures were reassessed to see if they had anything to offer to the modern reader (not much in most cases). Mark, remembering a feature on Thomas Hood called *So Much Comic, So Much Blood* which Charles had written some years previously, had rung and asked if there was anyone he'd like to reassess. The Paris diary being as unsullied by bookings as usual and his long-running hare and hounds race with the tax man reaching a point where the latter was no longer going to be fobbed off with any scraps of paper other than banknotes, he assented, mentioning, off the top of his head, Swinburne, whose works he had not glanced at since leaving Oxford nearly thirty years before.

He had enjoyed researching and writing the programme. It was a long time since he had become so involved in a project. And, after the strains of recording, he felt distantly confident that it had worked. A little enthusiasm insinuated itself into his mind. There was something there. Why shouldn't he turn it into a one-man stage show, as he had with *So Much Comic, So Much Blood*? Why shouldn't he write more for radio? The basic money really wasn't bad, and always a good chance of repeats. It was just a question of getting himself organised.

Simultaneous with this thought arrived what most frequently prevented him from getting himself organised. Mark handed it over. 'Cheers. Thanks for doing the programme. I think it really worked.'

Charles drank gratefully. 'Hope so.'

'No, I felt satisfied with it. All seemed to fit. Came out of the studio feeling we'd really made a programme. Don't often get that. The Beeb puts out so much rubbish these days.'

'I have to confess I don't listen much.' It was true. For a moment, Charles wondered why. The radio would be an ideal companion for those (increasingly frequent) days when he just mooched round his bedsitter. And yet it was hardly ever switched on. Maybe he didn't want to be distracted from his mooching.

'Radio Three and Four are okay, I suppose, rapidly going downhill, though. But it's Radio One and Two that are really awful.' Mark gave the little pause of someone about to swing a leg over his hobbyhorse. 'Yuk, "Nation shall speak piss unto nation."'

Charles smiled politely at this distortion of the BBC's motto, which Mark obviously kept polished in a little box for dinner parties, in the way his father might have kept pearl shirt studs. It was strange seeing Mark after all these years. Charles had forgotten the anti-establishment pose. Or at least, it had used to be a pose; now it seemed to have hardened into something beyond cynical phrase-making. But how old must Mark be now? Thirty-seven, thirty-eight? Perhaps he saw himself trapped, fully wound up, and pointed on an unswerving course towards his pension. In the old days he had always been complaining about the amount of dead wood at the top of the BBC; now perhaps he was feeling incipient Dutch Elm Disease himself. In the old days he had said he would never stay in the BBC. Only a couple of years, anyway. And then . . .

'Of course, I'm not going to stay,' Mark went on. 'As I say, today was good, but most of the time I'm producing totally predictable rubbish. I can't think when I was last surprised by anything I did. No, I'll get my own thing going, I don't know, I'll . . .'

He returned to his drink. Maybe he could have finished the sentence, but Charles had a feeling that there was nothing more to add. Mark only wanted the negative benefit of escape; he had no positive thoughts of where he could escape to.

Time to move the conversation on to a less morbid plane. 'How are the wife and kids?'

'Oh, they're fine, fine.' Mark Lear's mind was elsewhere. His eyes kept scanning the swirl of heads. Looking for someone specific? Or just looking. Yes, there was quite a lot of talent around. Another piece of Charles's memory of Mark fell into place. He'd always had a roving eye.

The eyes roved on as he continued, 'Vinnie is as ever, you know, full of good works, and the children are – well, you've had children . . .'

'One.'

'That's enough to know that they are alternately tiresome and endearing. And always present. You must come and see us soon. We're only up in Chalk Farm.' The invitation was given automatically, without expectation of acceptance. 'You haven't gone back to Frances, have you?'

'I see her sometimes.' Charles didn't want to be reminded of his own marriage. Not that he hated his wife. Far from it. He was probably as near to loving her as anyone else. But when they lived together, they bickered and things didn't work. And he stumbled into affairs and . . .

When it was all working, when he was secure of Frances's love in the background and he had some nice beddable little actress in the foreground, it seemed an ideal relationship. But the balance was rarely achieved. Recently, beddable little actresses had become rare enough to qualify as an endangered species. And Frances, who had just been appointed headmistress of the school where she taught, had developed a new career dynamism, which seemed to leave little time for an intermittent husband. Charles felt ruffled, fifty-one and failing.

He tipped his drink back, so that the ice clunked down on to his lips.

7

'Another of those?' he pointed at Mark's dry white wine. 'You haven't got to rush away?'

'Oh no.' The Producer grinned with primary-school slyness. 'I told Vinnie the studio was booked till ten. Since it's now twenty past six, that gives me a bit of time.'

Charles edged his way to the bar, elbow to the fore, wishing, not for the first time, that the human body had been built to a more triangular design. He achieved base camp of one elbow in a pool of beer, and immediately assumed his customary cloak of invisibility. Maybe the barmen really could not see him. Or maybe part of their induction into the mysteries of the BBC was rigorous training in recognising and ignoring people without grades and staff numbers.

A tall man in a brown corduroy bomber jacket appeared at his shoulder, immediately drawing a barman's eye. 'Yes, Dave, what can I get you?'

Charles turned to remonstrate, or rather, being English, turned to debate inwardly whether or not to remonstrate, but, fortunately, the man behind was a gentleman. 'I think you were ahead of me,' he said with a well-crowned smile.

The voice was clear and professional, with an overtone of some accent. Scottish? American? But it carried authority. The barman grudgingly supplied Charles's drinks, still resolutely ignoring his presence. 'Saw you on the telly last night, Dave. On the quiz show.'

'Oh yes. *Owzat*? Hope you liked it.'

'Certainly did, Dave. Thought it was very funny. So did the wife. Is it going well, Dave?'

'Pretty good reaction, I think. They seem happy with the ratings. Happy enough to book another series, anyway.'

'Good for you, Dave. Oh, you'll be leaving the radio soon, won't you?'

'No chance, no chance. Radio's where I belong.'

'I hope you're right, Dave. The wife'd certainly miss your *Late Night Show* if it came off. She loves that *Ten for a Tune* competition.'

'No danger of me going – unless the Beeb decides they've had enough of me.'

'Wouldn't worry about that, Dave. Now what can I be getting you?'

Charles saw that he had his drinks and change. The latter had been deposited in a little pool of Guinness. The barman didn't believe in handing money to people who were invisible.

The man called Dave gave his order. 'Perrier water for me – I have to work tonight. And what was it, girls?'

He turned to two women, hooked on either arm of a short man in a sleek toupée. 'Riesling please, Dave,' said the older one, pronouncing it 'Reisling'. Her inclusion in the appellation 'girls' was generous. She was a middle-aged lady of pleasant dumpiness, with long hair of a redness unavailable on the colour chart offered by God.

'Right you are, Nita,' said the man called Dave. 'And for you?' He turned to the second girl with a charm that almost disguised his ignorance of her name.

This one was much more a girl, a shapely little wisp in a cream crochet dress. 'Well, I'll –'

'No, I don't think we'd better have another,' interposed her thatched escort in a strong American accent. 'We're just about to go out to eat.'

'Right you are, Michael.'

'Then we'll come along and see the show go out. Would you like that?'

The girl giggled and said she would. 'As the guy's agent I don't get many perks, but at least I can organise that,' said the American with a laugh. 'And who knows, maybe I can twist his arm, to play you a request. Even get you the Dave Sheridan Bouquet.'

'Ooh.' The girl squirmed.

Charles shielded his cargo of drinks back to Mark, negotiating the rare stepping-stones of carpet through a maelstrom of handbags, briefcases and legs. Mark, predictably, was talking to a girl.

She was short, probably not more than five foot three, and dark. Centre-parted black hair, well cut, framed an olive face dominated by enormous brown eyes. Once you saw the eyes, you didn't notice the rest of her. Charles was vaguely aware of a boyish body in trim cord trousers and Guernsey sweater, but he was mesmerised by the eyes.

She was talking animatedly as he approached. 'But come on, of course it's a political issue. No education is apolitical. None of it's pure information; there's always some dressing-up, some emphasis . . .' She broke off and looked enquiringly at Mark.

'This is Charles Paris. Charles – Steve Kennett.'

'Hello.'

'Steve works in News. *The World Tonight*, that sort of thing.'

'What do you do on it?'

'Produce.'

'Ah.' Hardly looked old enough to listen to the programme, let alone produce it.

She didn't seem inclined to pick up her previous polemic, so Mark explained Charles's part in the feature on Swinburne.

'Algernon Charles,' she said.

'That's the one.'

She wrinkled her nose. 'The only thing I remember about him was . . . he was into flagellation, wasn't he?'

Charles smiled. 'He certainly had a fascination for the relationship between pain and pleasure.'

Mark recited,

> 'I would find grievous ways to have thee slain,
> Intense device and superflux of pain;
> Vex thee with amorous agonies, and shake
> Life at thy lips and leave it there to ache.

Good sado-masochistic stuff, isn't it?'

Charles was surprised by this sudden long quotation, until he realised that Mark was simply showing off. The resonant declamation was part of a cock-dance for the girl's benefit. Unaccountably, he felt a little twinge of jealousy.

But Steve didn't react to any sexual message there may have been in the quotation. 'Is sado-masochism an okay subject for Radio Four these days? I can never remember whether we're in the middle of a new permissiveness or a Reithian Puritan backlash—it changes from day to day.'

'Doesn't worry me,' Mark replied. 'We're on Radio Three. There is no smut on Radio Three – by definition. As soon as it's there it becomes Art. Anyway, we're Further Education. Anything goes if it's in a proper educational context.'

'Or if it's on *Woman's Hour*,' added Steve. 'They can get away with murder.'

'Murder.' Mark smiled. 'I heard rather a good line the other day – if there was a murder in the BBC, who do you think would have done it?'

'No idea.'

'The Executive Producer.'

'Why?'

'Well, he must have done *something*.' They laughed. Mark pointed to Steve's glass. 'What's that – a lager?'

'Yes, but only if you're getting one.'

'Certainly I am. Charles and I are going to get resolutely and gloriously pissed tonight.'

'You mean you're not going to the Features Action Group Meeting?'

'What?'

'You hadn't forgotten? John Christie's thing. Today's Thursday.'

'Oh shit.'

'You had forgotten.'

'Yes. Oh, Charles, I'm sorry, it had completely slipped my mind. I've got to go to this meeting.'

'Don't worry about it.' Charles was still determined to spend the evening drinking, and he felt confident he could find other companions. There's always someone to drink with in the BBC club.

'Oh shit,' said Mark again. He looked at his watch. 'At seven, isn't it? Well, if I've got to sit through that, I'm certainly going to need another drink.' He dived back into the crowd.

Charles raised a questioning eyebrow to Steve, who smiled and began apologetically, 'It's very BBC. You probably wouldn't understand it. The fact is, in the great glorious past of radio, back in the days when people actually listened to it, there was a department called the Features Department, which produced various landmarks in sound like *Steel* and *Under Milk Wood* and other forgotten masterpieces. It was full of various brilliant producers, who, so far as one can tell, spent most of their time drinking in the George and arguing about whose sports jacket Dylan Thomas had puked over most often.

'Well, like all good things, the department declined and, some time – in the early Sixties it was – it was disbanded. Since then, whenever anyone feels frustrated about the sort of work they are doing or about the general quality of radio programmes, they say, "Why don't we start up the Features Department again?" As if the clock could be turned back, the invention of television could be ignored, and England could once again become a nation of nice middle-class families sipping mugs of Ovaltine round the beaming bakelite of their wirelesses.'

'I see.'

'The latest in the long line of people to use this rallying-cry is that gentleman over there –' She indicated a man in his mid-thirties, dressed in pin-striped suit, bright silk tie and complacent smile. 'His name's John Christie. He's a BBC career politician.'

'I don't really know what you mean by that.'

'He is destined for some sort of greatness in the misty upper reaches of Management. His career has been textbook. Out of Oxbridge straight into the African service – I believe he speaks fluent Swahili, though I'm not quite sure when he gets an opportunity to use it. Then he went to Belfast and worked over there in some administrative capacity . . .'

'And that's good, is it?'

'Oh yes, lots of Brownie points for going to Belfast. The BBC doesn't forget its loyal servants who risk getting blown up in the cause of regional broadcasting. His reward was a post created in Drama Department. Coordinator, I think he's called. Coordinator, Drama Department. CDD. The BBC loves initials. But from there he's destined for greatness. Great greatness.'

'What, you mean he'll become editor of some programme or –'

'Good Lord, no. You are naive. The top jobs in the BBC don't have anything to do with the making of programmes. No, he'll end up as Chief Sales Inhibitor for BBC Publications or in some strange and powerful department like Secretariat.'

'What do they do there?'

'God knows.'

'You sound pretty cynical about the whole thing; I take it you are not involved in the meeting.'

'By no means. I'll be there.' The huge brown eyes looked levelly into his. Even if he could have broken the stare, he didn't think he would have wanted to.

The interruption came from a third party. A blonde girl came up and threw her arms around Steve. She was only a little over average height, but looked huge beside the other. 'Steve, look at me – still standing up.'

She carried a fairly empty wine glass and seemed in a state of high excitement. 'Have you managed to get any sleep, love?' asked Steve, with a trace of anxiety.

'No, I'm held together by alcohol and willpower and sheer animal high spirits.' The way she spoke suggested alcohol might be the dominant partner in the combination.

'Can't you get out of tonight?'

'No, I'll be fine.'

Steve remembered Charles. 'I'm so sorry. This is Charles Paris. Andrea Gower. She shares a flat with me. Just come back from a week's holiday in New York.'

Andrea giggled. 'Just back in time for the Wimbledon finals. And I'm still somewhere up on a cloud over the Atlantic.'

'Didn't you sleep on the flight?'

'Not a wink. I had a drink and another drink and then the movie and then another drink.'

'You should have got out of today's work,' said Steve, 'caught up on some sleep.'

12

'No, I'll do that tomorrow. It's my own fault. I stayed the extra day.'
Steve explained. 'She was due back yesterday to start work today. But she decided to stay on.'

'Ah, it was very important. I was finding out some very interesting things. I had to stay. It was necessary to the cause of investigative journalism.' She stumbled over the last two words. 'I have found something eminently worthy of investigation.'

'Are you a journalist?' asked Charles.

'No, just a humble SM. Today an SM – tomorrow ruler of the world or dead in the attempt.' She dropped into an accent for the last phrase. Charles revised his earlier opinion that she was drunk. She had had a few drinks, but her excitement was more emotional.

'I'm sorry, I don't speak BBC. What's an SM?'

'Studio Manager. Knob-twiddler, teacup-rattler, editor, tape-machine starter and what you will.'

'Ah. So what does that mean in practical terms? I mean, what have you done today?'

'Today? God, what day is it? Today started about forty hours ago with pancakes and bacon in a coffee shop on a very hot Lexington Avenue . . . But, coming up to date, having been met at Heathrow by my good friend, Miss Stephanie Kennett, I rushed to Maida Vale to record a music session for the famous Dave Sheridan . . .'

'Should I know him?'

'What, you mean you don't know the famous disc jockey? Him, over there – with Nita Lawson – she's his Executive Producer.' She pointed to the tall man who had deferred to Charles at the bar. 'The session was the usual Radio Two treacle – I say . . .' A new thought struck her. 'If you haven't heard of Dave Sheridan, can it be that you are a lover of real music? Real classical music?'

'Sorry. I'm afraid I'm not very musical at all.'

'Oh, never mind. It's just that in these degenerate days, lovers of real music have got to stick together. And fight the barbarian hordes who play Simon and Pumpernickel into the wee small hours of the morning.' She grimaced at Steve, who said 'Simon and Garfunkel' with automatic amusement. It was evidently an old joke between them.

'Anyway, where was I?' Andrea was so wound up that nothing could stop her flow. 'Yes, right, that was the music session, at which would you believe the great man Dave Sheridan actually put in an appearance. So we exchanged badinage. Then, after the session, I hopped into a taxi – which I can claim because I was carrying tapes and they can be wiped by travelling on the Underground – took them up to the Library and here I am. This evening I have to record – would you believe – a European Cup soccer match. It's not even my group. Someone's sick in the other lot and I'm on standby. The match is broadcast live from Munich at nine o'clock and I have to sit in a channel and record it. How long do soccer matches last?'

'I don't know. An hour and a half maybe.'

'Ugh. So, if I don't drop dead beforehand, half-past ten will see me staggering into a cab, telling the driver to take me to Paddington, taking a Mogadon and falling into bed for about a fortnight.'

'I'm sure you could get someone else to record this match for you,' Steve remonstrated. 'You look dead on your feet. Alick'd do it, I'm sure, if he's free.'

'I am booked for it,' said Andrea stubbornly, 'and I'll do it. I can do anything at the moment. I'm on an incredible high.'

'So it seems,' said Charles.

'Just try not to be around when the low comes.'

Andrea's ebullience was momentarily curbed by the appearance of Mark with the drinks.

'I'm sorry I took so long. I was talking to John Christie and . . . Oh, hello.'

Neither Mark nor Andrea seemed to be exactly pleased to see each other. 'How was your trip?' he asked after a pause.

'Fine. Smashing.'

'Good.'

'Yes, it was. Very good. Made me completely rethink my life, what I'm going to do.'

'Good.'

'I am going to unearth the truth. I think the truth's very important. Everyone should know the truth.' There was a pause. She swayed slightly with exhaustion. Then she grabbed Steve's hand and said, 'Come on, Roger and Prue are over there.'

Steve muttered an apologetic 'Goodbye' to Charles as the two girls disappeared into the crowd.

Mark studiously didn't comment on their departure. 'Look, I've just been talking with John Christie and he wants you to join this committee.'

'What committee?'

'This Features Action thing.'

'What are you talking about?'

'You see, the thing about it is, John doesn't want it to be just BBC staff. Thinks we're in danger of getting too insular. Says we should involve creative people from outside too. Well, Helmut Winkler had got

Reggie Morris set up – do you know him? – he did that big feature on Nietzsche which was nominated for the Italia Prize.'

'No.'

'It was called *Zarathustra Meets Übermensch* . . . ?'

'Still no. In fact, even more no.'

'Anyway, Reggie's suddenly rung through to say he can't make it – pissed, I imagine – so we haven't got anyone representing the writing end of Drama features. So I told John about the smashing job you'd done on Swinburne and he said, Great, you'd be ideal.'

One decision Charles had taken very early in life, in fact while still at school when he had been elected on to the committee of the Drama Society, was that he would never again be on any committee for anything. Committees he knew to be time-wasting, long-winded, inconclusive and mind-blowingly boring. One of few advantages of his footloose life as an actor was that he did not have to take part in regimentation of that sort. Committees should be left to that unaccountable group of people who actually enjoyed them.

So he started to make his excuses, but was interrupted by the arrival of the pin-striped suit which had been identified as John Christie. 'Charles Paris, I'm delighted you're going to be with us,' he said with the unctuous charm of a Tory MP opening a garden fête.

'Yes, well you see, the thing is . . .'

'John, shall I get a couple of bottles to take over? I mean we can have a drink at this job, can't we?'

'Of course, Mark, of course. I do want this to be totally informal. Not BBC at all. In fact I've organised a few bottles of the old Sans Fil over there.'

'Oh great. If we run out, I can come back for more. Come along, Charles. The meeting's over in BH. In John's office on the Sixth Floor.'

So Charles went along. As he caught up with Mark, he asked, 'What's the old Sans Fil?'

'BBC Club wine. It's French for "wireless".'

CHAPTER TWO

'So what we are saying is, okay, stuff Management. Let's forget all the old prescribed answers and see what we can come up with by just gathering a few of the real creators together. Let's think laterally. Are we going to do better by sticking with the current *ad hoc* way of making occasional features or by starting a department formed just for that purpose?'

As John Christie concluded his opening address, Charles was again struck by the political image. The candidate was still opening the fête, smiling at everyone, on everyone's side, concerned about everyone's minor ailments, defending everyone against Them and obscuring in a welter of solicitude his own identity with Them.

An earnest thin-faced young man picked up the gauntlet. 'The point is that in the current climate, none of us has any time to make features – certainly not in News. We're too busy producing the day-to-day programmes. If we ever got any thinking time, I'm sure we could come up with the goods.'

'Exactly,' said John Christie, though Charles felt he would have said that whatever opinion had been expressed. 'That is why we have here a representative selection of creative programme-makers to find out how that sort of time can be made.'

'Huh,' objected a girl with a grubby T-shirt and Shredded Wheat hair, 'you call it representative, but I notice there are only four women here.'

John Christie opened his hands in what was meant to be a disarming shrug. 'Sorry, love. When I said "representative", I didn't mean representative of society as a whole; I just meant representative of creative programme-makers within the BBC.'

That didn't go down any better. 'I see, you are saying that men are more creative than women.'

'No, I didn't mean –'

'Come to that,' objected a young man with wild eyes, beard and teeth, 'I don't see many black people here. Or gays.'

16

'Who's counting?' came a limp voice from down the table.

'No, but there should be some blacks. I mean, we live in a multi-racial society.'

'Yes,' said Mark Lear, 'but we work in the BBC, where, as we all know, our concession to a multi-racial Britain is one coloured newsreader, a doorman and half the canteen staff.'

The line came out rather crudely. Obviously it had been meant as a joke, and Charles wondered whether Mark was drunk. He had a vague memory from their previous acquaintance that Mark didn't hold his liquor well.

John Christie dispensed unction on to the ruffling waters of the meeting. 'Now come on, we're only at the stage of preliminary discussion. I'm sure when we get into more detailed work, we can decide what is the optimum composition of our work-force. This is just an exploratory meeting.'

The objectors shrugged back into their chairs with Well-don't-say-I-didn't-warn-you expressions and the chairman continued, 'Let's try as far as possible to keep the discussion to features and how they are best made. Don't let's get sidetracked. Any thoughts?'

'I think we're doing features already. We always have been on *Woman's Hour*; just don't give them fancy titles.' This was from a lady of a certain age and a less certain shape. 'I mean the programme we did recently on hysterectomy was a feature by anyone's definition.'

'Yes, yes, I'm sure. But the point at issue is whether that sort of programme would be improved by having more time and resources available for its production.'

'I suppose it might be a bit better, but on the whole things that just have to happen come out best. At least that's what we find on *Woman's Hour*. All that's needed to create good features is creative writers and producers. This moaning about lack of resources and time just sounds to me like bad workmen blaming their tools.'

The girl in the T-shirt wasn't standing for that. 'Even the most brilliant workperson in the world needs some sort of tools to play with.'

'I didn't know workpersons had tools; I know workmen do,' came a facetious murmur from Charles's right. They had been introduced before the meeting started. Nick Monckton, Light Entertainment. It seemed that everyone present felt obliged to slip into his or her departmental stereotype. Nick felt it his duty to supply the jokes.

The girl either didn't hear or chose not to hear the interpolation. 'And by tools, I mean not only time and money, but also cooperation and encouragement from above. I mean, I came up with this great idea for three one-hour features on force-feeding the suffragettes, and HSP(R) had the nerve to say he didn't think it fitted into a course on Parliamentary Democracy.'

Charles appealed silently to Mark and received the whispered gloss, 'Head of Schools Programmes (Radio).'

'I got the same reaction to my Buddhism in the London suburbs idea,' objected someone. 'H. CAMP turned it down.'

'Same thing with my radiophonic *Crucifixion in Space*. Both CR4 and CR3 were frightened of it.'

'Well, the Gogol musical idea got up as far as DPR. HDR just didn't understand it, basically. I think at one stage DPR was going to refer it to MDR, but AHDR reckoned that would be publicly questioning HDR's decision, so sweet F.A. happened.'

Charles was beginning to feel he had somehow drifted into a game of Etruscan Scrabble and was relieved when John Christie once again chaired them into silence. 'Look, I know we've all got lots to say, but let's try and keep it one at a time, shall we? And I do think it important that we keep the discussion as general as possible. I mean, I'm sure you've all got pet projects which would fall into the features category – indeed, I hope you all have, because that means that I've invited the right people – but let's try to keep off individual and departmental hobbyhorses for the time being. Let's just try to think how it would all work out in an ideal world.'

'In an ideal world we wouldn't work for the BBC,' said Mark Lear with surprising savagery. But the rest of the meeting took it as a joke.

A small man with a large moustache came in over the laughter. 'I think, I hope, that is, pardon me, but, speaking for a moment with my regional hat on, I think there is a danger that we are all going to forget the important creative resources we have in the regions. I don't know that we've all met, but I am, to those of you to whom I am unknown, not to put too fine a point on it, Harry Bassett from Leeds, and I do, er, hope that, when the chips are down, we won't ignore the veritable mines of talent which we have been, as it were, mining for some time in Leeds and the other regional centres, that is, in any discussion we are having to which what I'm saying might be of relevance, if you take my point. And I'm not just harking back to the days of E. A. Harding and Geoffrey Bridson in Manchester or Cecil McGivern from Newcastle. I'm talking about the, as it were, here and now.

'I mean, no one's denigrating the fine work done in London, but I think, in a sense, it always seems to me, speaking off the record, that London is only one of many centres of creative radio and there's an all-too-ready tendency to dismiss the regional contribution as something that is not, in any real sense, as it were, of great importance. I mean, we may be, in a manner of speaking, out of town, but we're by no means and not in any sense, out of ideas, if you take my point.'

It was apparent from the impatient expressions of the rest of the meeting that they *did* all regard the regional contribution as completely irrelevant, but John Christie, salting away votes for some future election, smiled charmingly and said, 'Yes, of course, Harry. I'm very glad you brought that point up. But perhaps we ought to start, before we get too deeply embroiled in production details, with the artists involved in the creation of feature programmes. I thought it very important, for this meeting, that we should spread our net wider than just BBC staff. There's a dangerous tendency for us to regard what happens here as something on its own, totally divorced from the general world of the arts. So I'm very pleased to have with us some writers and performers whose opinion on the true creative issues will, I think, be invaluable to all of us. We are lucky to have with us the composer – dare I say *avant garde* composer? – Seth Hurt and –'

'I don't really regard myself as part of any movement, *avant garde* or –'

'No, well, I don't think it's necessary to get bogged down in definitions. What I was –'

'Definition, and particularly self-definition, is very important to me as an artist. I regard the music I write as unique and I rather resent being bunched into some blanket category with a lot of self-indulgent experimenters, who –'

'Yes, well I'm sorry to have got you wrong there, but if I could just move on, we're delighted to have with us Dave Sheridan, who, I'm sure, will excuse me for describing him as at the more popular end of the artistic spectrum. . . .'The disc jockey inclined his head graciously.
'. . . But I do think it's important that we don't lose touch with popular culture. We also have Ian Scobie, whose work as a presenter and interviewer in the news field I am sure you all know, and the famous actor, playwright and great specialist in the poetry feature world . . .' He glanced at his notes. '. . . Charles Paris.'

Charles looked at the floor to avoid seeing them all mouthing, 'Who?'

'So I think it might be very instructive if we were to hear from some of them as to how, as artists who might be employed by the BBC, they would best like to see feature projects set up.'

Charles continued his scrutiny of the carpet tiles. The only thing he had to say was that he thought he probably shouldn't be there and was there any chance of one of the wine bottles being passed in his direction as his glass was empty.

But, fortunately, Dave Sheridan willingly took up the challenge. 'I think, speaking as a kind of outsider, who has worked in a great variety of different styles of radio all over the world, there is an excellence in BBC programming which is unrivalled, and this –'

'Oh, but there's a lot of shit too,' observed Seth Hurt, who, despite his unwillingness to be categorised, Charles had already pigeon-holed as a repellent little tick.

Dave Sheridan rode the interruption with dignity. 'If I may finish. Sorry, I have to go off in a moment to pre-record the opening of tonight's show, so I must be brief. The point I was coming to was that features are a wonderful way of bridging traditional gaps between popular and more esoteric forms of culture and I would hope . . .'

He continued to develop his theme with skill and coherence. There was a lot more to him than the public stereotype of a disc jockey. Beside him, Nita Lawson's head nodded to reinforce his points, occasionally murmuring, 'Right on, Dave.' But Charles found his mind wandering. He shouldn't have come. He knew that all he had wanted for that evening was to get drunk, and yet somehow here he was stuck in the spiralling tedium of a committee meeting in whose subject he had no interest at all. To compound his gloom, he saw the feminist up the table trickle the last of the wine into her glass. Good God, how long would this thing go on? Already an hour and a half had passed and they still seemed to be waffling round preliminary remarks. Surely they'd stop before the pubs shut.

He contemplated just getting up and leaving. After all, he didn't know any of them and he wasn't going to be of any use to them if he stayed. Maybe he could leave as if to go to the Gents and forget to come back. . . .

'. . . and maybe you have something to add, Charles?'

He looked up to see John Christie and the rest of the meeting focused on him. Dave Sheridan had finished his peroration and gone off to pre-record the opening of that night's show. Charles had been chosen as the next creative contributor.

'Um, er, well,' he said, like an art dealer valuing a Rembrandt. Then, reaching the appropriate price, 'No, I don't think I do have anything to add.' In case that didn't carry conviction, he added darkly, 'Not at this moment,' implying, he hoped, esoteric suspicions as to the authenticity of the Rembrandt in question.

'There are a couple of things I'd like to add to what Dave said, if I may.' The speaker was Nita Lawson. 'You see, Dave's talking about music, because that's the scene he's into, but I think, whatever your bag, features could still be where it's at, creative-wise, because it's a matter of vibes . . .'

The meeting continued relentlessly, but not forwards; its course was a tedious sequence of meanders and eddies, with every advance of common sense choked in tangles of interdepartmental jealousies. Moment by moment, Charles wanted to leave more, and then didn't have the nerve just to get up and walk out, and then suffered self-recrimination for his gutlessness.

A possible relief came when Mark finally suggested going over to the club to buy more wine. Charles welcomed the prospect of accompanying him. Once there, he could down a couple of large Bell's while deciding whether to return to the meeting or not. But when he made the offer, Mark said, 'Oh no, I can manage,' and left before there was time to argue.

Shortly after this diversion, John Christie himself had to leave the room briefly. He had been summoned by a phone call from the duty office; some crisis had arisen over a play that was being broadcast that evening.

His departure relaxed the mood, and people started talking in little groups. Charles grinned across at Steve Kennett and received the rich gift of a smile from her huge eyes. He supposed the mouth must have smiled too, but it was difficult to disengage the eyes and look. He hoped there would be time later to have another drink with Miss Kennett.

He glanced at his watch. Nearly nine. Maybe the meeting would just disband naturally after this partial break-up. He had a horrible feeling it wouldn't though. Of course there was nothing to stop him from walking out. . . . But he felt vaguely that he should at least say goodbye to Mark. And then if there was any chance of seeing Steve afterwards . . .

Sheridan returned and sat down beside Nita.

'Opening safely in the can, Dave?'

'Yes, sure thing.'

'Is Kelly there?'

'Just checking through the running order.'

'Good. All all right?'

'Just fine.'

'I'm sorry, Dave. Won't be able to drop into the studio tonight. Got to leave by ten to get the last train out to Watford.'

'Don't you worry, my love. You do quite enough looking after my

21

interests in the office all day without fussing about me at night.'

'I'll switch on when I get home. Hear the last half-hour.'

'Ah, what devotion.'

At that moment conversation was interrupted by the arrival of a new figure. The door burst open with such a bang that everyone turned towards it and, once there, their attention was held by the eccentric appearance of the newcomer.

The first impression was of Lewis Carroll's White Knight. A middle-aged man with the same affronted mane of white hair and pale lugubrious face. Spotted cavalry twill trousers and a grubby linen jacket also seemed drained of pigment. And, as the White Knight's horse had been cluttered with pots and pans and other impedimenta, so his facsimile seemed to be sprouting belongings in every direction. His arms were full of files and tape boxes, while from his pockets sheaves of paper and streamers of tape and coloured leader spilled in carnival disarray.

To compound the surrealism of his appearance, when the man spoke, it was with the thick German accent of a mad professor from a comedy sketch. 'Mein Gott, ven vill ve haf tape editorz in zis organization viz any sensitivity to ze English langvidge?'

His words were greeted by a ripple of affectionate laughter, which did not seem to worry him, and he subsided into a chair in a shower of belongings, like a building being demolished.

Charles raised inquisitive eyebrows to Nick Monckton, who, in Mark's absence, was proving a sympathetic interpreter.

'Helmut Winkler,' came the whisper back. 'Reputedly one of the greatest intellects in the BBC. And incidentally a complete loony.'

The little man next to whom Winkler had sat, earlier identified by John Christie as 'Ronnie Barron, a tower of strength from the Studio Managers Department, who's here to advise us on matters technical and to keep the minutes of the meeting', took issue with the newcomer. 'Now, Helmut, you can't just make allegations like that. Are you complaining of inefficiency on the part of one of the SMs?'

'Inefficiency, no. I did not say inefficiency; I said insensitivity. Yes, ze girl iss as efficient as a voshing machine – and viz ze same amount off imagination.'

'Well, listen, if you want to make a formal complaint, then you have to –'

But that particular argument was curtailed by the return of John Christie's bland smile. Soon after, Mark Lear came back loaded with bottles of Sans Fil. His flushed expression suggested that he had stoked up with a couple of drinks at the bar while making his purchase. Still,

Charles's jealousy soon passed when he had a full glass in front of him and he felt more able to endure the wash of irrelevance that eddied about him.

He sank into a reverie. Not his customary depressed brooding, but mildly cheerful visions. There was still a glow from the Swinburne recording and a pleasing irony in his presence at the meeting. He mused, content.

Anyway, the proceedings were drawing to a close. One or two people had had to leave. Dave Sheridan had gone off again at about half-past nine, because he was on the air at ten. A couple of others had snuck away, mumbling about trains to catch. Charles himself could have left easily, but he felt now he might as well stick it out. So long as they broke up by ten or soon after, there would still be time for a couple of drinks in the club.

The committee had already reached the conclusion that certain aspects of the features problem should be discussed in smaller units or sub-committees and possible dates for the next full meeting were mooted. Everyone got out diaries, which they scanned importantly, searching for elusive gaps in their work schedules. Charles didn't have a diary; the dynamism of his career rarely gave rise to the need for one.

'. . . and then, Charles, you and your sub-committee should be able to get together before that date and report back to us all. Okay?'

He looked up blankly into John Christie's inquiring eyes. 'Um, yes, possibly,' he said, pricing a second Rembrandt. And then, remembering his views on committees and their baleful offspring, sub-committees, he added, 'What I didn't quite get clear was who else was going to be on the sub-committee.'

John Christie didn't rate him for not paying attention, but urbanely supplied the list of names: 'Nick Monckton, Harry Bassett, Ronnie Barron and Steve Kennett.'

'Ah, yes, of course.' There were quite a few things he would like to be on with Steve Kennett and, until such time as they became possible, a sub-committee was a good start.

'Okay then? Next Wednesday all right for you?'

'Um, er, yes.'

'If you sort out the venue between yourselves.'

'Sure.' Charles feared it would stretch his credibility as a Rembrandt-assessor if he asked what the sub-committee was meant to be discussing.

The meeting broke up. Mark Lear said, 'See you over the road. I'll sign you in. Large Bell's, is it?' and vanished before Charles could reply.

The other contributors moved off in slow groups, some still talking animatedly. John Christie beamed in the doorway, a vicar congratulating himself on the holiness of his congregation.

To Charles's relief, Steve Kennett approached him. 'I can ring the others at work, but I haven't got your number.'

'Ah, it's –'

'Or, on the other hand, we can fix where the meeting is now.'

'Fine.'

'We'll have it round at my flat. Be a relief to get off BBC premises.' She gave him an address near Paddington. 'About eight, I should think.'

'Fine.'

'Not that I think we're likely to get far with the topic.'

'No.' Charles smiled. 'Well, it's that kind of topic,' he observed, masking his ignorance. 'Are you going over to the club for a drink?'

'Why not? I'll just pop in on Andrea in the channel and see if her wretched football match is over.'

'I'll tag along. I haven't worked out the geography of this building.'

The editing channel on the floor below was a small greenish room with sound-proofing fabric panels on the walls. But the thick door was open when Steve Kennett screamed and the sound rang along the corridor.

Charles rushed to the doorway and peered over her shoulder at the scene inside.

Andrea Gower was sitting on a tall chair in front of a green tape recorder as big as a fridge. But her head lolled backwards and her arms hung limp at her sides. Her skin was as white as the polystyrene coffee cup on top of the machine.

Next to the cup two razor blades were upended in a slot by the editing block. From them dried rivulets of blood like spilled cooking ran down the front of the tape machine.

And from gashes in her wrists as neat as cuts in fabric, darkening blood had flowed down her limp hands to the floor. The carpet tiles, designedly dull in colour so as not to show coffee stains, could not subdue the red deposit that had seeped into them. But the blood had ceased to drip; she had been dead for some while.

The football match was still on. The ten-inch metal spools on the tape deck turned inexorably, while the commentator and crowd in Munich screamed and sighed at the thwarted climaxes of the game.

'Oh, my God,' said Steve Kennett. 'Do you remember what she said? "I'm on an incredible high. Just try not to be around when the low comes."'

CHAPTER THREE

As THE TAXI approached Mark Lear's house, Charles remembered another detail about the producer which had slipped his mind – he had married money. Vinnie's father had been a wine shipper, sold out his interest just before his death, and left his beloved daughter extremely well-heeled. The house off Haverstock Hill was considerably more splendid than the average BBC producer's salary could buy. Anyone less embarrassed than Mark about his unearned wealth would have given his postal address as Hampstead, rather than Chalk Farm.

There were just the three of them – Mark, Charles and Nick Monckton, the young Light Entertainment producer. He lived nearby in Belsize Park and had said he would drop in for a quick drink. Charles also felt in need of one. He hadn't made it to the club. By the time the Duty Officer had been summoned and called the BBC Head of Security, who had reluctantly called the police, it had been long past closing time. Mark had come back into Broadcasting House to look for him and there heard the news of Andrea's death. He took it badly.

So it was about half past twelve when they got back. Mark's sitting room was smartly furnished, with a couple of tables and a desk of real value. What must have been Vinnie's family silver was arrayed in a glass-fronted dresser. The carpet was plush and the wood highly polished. Mark's contribution to the décor, an irregular shelf of records, a row of paperbacks loitering on top of the piano and a defiant poster of Lenin, seemed self-conscious and impermanent. Vinnie dictated what the room should look like, and her cleaning lady ensured that it kept its high polish, both literal and metaphorical.

Mark didn't speak as he went across to the well-stocked silver drinks tray. He looked too large for the room, very bull-in-a-china-shop in his jeans and the dark blue donkey jacket he had not yet taken off. There was a calculated incongruity: the gritty student thrust into the stately home, Jimmy Porter visiting the in-laws.

And yet even as the impression came, Charles knew it was illusory. The donkey jacket wasn't a real donkey jacket, but a well-cut coat in donkey-jacket style from a Hampstead boutique. And the jeans weren't worker's jeans, but expensively aged denim trousers, finished with curlicues of yellow stitching.

The image of social gaucherie was no more than an image, a reflection of Mark's anti-BBC pose. He might rail against the values of the class in which he found himself, but he was no more likely to leave the comfort of his home than he was the job he affected to despise. A studied nonconformity of dress, Labour stickers in the window at election time, a shrugging shift of blame to Vinnie whenever his children's private education came up, and Mark could live with himself.

Besides, Charles recalled, the whole act of the deprived orphan fingering the velvet curtains of the big house was a nonsense. Mark's parents, though not as wealthy as Vinnie's, had been comfortable middle class and, though it was rarely mentioned, he had been through public school and Cambridge.

He poured them all large measures of whisky in cut-glass tumblers, threw his donkey jacket with unnecessary untidiness on to the green velvet sofa, and slumped into a matching armchair. 'What's the toast?' he asked brutally. 'Absent friends?'

Nick Monckton took a drink and shook his head. 'I don't know. Jesus, though . . . Poor kid.' The last comment was a bit patronising, since he must have been three or four years younger than the dead girl.

'Did you know her well?' asked Mark.

'Saw her a bit. Occasional parties. She did a few shows for me, and editing, of course. She was in the Radio Two group, so I only saw her when Light Ent. were short. Didn't know her very well really. How about you?'

'Much the same. The odd editing session . . . you know.' Charles, having witnessed his encounter with Andrea in the club, felt that Mark was telling less than he might have done.

'How is it,' he asked, '– explain it to me simply, because I don't understand the workings of the BBC – that if she specialised in Radio Two music, she was recording a football match tonight?'

'The other group just got stuck,' said Mark. 'Needed someone to help out, and she got lumbered.' He saw Charles looking at him and added defensively, 'She told me in the club earlier this evening.'

'It's happening more and more,' complained Nick Monckton. 'It's impossible to get the same SMs for a series. And as for booking studios . . .'

He continued and Mark joined in the BBC-griping vigorously, finding comparable instances in Further Education. Rather too vigorously, Charles thought. The hurried explanation hadn't fooled him. He had witnessed their meeting in the club and knew Andrea hadn't mentioned her football recording in Mark's hearing. Perhaps there were other ways he could find out about it, schedules he could consult, but it seemed strange that he should show that amount of interest. Alternatively, he might have spoken to Andrea at some other point during the day. Though, if she had only arrived at Heathrow at lunchtime and gone straight to a music session at Maida Vale . . . Either way, it confirmed the impression that Mark had known the girl rather better than he implied.

Nick Monckton was leaving. 'Starting rehearsal at half-past nine in the morning.'

'What are you doing?'

'It's a sit. com. called *Dad's the Word*.'

'Fun?'

'Well, some of it's sort of all right.' He didn't sound very convinced. 'I mean, we suffer from doing lunchtime recordings, you know, just get an audience of old biddies, and the scripts are . . . well, not that great. . . . But it's okay.'

'You make it sound terrific,' Charles observed.

'Usual BBC tat,' said Mark automatically. 'Whatever happened to radio comedy?'

'It is getting better, actually.' Nick looked quite earnest. 'There are a lot of young producers and a better atmosphere for getting new ideas away, Mark. Really.'

'Not like the old days.'

'I'm going to go before someone mentions Tony Hancock.' Nick Monckton stood up. 'Thanks very much for the drink, Mark. No doubt see you around. And, Charles, nice to have met you. We'll meet again on this sub-committee, anyway, or somewhere else. . . .'

'Maybe.'

'I mean, you're an actor and I'm a producer.' He didn't sound very convinced about the second part of the definition. 'Do you do comedy?'

The question came as something of a shock. 'Yes, I suppose so. I mean, I have done. Even did a job last year as feed to the late, great Lenny Barber. I mean, I'm an actor. Most of us do most things. Or say we can and only reveal we can't after the contract's been signed.'

'Oh well, maybe I'll be in touch.' It was spoken casually, but its intended showbiz condescension was weakened by furious blushing.

27

'My God, how old is he?' Charles asked after the young man had gone.

'About eleven, I should think. No, I suppose he's twenty-four, something like that. A product of Light Ent.'s conviction that everyone who sang comic songs for the Cambridge Footlights or did an impression of the Chancellor of the Exchequer for the Oxford equivalent must be God's gift to the entertainment business.'

'I see.'

'It's probably as good a way of recruiting as any other. There have been successes.'

'Hmm. Do you know him well?'

'No, hadn't met him before tonight. That's the trouble with the BBC – people in different departments never meet each other, never listen to each other's programmes. It's awful, a series of little islands with no ferries between them. No one can talk about anything but their own department. I mean, in FE . . . I've never met such a single-minded lot.' Mark was talking for the sake of talking, fencing really. They both knew there were more important topics, but Mark seemed unwilling to move the conversation above this level. Charles decided that that was his friend's privilege; if Mark wasn't going to bring it up, then he wouldn't.

The producer continued, 'Yes, if Smoothie Christie's little plans lead to nothing more – and I shouldn't think they would – he has at least introduced a few of the different islanders to each other. Can I top that up?'

Charles handed over his glass and decided that the conversation wasn't going to change gear. He would just have one more quick drink and then go. He felt exhausted.

But just as he reached this decision, the gear change came. Not smoothly and silently with benefit of synchromesh, but with an awful crunch. A glass dropped loudly on to the drinks tray and Mark's back started to shake convulsively as the sobs broke through.

Charles led him gently to a chair and finished pouring the drinks. He waited till the crying subsided before proffering one. Mark took a savage gulp, as if to bludgeon himself into composure. 'I'm sorry.'

'Andrea?'

He nodded. 'Yes, I feel responsible. I just . . . I didn't think I'd feel like this.'

'Do you want to talk about it?'

'I've got to. I mean, I won't be able to talk about it, when . . . I've got to talk about it now.'

'Okay.' Charles sat down and took a long swallow, but Mark didn't initiate anything. So Charles fed gently, 'I take it you had had an affair . . . ?'

'Was it that obvious?'

'No. There seemed to be some tension between you when you met, but it's only from seeing the state you are in now that I make that assumption.'

'Well , yes, you're right. The fact is that Vinnie is fine, you know, we get on pretty well, but I've always felt kind of claustrophobic, that I was only half alive, that bits of me, parts of my character, were just starved and cramped in a marriage situation and –'

'You don't have to justify yourself to me. I know exactly what you mean.'

'Yes, well of course you've been through it.'

'Just tell me what you want to tell me. I'm not going to judge you. My own eyes are fuller of beams than a mock-Tudor pub, so I can't even see your motes.'

Mark smiled lightly. He was calmer; he just needed confession and Charles was sufficiently uninvolved with him to take the role of priest. 'Right, okay, I'll tell you a bit to expiate some of my guilt. I'll try not to bore you with details.

'It happened in the usual way. I'm sure there is a standard way that all extramarital affairs start, but perhaps we are more prone to temptation in this business. You know, working late, that kind of thing. I had some crisis on, because I'd done a programme which contained critical references to Tony Crosland, you know, the late Foreign Secretary. Then he died suddenly and HFE(R) – that's my boss – he said it should come out. I argued, because I felt that the criticism was valid, regardless of whether the bloke was alive or dead, but, you know, we are the BBC, decorum must be maintained.

'Anyway, the result of all this was that a rush editing job was called for and there weren't any SMs around from our usual lot, so Andrea was booked to do it. She worked bloody hard and so I took her out for a drink afterwards. Well, the drink led to another drink back at her place and that led to . . . I don't need to fill in the details. I know I'm making it all sound shabby and calculated, but it wasn't. At the time it was . . . you know, some things just work.'

'Yes. Crosland died over a year ago, so I take it the affair went on for some time.'

'Yes, it did. Look, I loved her for God's sake!' This outburst had a staged quality to it, which Charles couldn't help observing. As if Mark needed the melodrama of the situation. As if an ex-mistress's suicide

29

gave him some kind of perverse cachet. The impression was reinforced when he went on. 'I can't get that Swinburne out of my mind:

> The small slain body, the flower-like face,
> Can I remember if thou forget?'

'From *Itylus*. I think you're taking it rather out of context.'

'I know. It's just the words. They keep repeating in my mind. That, and "sweet red splendid kissing mouth". They seem to be part of the confusion I feel. I mean, to think that she's dead, that she's lying there in some morgue and that that body I used to touch –'

Charles cut across the self-indulgence in this morbid detail with some savagery. 'But I gather your affair was already over.'

'That doesn't mean I don't feel anything.'

'No, of course not, but it must lessen the impact. The shock is still there, but it's not as if she was going to be part of the rest of your life.'

'I don't know.' Mark was aggrieved, unwilling that Charles should diminish his *grand amour*. 'We had broken up, but I still loved her. It was she who broke it off.'

'Can I ask why?'

'I suppose so.'

'Not if you don't want to tell me.'

'I'll tell you.' Mark's haste betrayed his unwillingness to let the subject drop. Charles had noticed in other friends an obsessive desire to talk about their infidelities. Partly he knew it was because he was uninvolved, because he was a handy confidant, slow with judgment, quick with reassurance. But he also often felt that confession was part of the attraction of affairs, that their secrecy was claustrophobic and such relationships only took on three dimensions when their enormity was confided to a third party. In a childlike way, there was no fun in a truancy that no one knew about. Anyway, Mark seemed more than willing to talk.

'She wanted it to end, because she couldn't see any future for us. It wasn't that she didn't love me, there was no one else, it's just that she reckoned the relationship couldn't progress. I argued with her. I mean, as I say, I loved her. God knows, I loved her.' The repetition sounded melodramatic and false. 'But she felt we'd be better off apart. She saw herself getting older, no chance of our ever getting married or anything. She felt it was hopeless to continue.'

'Why couldn't you get married if you loved her?'

'I couldn't do that to the children.'

A pattern was emerging, a cliché of an affair. 'What did Vinnie say about it?'

Mark seemed genuinely surprised at the question. 'Oh God, she didn't know.'

'You never discussed it?'

'No, she wouldn't have understood. And it would have been dreadfully upsetting for the children if we started to have rows and things.'

'Of course. And did Andrea know that Vinnie didn't know?'

Mark was evasively casual. 'I'm not sure. I suppose she did. We never discussed it.'

'I see.' And he did see. It was such a familiar scenario that he couldn't help seeing. Of course Mark hadn't told his wife. Why should he? He was sitting pretty, with her money and no doubt some of her affection. Probably a darned sight more of her affection than he ever admitted to Andrea. Yes, a nice domestic little marriage.

Meanwhile, with his mistress, another nice little set-up. Clandestine visits to her flat, maybe the occasional daring trip to a restaurant where he was unlikely to meet anyone, good sex, constant complaints that they couldn't meet more often, and the uncluttered relief of driving away from her at the hour when his studio booking or ideas meeting or other specious excuse ran out.

Charles could fill in all the details. He could also see why Andrea had eventually stopped and tried to back out of the cul-de-sac. No doubt they had discussed marriage, no doubt Mark had at times said he'd leave his wife, no doubt he'd said he'd talk to her. But every time something had happened, some crisis with the children maybe – yes, that was always an unanswerable excuse – and somehow the confrontation hadn't happened. Of course the relationship couldn't progress. One of the partners had no desire for it to progress; he was doing very nicely with it static.

What he saw so clearly made Charles cross. He would have liked to challenge Mark with the facts . . . but perhaps this wasn't the moment. Mark was obviously genuinely upset by what had happened. Charles was upset too, upset because he could see his friend already processing the memory, sweetening the pain, packaging it into a story that in a few months he would confess over a drink, about the girl he had had who had killed herself because of their star-crossed love. It was all too predictable and cruel.

Mark had now moved into a phase of crucified nobility. 'The worst thing is,' he said, 'the inability to grieve properly. That's why I'm going on to you about it, I can talk to you, pour out my feelings. Whereas tomorrow morning I have to sit at breakfast with Vinnie and the kids, spoon Weetabix into the little one and keep up cheerful chat about what's on the front page of the *Guardian*. Whereas inside I'll be . . . Oh

31

God. I won't really be able to grieve till next Monday when Vinnie takes the kids off for a week at her mother's. Next Monday – Jesus, just to keep it from Vinnie till then. Since she never even knew I knew the girl, she would never understand why I was so cut up about her death.'

'Shock would be a legitimate emotion, surely, after you'd been on the premises when her body was discovered.'

'I suppose so. But I wouldn't trust myself. I don't know, if I just mentioned her name, I might . . . Oh God.' He was near to tears again, but this threatened outburst didn't seem quite so spontaneous. Maybe, Charles reflected cynically, the first lot had been manufactured too. 'Then why don't you tell Vinnie?' he asked gratuitously, just to hear the shocked reaction.

'Tell her? What, you mean tell her all about Andrea and . . .'

'Why not? She can't possibly worry about the affair's continuance. Most women love the opportunity to prove how understanding they are of their men's weaknesses. It gives them an untouchable moral ascendancy.' He was surprised at his own cynicism. It was a reaction to Mark. The whole revelation of his selfish affair, juxtaposed with the recent image of the dead girl, filled Charles with anger.

But Mark had gone white as a sheet even at the mention of the idea. 'Good God, no. You don't know Vinnie, you don't know what it would be like. I mean, it'd be the end of . . .' He gestured ineffectually. '. . . Everything.' Somehow his gesture seemed only to encompass the prosperity of his surroundings.

Irritation pushed Charles on to another barb. 'You might as well tell her. It's going to be fairly difficult to keep it from her when the police come round to interview you.'

That winded Mark like a punch in the stomach. 'Police,' he gasped. 'What do you mean – police?'

'Andrea's was a suspicious death. I would think it unlikely they'd just let it pass without talking to the people nearest to her.'

'But I wasn't nearest to her. I mean, as far as anyone knew.'

'Oh, come on. In the BBC? There is no way you could keep an affair a secret in a place like that.'

'Well, okay, maybe one or two people knew, but not anyone who . . .'

'Look, I believe Andrea shared a flat with Steve Kennett. She'll be the first person they interview about her state of mind. You're not going to tell me Steve didn't know what was going on.'

Mark spoke slowly, planning, calculating. 'No, no, she knew. I wonder . . . Oh God, this could ruin everything. I mean, to have kept it a secret this long and for Vinnie to find out just at the moment when there was nothing actually to worry about.'

'You don't regard Andrea's death as anything to worry about?' He couldn't resist it.

'I didn't mean that.' Mark wasn't really listening; he was still working things out. 'I know. If the police come and see me at work, Vinnie need never know. That's it. They're more likely to interview me at work, aren't they? I mean, because that's where it happened?'

Charles felt very tired. Why not give him that comfort? 'Yes, yes, Mark, I'm sure they'll interview you at work.'

The shock of the girl's death had passed and he now felt the exhaustion of reaction and the depression of waste. She needn't have died. If she hadn't got mixed up with a selfish shit like Mark, she needn't have . . . Oh, what was the point? She was dead. 'I must go. Thank you for the drink.'

'And thank you for letting me go on like that. I'm sorry, but I had to. You see, I did love her.' Yes, maybe after all, in his way he did. 'I suppose I'll survive without her. It won't be easy.'

Charles bit back an unsuitable rejoinder to this maudlin play-acting. But worse was to come. 'It's Swinburne again,' Mark went on. '"I shall never be friends again with roses." That sums up the sort of emptiness I feel at the moment.' Already the loss had become fictionalised, drained of blood and embalmed in the mausoleum of Mark's memory.

'My feelings would be summed up in a different passage.' And Charles recited, not without irony:

> 'I am tired of tears and laughter,
>   And men that laugh and weep;
> Of what may come hereafter
>   For men that sow and reap:
> I am weary of days and hours,
> Blown buds of barren flowers,
> Desires and dreams and powers
>   And everything but sleep.'

Mark nodded lugubriously. 'Yes, Charles, yes.' Irony was wasted on him.

There was a note by the payphone when Charles got back to the house in Hereford Road where he had a bedsitter. He recognised the scrawl of one of the Swedes. All the other bedsitters in the house seemed to be occupied by Swedish girls. But not Swedes of lissom thighs and sauna baths and after-shave commercials; these were more like the vegetables.

The timed light on the landing went out as he took up the paper, and he fumbled for the switch. The note was full of the usual Swedish misspellings, but its message was clear.

FRANCIS RING. URJENT. RING WENEVER YOU COME BACK.

Oh God, no. Not Juliet. His first instinct was for his daughter. Maybe it was having seen Andrea dead that evening, Andrea, who must have been about the same age as Juliet. Suddenly he felt again that awful panic, like when she was a tiny baby and he had woken in the morning with a terrible rush of fear and torn into her bedroom to see that she was still breathing.

He was almost praying as he dialled the familiar number in Muswell Hill. The phone was picked up on the first ring. 'Yes?' Her voice was tight almost to breaking.

'Frances.'

'Oh, it's you.' A degree of relief. 'I thought it was America.'

'America? Why, what's happened?'

'It's Mummy. She's had a heart attack. Rob rang about seven this evening. He was practically beside himself.' Charles breathed again with a guilty feeling of relief. He was fond of Frances's mother, but at least she was of a generation where illness might be expected. Not like Juliet. He was surprised by the power of his feeling for his daughter. It was a feeling that he had never had much success in expressing in her company. Still, nice to know it was there.

Frances's father had died some twenty years previously and her mother married a charming American art dealer called Rob some four years later. They now lived in Summit just outside New York. Charles hadn't seen them for at least ten years.

Frances filled in the details. Apparently her mother had suffered a severe heart attack while out in the garden that morning. She was in hospital, still alive, but the doctor was afraid she might have another one. Frances was just waiting further bulletins.

'It's awful being so far away. I feel there's something I should be doing and yet . . .'

'There's nothing you really can do, love.'

'I know. I may have to go over, I don't know, see how she is. I'm incredibly busy at school with the end of term coming up, so I don't know if . . . Oh, it's impossible to plan anything.'

'Yes.'

They talked further and Charles felt very close to her, as if they were still properly married. In a crisis they were. He felt he needed to be near her, to protect her.

She sounded calmer, talking to him had helped. She said they'd better get off the line in case Rob was trying to ring through.

'Is there anything I can do, love?'

'No, it's all right, Charles. Just ring me. Keep in touch.'

'Of course. Are you sure you don't want me to come up to Muswell Hill and . . . ?'

She paused for a moment, and then said firmly, 'No, no, I'm okay. Just ring me in the morning.' And she rang off.

He topped up his whisky level straight from the bottle and went to bed. Rather to his surprise, sleep came. But dreams came too. He was in an American hospital like something out of *Dr Kildare*. On a stark white bed, with her wrists being systematically bled into huge transfusion bottles, lay Andrea. But her face was Juliet's.

CHAPTER FOUR

HE WAS WOKEN by a Swede thumping on his door. He had slept late. Half past ten. He must have been exhausted.

'Telephone. Telephone,' sang the voice outside. He staggered out. A lardy Swede in a blue nylon quilted housecoat scurried upstairs, mortally shocked by the sight of his pyjamas.

He picked up the dangling receiver and said a gravel-voiced 'Hello'. Always good at Orson Welles impressions first thing in the morning.

'Charles, it's me, Maurice. How are you, dear boy?' His agent. The 'dear boy' assorted ill with the shabbiness of Maurice Skellern's outfit.

'Not so bad. What is it?' It was almost unprecedented for Maurice to ring. It certainly couldn't be that the agent had actually found a job for him; that never happened; someone must have rung in an enquiry.

And so it proved. 'Listen, Charles, something I've been hoping for's come up. Part in a radio thing. Sit. com. called . . .' A note was consulted. '. . . Dad's the Word. Not a big part, but a nice little cameo. Thought it could be right up your street. I was glad to get the call, because it means my new policy's paying off.'

'Policy?' asked Charles drily.

'Yes, you know, I keep mentioning your name around when I hear series are coming up and . . .'

'Sure.' Charles was used to Maurice's protestations of how much work he did for his clients. And equally used to the fact that he never did anything at all. This booking was obviously a result of Charles's meeting with Nick Monckton the night before. Maurice, as usual, had had nothing to do with it. What surprised Charles, though, was the promptness of reaction. Nick must have put the call through as soon as he got in. And of course he'd been going straight in to rehearse an episode of Dad's the Word. God, maybe somebody hadn't turned up that morning. 'Is it for today, Maurice?'

'Today? Good Lord, no. It's in about ten days. Monday week. I just had a call from the producer, pleasant young man called . . .'

Charles saved another recourse to the notes. 'Nick Monckton.'

'That's right.' Maurice showed no curiosity as to how Charles knew. 'I haven't heard from the booker yet, but he hoped they'd be through within the day. I'm not sure what they're likely to offer. I know the rates have gone up recently, but it's some time since you've done a radio, so I don't know what your fee is.'

'Well, I was in doing something yesterday and –'

'What?' Oh, damn, fatal mistake. He had been determined not to tell Maurice about the Swinburne thing. Since it had been set up privately between him and Mark, he didn't see why he should give his agent ten per cent of a fairly modest fee for doing absolutely nothing. He always made resolutions that he would only let Maurice get commissions on things that he had personally set up. But if he were to do that, the agent would never get anything. Charles often wondered why he had an agent. But always, as on this occasion, when he heard Maurice's aggrieved 'What?' down the phone, his resolution crumbled.

'Oh, it was a feature on Swinburne. I was going to tell you about it.'

'I see.' Maurice sounded hurt and, to his fury, Charles felt guilty. Guilty, for God's sake. 'Swinburne, Swinburne . . . ? That's where they do all the operas out of doors, isn't it?'

'No, that's Glyndebourne. Swinburne was a nineteenth-century poet of considerable lyrical virtuosity and mental confusion.'

'Oh, *that* Swinburne,' said Maurice, hearing the name for the first time. 'So, well, no problem about this thing, is there? Nothing else in the diary for Monday week?' He didn't even pause for the answer he knew so well. 'It's a nine-thirty call for a lunchtime recording. You'll be through round two.'

'Only possible thing that might be a problem is that I heard last night Frances's mother's pretty ill in the States. I suppose if the worst happens, I might be involved in funerals and things. But can't really predict about that. Accept, anyway.'

'Right. Shall I be difficult about money?'

'Not too difficult. The BBC hasn't got any.'

Having reminded himself of Frances's mother, he rang the Muswell Hill number. There was no reply, which either suggested that everything was okay and Frances was at school as usual, or that the crisis had worsened and she was already on a plane across the Atlantic.

So he rang his daughter Juliet down on her executive estate in Pang-bourne. She was busy doing something with his two-year-old twin grandsons and sounded more than a little preoccupied. But yes, Mummy had heard again from Rob. It seemed that Granny's condition had stabilised and the worries of the night before were partially allayed. So Mummy had gone off to school as usual. And yes, they were all fine and he really must come and see them soon and oh God, she'd have to ring off because Damian was about to pour a tin of Golden Syrup over Julian's head.

After the panic and dreams of the night before, Charles felt let down to speak to the real Juliet. She sounded as distant as ever.

And when he spoke to Frances that evening, to confirm that there was no change in her mother's condition, their closeness of the night before seemed to have dissipated too.

The Paddington address was not far from Hereford Road, so Charles walked round on the Wednesday evening for his Features Action Group sub-committee meeting. He tried to pretend that was the reason for his going, but, self-confronted with his frequently expressed views on committees and the fact that he had never found out what this one had been assembled to discuss, admitted that really he just wanted to see Steve Kennett again.

And maybe to find out a bit more about Andrea Gower and why a pretty girl of twenty-seven should want to kill herself.

It was one of those big frontages with Palladian porticoes, built as family houses in more gracious days. Since now only a millionaire family could afford to live in one, they had all been converted into hotels with very British names for German tourists, private nursing homes for Arabs or, like this one, honeycombs of small flats.

Only the name 'Kennett' appeared in the little window by the Entryphone button. Charles wondered for a moment if the 'Gower' had been removed as a prompt mark of respect, but the dust on the plastic suggested that it had been that way for some time. He pressed the button.

'Hello.'

'It's Charles Paris. I've come for this sub-committee meeting.'

'Oh.' There was a reservation in the crackly voice. 'Oh, well you'd better come up.' There was a buzz and he quickly put his shoulder against the door.

Steve was standing on the second landing, holding open the front door of the flat. A heavy white-painted fire door, matching the bareness of the staircase and landings, clean and lifeless. She grinned as she saw him. 'I'm afraid you've had a wasted journey.'

38

'In what way? Have you managed to create a Features Department without me?'

'No, but I'm afraid our meeting's been cancelled. Ronnie Barron's tied up with some farewell party he'd forgotten about and Harry Bassett's got some emergency in Leeds. So I'm afraid it all got called off. I wanted to contact you, but no one seemed to have your phone number.'

'Mark Lear would have had it.'

'Yes, I didn't ask him.' It was said casually enough, but she hesitated and there was a slight edge to her voice.

'Oh. Oh, well, thanks.' He hesitated momentarily. 'I'd better be off then.'

'No. At least come in and have a drink, now you've dragged yourself all the way over here,' she said, exactly as she should have done.

Charles didn't point out that 'dragging himself all the way over' meant a pleasant five-minute stroll, bit back his disappointment at not being able to participate in a Features Action Group Sub-Committee meeting that evening and, almost too readily, said he'd love a drink.

The drabness of the landing was sharply contrasted by the skilful use of colours inside the flat. The walls were yellowish-brown, which offset the brightness of the multiplicity of hangings on them. Crude rugs from North Africa, bark paintings from Mexico, a blood-red shawl with mirror decoration and two Italian string-puppets in silver armour mixed with a wealth of posters and prints. Old *Good Housekeeping* covers, a couple of Norman Rockwells from *Picture Post*, a map of the world, a metal advertisement for *Virol: For Anaemic Girls* and, over the fireplace, a huge print of Hieronymus Bosch's *Garden of Earthly Delights*. On the wall furthest away from the window, orange plastic milk crates had been stacked to make storage units for records, stereo equipment, books, telephone directories and so on. In this structure a desk surface had been cleared. A typewriter nestled there with a half-finished sheet of paper in it.

On the tiny balcony outside the tall open window was a rich profusion of geraniums. Their dry scent permeated the room.

The lack of co-ordination amongst the objects in the room should have made for a terrible mess, but they had been disposed with such skill that it worked.

'I'm afraid I can only offer you wine,' said Steve, picking up a one-and-a-half litre bottle of Frascati. 'Just come out of the fridge, so it's still pretty cold.'

'That's lovely. Thank you.'

She poured him a healthy measure into a high bell-like glass and topped up her own. Then disappeared to put the bottle back into the fridge. When she came back, she raised her glass. 'Cheers. Sorry there's no meeting.'

'I'll survive. I hope I'm not keeping you from anything.'

'No, I was just doing the odd letter. Nothing important.'

Charles sipped the cool wine. It was pleasant sitting there with an attractive girl. Oh dear, immature again. He had seen enough of Steve to recognise that she was at ease in a man's world, that for her being alone with a man would not carry the overtones it had for someone of his generation. A good career girl with a mind uncluttered by old sexual stereotypes. He must try to attain her maturity and not keep thinking in sexual terms. Which was easy enough to do in principle – good God, he had worked with enough women, actresses and so on, for whom he had never had the slightest sexual interest. That was easy. It was only when he fancied them that he got all these immature thoughts. And he did fancy Steve very much.

Partly to get away from such distractions, he broached the subject of Andrea. They were going to get round to her sooner or later. Why not sooner? 'I'm still pretty shaken by what happened last week.'

Steve nodded. 'So am I. It's strange not having her around the flat. I mean, we never saw that much of each other, we led completely different social lives, but, you know, she was . . . around. I find when I go to sleep at night, I'm sort of half expecting to hear the door when she comes in. I don't think I've really taken in that she's dead.'

'It must be very sad.'

'I suppose so. Sad isn't really the word, though. I haven't felt sadness, not sort of weepy sadness. Just a strange sort of . . .' Her hands felt for the word. 'Disbelief. I keep thinking it didn't really happen, that I just imagined it. And then something forces me to know, or face the fact that it is true, it did happen. And then I just get furiously angry at the injustice of it, how unnecessary it was. But I don't feel sad. Yet. I suppose I will in time.'

'How long had you known her?'

'Since university. What, six, seven years. We were both at Cambridge and did lots of journalism there. That's how we met. Then we both applied for the BBC and I was lucky and she wasn't.'

'How do you mean?'

'I went straight into production, got a trainee course, and she became an SM. Just luck really. We had pretty much the same qualifications.'

'I don't fully understand what you're saying.'

'Well, round that time, they were saying at the Beeb that if you wanted to get into production, the idea was to get in as an SM and then, after a little while, you'd make the jump to producing.'

'But the jump wasn't as easy as it sounded.'

'Some people made it. But it was all tied in with the economic situation. The BBC was hard up, had to make economies, even cut down on staff. It meant there was less job movement, so people tended to get stuck with whatever they were doing.'

'So Andrea stuck as an SM, with all the frustrations that entailed.'

'Yes. I mean, she quite enjoyed it. It's not a bad job and the people are nice, but I think she did get frustrated a lot of the time. She used to be quite ambitious. You know, in journalism. She was very intelligent.'

'Yes.'

Steve Kennett stretched her small body and blinked her enormous brown eyes. 'I'm quite glad to talk about her, you know. I mean, just about her. At work everyone is either treading on such discreet tiptoes that they won't even mention her name, or else gossiping so shamelessly that . . . Hmm. And when the police asked me about her, they didn't seem to be talking about a real person, just some sort of specimen or courtroom exhibit.'

'Did you have long with the police?'

'I suppose so, yes. They have to, don't they? Have to find out why. I suppose an apparent suicide could be a murder disguised.'

'Could be. Did they seem to think this one was?'

'Oh no. I think they were just eliminating possibilities.'

'And what about you?'

'Me?'

'Yes. What do you think?'

'You mean whether Andrea really did commit suicide or not?'

'Yes.'

This was a new idea. 'Well, I'd assumed she did. It seemed pretty inexplicable, but I can't really see any other explanation. Particularly when you consider the alternative. Andrea wasn't the sort of girl who made enemies; she made friends. She had a unique ability to make friends. So no one would have had a motive to murder her. Okay, some murders are committed without motive, but they tend to be psychopathic ones and I don't think a psychopath would have set up such an elaborately disguised crime.'

'Depends on the psychopath. But no, in principle I agree with you.'

They were silent. Steve seemed to be thinking round the possibility.

41

Charles continued, 'One thing you just said interested me. You said Andrea's death seemed "inexplicable".'

'Yes, I meant, knowing her, it seemed very strange. She didn't really have any reason to do it.'

'The affair with Mark was completely finished, was it?'

The brown eyes looked at him shrewdly. 'I didn't know you knew about that. Did he tell you?'

Charles nodded. 'The night she died. I had it all poured out.'

'Yes, I'm sure he made a meal of it. He likes doing the poor suffering misunderstood routine at the best of times. Given a real tragedy like that to be upset about, I'm sure he –' She stopped apologetically. 'I'm sorry. He's a friend of yours.'

'Yes, but don't worry. You seem to have a fairly accurate estimate of how he works.'

'Oh, he made me so angry!' The outburst revealed a longstanding irritation. 'Needless to say, I saw a lot of him round here while the affair was on. Well, okay, they hadn't anywhere else to go at first and I didn't mind. But it went on for over a year. And this flat wasn't really designed for two, let alone three. I took Andrea in when her marriage broke up, and we got on pretty well, but I hadn't counted on Mark mooning round trying to look attractive and interesting all the time.'

'I didn't know Andrea had been married.'

'Oh yes, to Keith. A fellow SM. At least he was. He's got an attachment.'

The instant image was of some artificial limb or aid to continence. Charles mumbled that he was sorry to hear it.

Steve looked at him blankly for a moment and then, when she understood, burst into an unexpectedly childish peal of laughter. 'No, no, he's got an attachment as a producer. He's producing in Radio Two for six months. If it works out he might stand a chance of getting a permanent producer's job.'

'I see. I'm sorry, I still need an interpreter in BBC matters. How long were they married?'

'Oh, I think it dragged on for a couple of years. It was a bad time for Andrea. Keith, whatever his other virtues – and, come to think of it, I don't think he has any – was not given to fidelity. Very immature, as if he had just discovered sex and wanted to see just how many little girls he could have in the shortest possible time. A purely quantitative approach to the subject. He should never have got married. I must say, poor Andrea did pick them.'

'Yes, I have a theory that there's a kind of girl who almost deliberately

42

goes in for kamikaze relationships with unsuitable men. It's some sort of deep self-hatred, as if they feel they should be punished for their own sexuality.'

He had hoped this might elicit some information from Steve about her own relationships with men, particularly her current state of attachment, but it didn't. 'Yes, I'm afraid Andrea did seem a bit like that. With men she had this – I was going to say "death-wish", but it's rather uncomfortably appropriate.

'You see, that's what I find so strange, that's why I said her death was inexplicable. I mean she'd had a really rough time over the last four years – first when she was married to Keith, then when they broke up, then more or less straight into the interminably unsatisfactory affair with Mark and then an awful patch when that finally came to an end.

'Throughout all those times she'd come and have sob-sessions with me and often I'd see her in a really low state. Then she'd talk about suicide, but not in a real way, just as a kind of intellectual resolution to whatever impossible situation she was in at the time. Even then, when she was at her most abject, I never worried about that. I never really thought she would do it.' She shrugged. 'Well, I suppose that shows how wrong you can be.'

But this conclusion didn't satisfy her and she continued, 'What I think I'm saying, in my long-winded way, is that, if she was going to commit suicide, I would have been less surprised had it happened on any one of a dozen previous occasions, when she was in a really bad state. But she seemed in such good form when she came back from the States.'

'As she said, on a high.'

'Exactly. She was talking so much more positively than she had for months. As you know, I drove her back from the airport and she talked non-stop. She was in an incredibly optimistic state, really excited about things she wanted to do. She was going to steer clear of men for a bit and just concentrate on her career. It wasn't the talk of someone about to do away with herself.'

'She seemed pretty manic when I met her.'

'Yes, I suppose that's it. The mood swung round and she couldn't cope with the depression. Being back at work, sitting on her own for the first time, exhausted after the flight, it must have all just seemed too much.'

'I suppose so. That seems the only solution.'

'The police were evidently happy with it. It tied up all the loose ends.'

'Yes.' Charles took another sip of his wine and looked out at the geraniums. 'Did you find out anything from the police . . . I mean anything you didn't already know?'

'Not much. Except medical details. I mean, like that Andrea had taken a couple of Mogadon before she did it. Apparently she'd crumbled them up in her coffee and taken them that way. With those and the alcohol and lack of sleep, she must have been in a pretty woozy state. I suppose that's what they mean by the balance of the mind being disturbed.

'Yes. You weren't surprised that she had the Mogadon on her?'

'No. She always carried them. Her doctor prescribed some when she was going through a rough patch just after the marriage ended, and I'm afraid it was repeat prescriptions ever since. She always had difficulty sleeping, especially when she was emotionally upset or excited.' Apparently reading some sort of disapproval in his eyes, she added, 'I'm sorry, I'm making it sound a real *Valley of the Dolls* set-up.'

'Don't worry. But basically you don't reckon her taking the Mogadon was strange? At that time.'

'No, she had said she'd take some. They take a bit of time to work, so it's quite likely that she would have had a couple to ensure that she went straight off to sleep when she got home.'

'Except that presumably it wasn't her intention to go to sleep, or indeed to go home.'

'No, of course not. I was forgetting. I suppose she must have taken them to make it that much easier. Or perhaps she took them with a view to going home and then was seized with such a terrible wave of depression that she cut her wrists on an impulse.'

'Maybe.' Charles didn't feel it all made sense yet. 'But it was quite carefully set up. I mean, the razor blade was placed in position. Anyway, I can understand somebody slashing one wrist on an impulse, but it seems to me the sight of all that blood might stop them short before doing the next one.'

'I agree. The whole thing is odd. But what else is there to think?'

'I don't know. That something happened to change her mood.'

'I don't follow.'

'Well, what's the situation? We both saw her, just back from the States, in an almost manic state of euphoria. If we assume that there was no outside influence, we must take it that that mood shifted and turned to a depression of suicidal proportions. That's the bit you described as inexplicable – right?'

'Right.'

'Well, the alternative, which might explain the inexplicable, is that she talked to someone, met someone, had a phone call from someone, and whatever they said turned her suicidal.'

'I'm with you. But who?'

'It's pure conjecture. It could be anyone. . . . Presumably she was just sitting alone in that recording channel and anyone could have gone in and talked to her.'

'Yes.'

Charles paused, then spoke more slowly. 'It seemed to me that Mark Lear took rather a long time to get that wine from the club. We know from the geography of Broadcasting House that he could easily have walked past Andrea's channel on his way.' He tried not to make it sound like an accusation, tried to make it sound like one of many hypotheses to be sifted and eliminated, but he still felt slight guilt towards his friend.

Steve nodded slowly. 'Yes, it's quite possible. I hadn't thought about it before, but Mark must have known she was there. It would be very much in his character to go and assert his continuing existence and shatter any new security she may have built up. He treads always with the sensitivity of a blind elephant.'

Another, more disturbing explanation of Andrea's 'inexplicable' suicide was taking shape in Charles's unwilling mind, but he dismissed it for the moment and continued, 'That might make some kind of sense. She feels all revived and changed – actually confronted with the man whom she hoped she had got over, she crumbles and feels as bad as ever – he goes – she thinks, what the hell, it's hopeless, fixes the razor blades in the slot and – geech!' He made a guttural sound and mimed the violent movement of a hand across the blades. Immediately he regretted the gesture. He had forgotten for a moment how close Steve had been to Andrea, and the pause before she replied showed how he had shocked her.

'Yes, that certainly makes a more convincing explanation than anything else that's been suggested.' She sighed, trying to shrug off the brutal reminder of the reality of her friend's death. 'Oh well, if that did happen, no doubt the police will get the details out of Mark and tie up the few remaining loose ends in their neatly woven fabric.'

'They've talked to Mark?'

'Oh yes.'

'He was very anxious that they should contact him at the office.'

'They did. He need not worry about that.' Steve Kennett's brown eyes focused on Charles wryly. 'So he never told his wife?'

'No.'

'I knew it. But, God, even so it makes me sick. The two-faced bastard. Needless to say, a constant theme of Andrea's outpourings to me was how Mark was going to leave his wife, she knew all about it, they were just trying to sort out the timing of the final break.'

'But every time it was about to happen, one of the children got ill, or . . . that sort of thing.'

Steve nodded. Charles felt satisfaction at having his conjecture confirmed, but he said, 'I apologise. On behalf of my sex.'

'You mean you've been through that sort of subterfuge?'

'Been through it and hated it. It was to avoid going through it again that I left my wife.'

'But not for someone else?'

'No. For the idea of all the women who up until that point had seemed unattainable because I was married. And who subsequently proved to be unattainable because they were unattainable.'

'I see.'

'I left my wife for an idea of freedom. A cliché of freedom, perhaps. Certainly an accepted stereotype of freedom.'

'And found . . . ?'

'That I had to redefine my concept of freedom.'

Steve Kennett nodded but said nothing. Charles felt they were nearer to a sexual context than they had been all evening. Equally, he didn't want to pursue any sexual disadvantage, or perhaps to make trial of the existence of any sexual advantage. He wanted to continue to know this girl, not to end their acquaintance on some dislocating rebuff to an ill-timed advance. He was relieved when Steve broke the drift of the conversation by offering him another drink.

'I'm afraid the answer is yes. As usual. But only if you are sure I'm not keeping you from anything.'

'Yes and no. You are keeping me from something, but it's something I am not looking forward to, and the idea of having a bit more Dutch courage before I face it is very appealing.'

His expression was only of mild enquiry; if she didn't want to tell him more, that was her privilege. But she supplied the explanation. 'Andrea's mother is coming down tomorrow to pick up her things. I feel I should go through them before she arrives. It's not a task I relish particularly.'

'No. I can see that. If it's a task that could more easily be done by two, I'd be more than willing to . . .' He hoped the offer wouldn't be thought of as presumptuous, of him muscling in on a private grief.

She didn't take it that way. 'Very sweet of you, but it really won't take me long. Just shove all the clothes into a suitcase without looking at them. It's the small things that I'm more worried about. Knick-knacks on the dressing table, oddments in old handbags, that sort of thing. Those are the ones I'm really going to have to look at, and I'm not sure that I feel strong enough for that. I've a feeling it's going to be many breaks for weeping.' She spoke as callously as she could, but she was not relishing the inevitable emotions that this sifting through of her friend's belongings would cause.

'Well, mine's a good offer . . .'

'Which I just might accept. Let's finish this drink and I'll see how strong I feel. Maybe two of us, with constant alcoholic fuel, could swan through it unaffected.'

'Who knows? We might also find an explanation of the inexplicable.'

'You mean a note or something like that?'

'It's possible.'

'I doubt it. We'd be following a path that's already been scrupulously trodden.'

'The police?'

Steve nodded. 'They've been through everything. And apparently found no expression of intent. They were very thorough. I gave them the key and they did the lot while I was at work on Monday. And, bless their little hearts, they put everything back exactly where they had found it. If I'd been here, I'd have asked them to leave it all in neat piles to save me the unappealing chore I have to do tonight.'

'Well, you never know. We may find something. At least looking for it gives us an objective other than maudlin sentiment.'

'True.' Steve drained her glass. 'Okay, let's start. In half an hour we'll have a break and reward ourselves with another glass of wine.'

They were finished well within the half-hour. The clothes were packed in a couple of suitcases and the other oddments filled a cardboard box that had once contained cans of ravioli. A whole young life fitted into two suitcases and a cardboard box that had once contained cans of ravioli.

They were both struck by this thought, but both resisted the slide into anger or depression. 'Thank you,' said Steve. 'Having you here did make it easier.'

'My pleasure. I'll get the drinks. Sit down.'

She didn't even make a token remonstrance, but sank into a chair, looking drained. Maybe a few tears would have made the ordeal less painful.

But when he came back into the room, she was on her feet again, rummaging in a cupboard by the front door. 'Her hand baggage,' she explained. 'What she carried on the plane. She just threw it in here when we got back from the airport.'

Charles felt a little surge of excitement. 'Would the police have seen it?'

'I don't know. It depends how thoroughly they searched. I didn't tell them it was here. I'd forgotten.'

It was one of those black plastic shoulder-bags designed for air travel. One of those with diminishing zip pockets which you have to remember to fill from the outside in or nothing will fit. It still carried the airline labels and seemed more evocative of Andrea's presence than all her other possessions.

The contents implied an unfinished life, a life that was about to be picked up again. There was a library book by Alison Lurie with a bookmark about two-thirds of the way through, an open and crumpled packet of tissues, a half-eaten Hershey Bar, an almost empty Fidji scent spray. They were all signs of a life about to be resumed, not one soon to be deliberately ended.

There was also all the tourist memorabilia. Criss-cross maps of New York, a souvenir programme from Radio City Music Hall, a couple of unused postcards of the Manhattan skyline, a catalogue of the Frick Collection, some theatre programmes, ticket stubs. All expressive of a busy and lively week in one of the busiest and liveliest cities in the world. And all now overcast with an unanswerable sadness.

Steve was very brave, still keeping a studied matter-of-factness in her voice, until she came to a professionally gift-wrapped package, whose accompanying card read, 'To Steve, With Lots of Love and Thanks for Putting up with Me, Andrea'. She was very white as she undid the ribbons.

The present was a denim bag, made in the shape of a pair of shorts. Its silliness was too much for her. Its choice expressed the reality of her friend's character in a way that all her familiar possessions hadn't. The tears that had been contained all evening burst through. The huge brown eyes filled and spilled. Charles put a gentle arm round her tiny shoulders and led her back to the chair.

She was a strong girl and after a couple of minutes had control of herself again. 'Is there anything else?' she asked in a businesslike voice, dismissing her weakness without apology.

Charles looked down to the bottom of the bag. There was a Macy's carrier which contained a set of table napkins. 'For her mother, I'm sure,' said Steve.

Then another paper bag full of cassettes. 'She could never stop herself from buying them. Even though she had access to the BBC library and could have copied anything she wanted on to blanks, she was always buying new ones. All classical, I daresay. Wouldn't pander to my de-based tastes and buy anything vaguely pop. She got enough of that at work, anyway.'

Charles sifted through the pile. There were about half a dozen. Yes, all classical. Mozart, Brahms, Vivaldi . . . all but one. 'Good God, what's this?'

The cassette was in a box marked Musimotive with an address on W44th Street, New York, and beneath that was printed, 'Neutral Mood, 90 minutes, suit working environment'. Steve came over and looked at it. 'Some sort of Muzak tape isn't it? Background stuff.'

'I suppose so.' Charles felt a sudden irrational detective excitement. 'Unless there's something recorded over it.' . . . Her suicide message perhaps.'

Steve caught the excitement. 'Let's put it on.' She went over to a music centre which was ensconced amid the milk crates and fed in the cassette.

Their excitement didn't last long once the music started. It was exactly what the labelled contents had suggested, neutral mood music, that kind of aural candyfloss that trickles out in lifts and bars and hotel lobbies and airports and factories and stores all over the world. Harmless, soulless, dull.

'You don't think she brought this back for you, Steve? Pandering to your popular taste.'

'Give me a bit of credit, Charles. My taste isn't this debased. Maybe she brought it back for me as a joke, a reinforcement of her oft-stated view that all pop music sounds the same.'

'Would that be in character?'

'Not out of character. Or maybe she brought it over for one of the other SMs. Some technical quality that she knew would interest one of the sound buffs. There are some great specialists among that lot.'

'Yes, maybe.' Charles sighed. 'Still, I suppose we'll never know. Anyway, it doesn't sound like an explanation for suicide.'

'I don't know.' Steve was now sufficiently in possession of herself to make a joke. 'If I had to listen to that sort of stuff for long, I think I'd pretty soon get suicidal.'

They flipped through the tape, playing little bits to see if it changed, but the same unremitting treacle covered both sides. Charles ejected the cassette and made to put it back in its box.

As he did so, he stopped. There was something on the inside of the paper cover. He pulled it out. It was written just below the address of Musimotive, the firm which had perpetrated the music.

DANNY KLINGER, 4th–11th NOV, 1977. 14th–22nd APRIL, 1978 AND NOW.

Steve had come to look over his shoulder. 'Is it her writing?' he asked.

She nodded.

'Then what the hell does it mean?'

'God knows.'

'Did she know anyone called Danny Klinger?'

'Not to my knowledge.'

'Do you think maybe she met this man, had an affair with him in New York and that's why she suddenly got so depressed when she got back?'

'All things are possible,' Steve replied drily, showing up the flimsy nature of his conjecture.

'Yes, and what could the dates mean?'

They discussed the possibilities for another half-hour, but they didn't get anywhere. Andrea's connection with Danny Klinger, whoever he might be, remained as 'inexplicable' as her suicide.

Shortly after, Charles left. 'I hope tomorrow's not too bad,' he said as he stood in the doorway. 'With Andrea's mother.'

'I'll survive.'

He mused, 'It's strange. Everything you've said tonight about Andrea makes her seem a less likely candidate for suicide.'

'I know. If you had asked me a week ago if I thought her likely to do it, I would have said, under no circumstances. But we are all constantly being proved wrong. I mean, she did it, didn't she?'

Charles nodded glumly, but as he walked back to Hereford Road, a little voice in his mind kept saying, 'Did she?'

CHAPTER FIVE

WITH THE PASSAGE of time, the suspicions that had been germinating in Charles's mind started to shrivel from lack of nourishment. For the rest of that week he heard nothing more from anyone at the BBC, except, through Maurice, the confirmation of his booking on *Dad's the Word* (and yes, radio fees had gone up a bit, but not that much).

He began to think that he had been romanticising about Andrea's death, excited by its recent shock and the crusading spirit which Steve's brown eyes had inspired in him. The next morning, the Thursday, he had woken up full of St Georgishness, determined to track down the dragon which was distressing that particular damsel, but as the day passed, it was his determination rather than his knighthood which proved errant. By the Friday morning he had forgotten any idea of a quest, or perhaps he had come to see through it as a simple ruse to keep in touch with the damsel.

So he did nothing in the way of investigation. The idea receded and the arrogance which had made him think of pursuing the girl shrank into lethargic self-distaste. What had a fifty-one-year-old man of diminishing charms to offer to a girl like her? He was far too old. He was glad he hadn't made any advance; he had thus saved himself the embarrassment of her puzzled and gentle but inevitable rebuff. And to think of using the suicide of her friend as an excuse to wriggle his way into her affections was shabby, the trick of a dirty old man.

No, Andrea Gower's death had been no more than it appeared. The poor girl, to whom life had dealt more than her fair share of knaves, couldn't face the descent from the manic happiness of her trip to New York and had taken her own life. Whether Mark Lear or anyone else had spoken to her just before the suicide was not particularly important. It hadn't affected the outcome.

Andrea Gower had committed suicide. There was nothing else to think.

Two things happened on the Friday afternoon to change that conclusion. The first took place, with the perversity that dramatic revelations have for choosing undramatic settings, in the launderette.

Charles didn't visit the launderette as often as he should. The little sink that lurked behind a plastic curtain in his bedsitter was good enough for drip-dry shirts, Y-fronts and socks. And such items dried satisfactorily from hangers by the window in summer, or on a Heath Robinson system of strings over the paraffin heater in winter. These methods, and occasional trips to the dry cleaner with jackets and trousers, could keep him reasonably nice to be near for most of the year.

But the bedsitter really couldn't cope with sheets. They wouldn't fit in the sink, they took up too much space when hung up and they took too long to dry. A fellow actor of similarly unambitious domestic habits had recommended that he buy fitted nylon sheets, which, the sponsor assured him, would dry in no time and could be put virtually straight back on to the bed after washing. Charles did actually buy some, but, after one night of feeling like a kipper fillet sealed in its individual polythene bag, relegated them firmly to the bottom of his wardrobe. The action gave him the righteous feeling that he still had some standards left.

But rejecting the nylon solution made the launderette inevitable. Every now and then he had to take his prized cotton sheets down to be washed and, more importantly, to be dried. The gaps between the now and the then were longer than those recommended in most books of household management, but at least the visits always happened eventually.

Westbourne Grove was the setting for his nearest launderette, which he often considered must be the most depressing place in the world. A few other candidates – one particular lino-floored pub in Edinburgh, the waiting room at Victoria Station, the Regent Palace Hotel, the South Bank Arts complex and all of Wales – occasionally vied in his mind for the title, but usually the launderette won.

It wasn't that it was dirty. It was regularly swept and the pervasive smell of detergent suggested cleanliness. But the dejected row of plastic-covered metal chairs, the piles of blue plastic baskets and the instructions unevenly printed out in felt pen suggested the set of some Beckett paean to despair. The characters who inhabited this bleak landscape matched.

Perhaps they weren't all miserable, perhaps they hadn't all just been kicked out of loving marital homes or recently widowed, hadn't just had their illegal-immigrant status discovered, and weren't facing imminent deportation; it's just that they all looked as if they had. As soon as he walked into the place Charles felt he had joined the shifting and shiftless population of London, the sort about whom earnest reports keep appearing in the *Guardian*. What made him feel guilty was that he rather enjoyed being there. Such total abnegation of human hopes had a perversely cheering effect on him.

Two things never changed when he went to the launderette – first, he always forgot to take his own soap, and, second, he always forgot to take whatever book he was reading. It was not from lack of foresight. He would put out the packet of detergent and the book long in advance of his departure; he would even sometimes put them just in front of the door of his bedsitter, so that he could not leave without tripping over them; but, whatever form of physical mnemonic he used, the result was always the same. He would arrive at the launderette clutching only the broken handle of his polythene bag of dirty washing.

This meant recourse to the soap machine. Since he never had the right change and could never find anyone else there who either had it and was prepared to part with it, or who spoke enough English to understand what he wanted, it usually took some time to get his soap. Often he would have to forage abroad for change and return with piles of matches and chocolate bars which he had bought rather than ask directly for what he wanted. He would then, having set his machine in motion, sit bored out of his mind, wondering why the hell he hadn't brought his book, and feeling agreeably abject, a contented piece of flotsam beached by the sea of humanity.

He should have known that something special was going to happen on that particular Friday, because as soon as he arrived at the launderette and made the regular discovery that he had left his soap at home, he found the right coin for the machine in the lining of his sports jacket. (There had been a hole in the pocket for so long that he reached his hand into the lining automatically.) To add to this serendipity, after he had started his wash and made the regular discovery that he had left his book at home, he found an abandoned newspaper on the chair next to him.

Here was riches indeed. A copy of the previous day's *Mirror*. He looked round to see if the newspaper had a potential owner, but decided that neither of the two impassive Chinese nor the dauntingly beaked Arab girl was likely to want it. He settled down to the luxury of reading every word. There was nothing else he could do. That, he decided, was probably why he liked the launderette – all the normal imperatives of life were suspended for half an hour, obedient to the inexorable sequence of rinses and spins.

As always with an unfamiliar newspaper, the *Mirror* seemed to have discovered a completely fresh hoard of news which his regular *Times* hadn't been told about. Or maybe it was just a difference of emphasis and style that made the stories seem unfamiliar. Or maybe (and this he suspected probably to be the real reason) he didn't actually take in anything from *The Times* as he flipped through it over his morning cup of coffee.

The item which shook him rigid appeared on Page 7. Had he not had time to read every word he would not have stopped for it. The headline read 'WOODCOTE CAR BODY IDENTIFIED' and underneath was this report:

> The man found dead yesterday in a car in a lonely wood near Wood-cote, Oxfordshire, has been identified as Daniel Klinger, an American record producer who had recently arrived in this country from New York. Police, who removed a length of plastic tubing from the hired car, say they do not suspect the involvement of another person in the death.

He read it again to make sure that he hadn't jumped to conclusions, but the main facts didn't change. Someone called Daniel (or quite possibly Danny) Klinger had arrived recently from New York and (the tubing the police removed suggested) had committed suicide. This had happened less than a week after Andrea Gower had returned from a holiday in New York and had committed suicide. And she had had Klinger's name written on a cassette she had brought back from the States.

It wasn't enough information to produce any meaningful conclusion, but it was at least an interesting coincidence.

And, from the limited facts at his disposal, Charles could reconstruct events in a variety of ways. All were based on the premise that Andrea had met Klinger while in New York, and most on the assumption that they had had an affair. Thereafter the possibilities were diverse.

Maybe Klinger had said it was just a holiday romance and it was despair at having met another unreliable man that drove Andrea to suicide. Klinger had then changed his mind, decided he couldn't live without her, followed her to England, heard about her death and killed himself from remorse. . . .

Hmm. That one was a bit novelettish. Try again.

Maybe . . . they had come over to England on the same flight, then he had revealed he was married/had a girl friend/had lost interest in her, she had killed herself and a week later, tortured by remorse for what he had set in motion, he killed himself. . . .

Still a bit flimsy. It was all this remorse that made them sound such feeble theories. Remorse was linked in Charles's mind with broken hearts and heroines with brain fever and other motivations which belonged in the exotic pastures of romantic fiction.

All right, maybe . . . Klinger had wanted to keep his affair with Andrea (or something else about himself) a secret from . . . a person or persons unknown – Andrea had insisted that she was going to tell – so he had staged her suicide and killed her. Then a few days later, tortured by remorse . . .

No, whichever way he did it, remorse kept pushing its way in.

One more try. Suppose . . . Andrea and Klinger shared a secret that A Third Person had to keep quiet at all costs and so A Third Person had killed both of them, making the deaths look like suicides . . .

Well, at least it got remorse out of the way. But, even so . . . And it did raise a lot of other questions. And leave rather a lot of blanks (like, notably, who was A Third Person?).

Basically, he just hadn't got enough facts. He could go on producing theories for days, but until he knew a bit more about Danny Klinger, the theories would be worthless.

Still, he thought as he noticed that his wash had stopped, leaving stalactites of sheet across the window of the machine, there were ways of finding out more about Mr Klinger.

'*Evening Standard.*'

'Could I speak to Johnny Smart, please?'

There was silence from the other end of the line. Charles looked at his watch. Nearly five o'clock. Even Johnny should have finished lunch. On the other hand, it was a long time since they had met and Johnny's drinking habits had been heavy then. Perhaps now his lunches went on even longer. Or perhaps he'd gone home. It was Friday afternoon; in most offices that meant POETS (Piss off early – tomorrow's Saturday).

'Johnny Smart's phone.'

'Could I speak to its owner or is the phone the only one there?'

'Who's speaking?'

'Charles Paris.'

'Just a minute. I'll see if he's about.'

There was a muttered conference at the other end of the line to decide, a) whether Charles Paris was someone whom Johnny Smart would speak to, and ,b) whether Johnny Smart was sober enough to speak to anyone.

He came straight on the line, so the answer to a) was yes. The answer to b) was 'just'.

'Charles, Charles, my old body – I mean, my old buddy, what brings you to contact me after all these years? If you're suggesting we should meet up and drink seventeen bottles of wine one of these days, the answer is yes.'

'That would be good. In fact, the reason I rang –'

'Oh, of course, it's favour time. You want me to find something out for you.' Johnny spoke without resentment.

'That's right.'

'What is it this time, Charles?'

'It's something one of your crime reporters might be able to help me on.'

'Crime, eh? That rings a bell. Didn't I hear from someone you're setting yourself up as a bit of a private investigator these days?'

'Hardly. I just seem to have stumbled into one or two things. Murders, you know.'

'I see. Is it more profitable than the acting?'

'I don't make any money from it, Johnny. I still live from my acting – no, let me rephrase that. Any money I make comes from acting.'

'Oh, I thought you'd given it up. I haven't seen your smiling face on the telly for a bit.'

'Come to that, it's a year or two since I've seen your by-line in the paper.'

'Oh, good Lord, Charles, when you get to my eminence in the journalistic profession, you don't actually *write*. You have little men to do that for you. Anyway, as the South African said, enough of this idle Bantu. I'm a busy man. I have an important meeting at half-past five with –' He broke off as some unintelligible ribaldry was shouted at the other end of the phone. 'Sorry, sorry, I shouldn't say meeting. Brands me as old-fashioned. What I should say is, I have an important and meaningful interface at five-thirty . . . with a wine bottle. So what is it?'

Charles asked if he could have any information available on the death of Daniel Klinger. Johnny said he'd try to find out who had covered the story and ring him back.

The call came through at twenty past five. Johnny was still going to make his 'important and meaningful interface' at five-thirty. 'There's not a lot known, but I'll give you what there is. Reporter who covered it says there'll be more after the inquest. Early next week.

'Anyway, this guy Klinger was apparently a record producer in the States. Had his own outfit called Musimotive. Sort of background music company, I gather. It seems that the firm's under some sort of investigation. Fraud, I suppose. That is unofficially thought to be the reason why he killed himself. Presumably he knew something nasty was going to come out.'

'Any idea when he arrived in this country?' Johnny gave the date, three days before Andrea's return from her holiday. That meant if they had met and had an affair during her week in New York, it was an extremely brief one.

'What about the actual death?'

'He'd had a lot to drink, huge amount to drink, presumably to soften the blow. Police reckon he had got through a whole bottle of whisky – and just to make sure, he'd crushed a couple of sleeping pills in with it. So, properly juiced up, he got this bit of tubing, fixed it to the exhaust, round into the back window, got in the driver's seat, switched on the ignition and the radio – for company perhaps – and waited. With the amount he'd had to drink, and the pills, the police doctor reckoned he was probably asleep before he died. Quite a painless way out, I gather.'

'What were the pills?'

'Mogadon.'

Hmm, a coincidence. At least a coincidence.

'When did it happen?'

'Tuesday night. He was staying at the Kensington Hilton. Seems he left there about quarter to ten in the evening, got into his Avis hire car with a road map, and drove off into the night till he found somewhere suitably lonely to end it all.'

'And where was that exactly?'

'Place called Greenmoor Hill. Near Woodcote. Very lonely. He'd driven the car into the woods. Found the next morning by some kids truanting from school.'

'And do the police know when he died?'

'Not exactly. Sometime during the night. The tank was empty and the ignition switched on, so presumably carbon monoxide just kept on pumping into the car until it ran out of petrol.'

'Right. Well, many thanks for all that.'

'It's extremely unethical, you know.'

'I know. You'd better get off for your interface.'

'Yes. Why don't you join us? We could be there some time.'

'Why don't I? You know, I might. Is it still that Mother Bunch's place?'

'No. Mr Barretta's.' Johnny Smart gave the address and Charles said he'd be along in an hour or so.

As he put the phone down, Charles assessed what new information he now had. The first, and most important, fact was that Danny Klinger

57

who had killed himself in the backwoods of Oxfordshire was almost definitely the same one whose name Andrea Gower had written down. The link with Musimotive made any other explanation too much of a coincidence.

Beyond that, he felt sure that he had other new information which was relevant, but he couldn't sort it out in his mind yet. He needed time, time for his subconscious to work while he was doing something else. Like, say, having an important and meaningful interface with Johnny Smart and a wine bottle.

He took all the money he could find in the bedsitter. It was going to be an expensive evening. He hadn't got much. There hadn't been a great deal of work recently and ever at his back he heard the Inland Revenue's winged chariot hurrying near. Still, he had enough cash for one last fling. Start saving tomorrow.

As he was passing the payphone on the landing, it rang, and he received the second jolt to all his previous thinking on the case.

It was Steve Kennett. 'Charles, I've found something new.'

'What?'

'A letter from Mark to Andrea. I was tidying up her bed this morning and I found it slipped down the side. I didn't want to ring you from work, because there are always so many people eavesdropping. But I've just got in.'

'What does the letter say?'

'It dates from just after Andrea broke off the affair. Mark was writing to try and get her back. It's all a bit melodramatic.'

'That's Mark's style.'

'There are various protestations, recriminations and so on. But there's one bit that seems more relevant – or more worrying, maybe – in retrospect.'

'What does he say?'

'Well, like I said, it's all a bit melodramatic.. . .' She was losing confidence, wondering whether she should have rung to tell him of her discovery.

'Go on.'

'He writes: "I suppose I could learn in time to accept the fact that I haven't got you, and learn to live without you. But what I don't think I could ever accept is the thought that someone else has you, that someone else makes love to you. If I ever found out you had another lover, I would not be responsible for my actions. I couldn't stand it. I would kill you both."'

There was a pause. Charles decided to make light of it, though his mind was reeling with possibilities. 'As you say, very melodramatic.'

'Yes. I mean, knowing Mark, as you say, it's very much his style. Dog in the manger.'

'Yes.'

'It's just . . . now that Andrea's dead . . .'

'I know, everything takes on new meanings.'

'Exactly.'

'I've had a few other thoughts actually, got something new on Danny Klinger. Maybe we could get together and talk about it.'

'Sure.'

He suggested a time, but she was spending the weekend away, so it was left that he would ring her the next week.

As he put the phone down, he wondered if he had been hypersensitive to detect in her voice a slight unwillingness to meet. He really must stop this, a grown man behaving like a teenager over some girl who was totally unaware of his feelings.

He didn't want to think about it. Nor, for the moment, did he want to complete the simple deduction that Mark's letter could produce. He saw no reason to change his previous plan, and set off for Mr Barretta's.

CHAPTER SIX

FOLLOWING THE INSTRUCTIONS on his contract, Charles presented himself at the Paris Studio in Lower Regent Street on the following Monday just before the nine-thirty rehearsal call for *Dad's the Word*. It was the first morning he had felt that all his body fitted into the skin provided since the Friday's heavy interface with Johnny Smart and friends.

He had read his script over the weekend. He didn't find it particularly funny, but put this down to the fact that he could never judge comedy material and, anyway, since this was one of many, perhaps appreciation depended on familiarity with previous episodes. He recognised the name of the writer. Steve Clinton had been responsible for some of the script of *The New Barber and Pole Show*, a somewhat unwieldly vehicle in which Charles had made a brief journey into television comedy. He hadn't found much of that script very funny either.

Dad's the Word chronicled the misadventures of a middle-aged man, who, after a lifetime abroad, returns home to find he has to look after three young children, who call him Dad. Whether he was actually their father, what had happened to their mother, what had brought him back to England (and indeed why he didn't just stay abroad), the script did not make clear, and Charles thought it impolite to ask. The programme was merely a showcase for the talents of a once-loved radio comedian, Dave Stockin (famous in the Fifties for his riotously witty catch-phrase 'This is Stockin knockin').

Stockin was one of those dated characters whom radio management love and from whom the radio audience has slowly drifted away. Nick Monckton was the latest in a long line of producers faced with the challenge of putting Dave Stockin 'back where he ought to be' (as the young producer's boss had put it to him). Nick had more brutal ideas of where the comedian really ought to be, but he was too diffident to suggest them.

Charles hadn't realised on first acquaintance just how shy Nick

Monckton was. But during rehearsal he was uncomfortably aware of the young man's constant nervous movements and sweating brow. The whole thing was a frightful ordeal and the producer was patently scared witless by his star. The tentative notes he gave on lines and performance showed a good sense of comedy, but, if Dave Stockin disagreed on any point, Nick immediately recanted. The comedian had an unpleasantly snide way of asking, 'Look, do you want me to do it your way, or do you want me to do it right?'

Stockin worked in a little sealed unit of his own ego. Charles, with experience of other stars, had been wary, knowing how capricious some could be in their reactions to their supporting artistes, but he need not have worried. Dave Stockin was totally unaware of the other people in the show; he only thought about his own lines and how he could get more of them.

His three children were played by an actress of thirty-seven, an actor of thirty-three and an actress of fifty-four (who took the part of the six-year-old boy). A character actor called Toby Root (one of that band of highly skilled character actors who are never out of work and who, in their quiet way, probably make as much in the long run as most stars) played a travel agent, and Charles Paris had the small part of a second travel agent. The script revolved, needless to say, about Dad's efforts to take the three children away on holiday, with all the predictable mix-ups that might involve. After the ups and downs of a disastrous trip to Skegness, Dad had a brief scene with the second travel agent, in which he tried to book a holiday to the Chamber of Horrors, 'or anywhere else where kids aren't allowed'. The script could have been written twenty years before and, knowing Steve Clinton's zealously conservationist approach to comedy material, probably had been.

The cast assembled for the read-through in the small Narrator's Cubicle, off the main studio, with the communal gloom of people all serving the same sentence for the same crime. They read with lethargic precision and funny voices. Steve Clinton roared hugely throughout and Nick Monckton smiled terrified encouragement.

Compared with television, Charles's most recent experience of this sort of work, it was all refreshingly quick. With the audience arriving at half-past twelve, there was only time for one read-through, notes, a run on mike, more notes and a short break before the show was actually performed. He felt that the script, like some poisons, would be in and out of the system so quickly that it wouldn't have time to do any harm.

After the read-through Dave Stockin, took Nick Monckton on one side to tell him all the lines he was going to change and all the long-

61

remembered jokes he was going to insert into the script, and the cast started desultory conversations among themselves. Like people at a funeral, they spoke of anything but the corpse (or in this case, script).

Charles discovered that he knew one of the actresses from way back. Or at least she knew him. 'Charles, darling, I haven't seen you since *Hot and Cold Running Water* in Cheltenham.'

'Ah yes.' He remembered the production vaguely. ('I don't know who this show was meant to appeal to. Certainly not me, and judging from their reaction, not last night's audience either.'—*Gloucestershire Life and Countryside.*)

The actress then revealed that she was on the BBC Drama Rep. 'Lucky to be working on this series for Light Ent.,' she confided. 'Usually it's difficult to get regular bookings, because of course Drama has first call.'

'Ah.' Charles nodded wisely. He looked at her covertly and with a little surprise. He had long had a private joke with himself that the BBC Drama Repertory Company was made up entirely of actors and actresses so handicapped and disfigured that they could only act on radio. He knew it was untrue, but the fantasy had taken root in his mind and he had difficulty in shifting it. It was a surprise to find the girl had the normal complement of arms and legs.

As they were talking, a young man came in with some enquiry for Nick Monckton. He could have stepped off a pop LP sleeve. He had smartly cut long black hair and wore tight blue jeans and a black T-shirt with 'Sardi's' written in glitter on the front. His expression was one of contempt for his surroundings. When he looked at Nick Monckton, that contempt seemed to grow, and the young producer was aware of it. The nervous movements intensified.

The newcomer turned to go, his query answered, but the Drama Rep. actress called out to him, 'Hello, Keith, back with us then?'

'For a bit.' He spoke without enthusiasm. 'They were short. I basically do Radio Two stuff now.'

'Oh, and, Keith, sorry to hear about . . .' She shrugged helplessly.

He gave as little acknowledgement of the sympathy as he could without actually being rude, and left the room. Charles looked up enquiringly, but got the information unprompted. 'Poor boy, his wife died last week. Well, I say died – committed suicide, actually. I think they were separated, but it must still be a shock for him.'

Charles asked the wife's name and got the answer he expected. So now he had met another of the people in Andrea Gower's life. He raked through his memory for anything Steve might have told him about the husband. Only that his name was Keith and that he had been on an 'attachment'. Presumably if he was back working as a Studio Manager, his attachment had been detached.

Charles got confirmation of this just before the run on mike. Dave Stockin had formed another little huddle with Nick Monckton to graft some more moribund jokes on to the script and everyone was kept hanging around. The rest of the cast started discussing the commercial voice-overs they were doing or the books they were going to record for the blind (Charles hadn't before registered the specialisation of actors who worked mainly in voice), and he wandered through the curtained area at the side of the stage, where he found Keith sitting disconsolately by a table loaded with unlikely objects. 'Are you doing Spot?' asked Charles, remembering the technical term, Spot Effects, for the sounds made at the time of recording.

Keith nodded ungraciously and Charles decided to lay on a little theatrical naïveté. 'I'm fairly new to radio. Is this all the stuff you make the noises with?' He pointed to the table.

Again Keith inclined his head.

'I'm Charles Paris.'

He received a grudging 'Keith Nicholls'. Ah, so Andrea had reverted to her maiden name when the marriage broke up. Or perhaps she had never changed it for work purposes.

Charles looked at the table. 'It's obvious what some of this stuff's for. I mean that bell on a spring must be for a shop doorbell.' Keith regarded this as too obvious to be worthy of confirmation. 'And these buzzers are for other doorbells. . . . And the telephone's self-explanatory. But what the hell's that for?'

He pointed at what appeared to be a shoe box covered in brown paper and sticky tape. He had judged his quarry right. The opportunity to demonstrate his skills to the ignorant prompted some reaction from Keith, who picked up the box.

'It's for marching. Listen.' He placed one hand on either side and shook it rhythmically.

The sound was startlingly like a squad of soldiers on a parade ground and Charles said so. 'Is that how you usually do the Effect?'

'Yes. Cheaper than getting a real lot of soldiers into the studio and the BBC's always keen to find the cheapest way. It's just sand and gravel inside. You can do all kinds of other Effects with it. Listen. . . . Halt. Or, if you like, a ragged halt. Stand at ease. Present arms.'

He illustrated each order with the appropriate twitch of the box and, for a second, looked mildly interested in what he was doing. 'Of course,' he said, 'this studio isn't really designed for Effects. Some of the Drama studios have got steps and gravel pits and rows of different sorts of doors and stuff. I used to do a lot of Spot before I got into the Radio Two group.. . . .'

He seemed to lose interest. He put down the marching box and his expression of lethargic distaste returned.

'That's for a bit where the family goes to the holiday camp run on military lines?' Charles tried to keep the conversation going.

'Yes.' Keith expelled the word as a long sigh, expressing what he thought of the script and life in general.

'It must be an interesting job,' Charles offered.

Keith just looked at him, and he backed down. 'I mean, not all the time, but it must be quite interesting sometimes. And no doubt it's a step in the right direction of production if that's what you want to do.'

'For the last six months,' Keith reflected bitterly, 'I have been working as a producer. This week I'm back here banging doors and rattling tea-cups. Not even doing music, which is what I specialise in.'

'Oh, did something go wrong?' asked Charles, deciding not to appear to know too much.

'Not really. It was just a six-month attachment, working for Radio Two. Now I have to sit and wait for a job to go up on the board and apply for it and . . . oh, shit, it goes on for ever.'

'Did you enjoy producing?'

'I liked the music sessions. The rest was okay. The money was nice. Mind you, you're really cheap labour on an attachment.'

'Oh well,' said Charles comfortingly, 'I expect a job will come up soon.'

'I suppose, if I'm still here, I'll apply for it.'

'If you're still here . . . ?'

'There is a world of commercial-music production of which the BBC seems unaware. In fact, so far as I can tell, the BBC is a conspiracy devoted to keeping from people their market value in the world outside.'

'Perhaps, but a lot of people seem to like working for it. Commands strong loyalty.'

'Not from me it doesn't. And I'm not going to let the BBC or anything else stand in the way of what I should be doing.' This outburst had a sudden intensity. Keith Nicholls was very ambitious and had the share of ruthlessness that that kind of ambition needs.

Charles steered the conversation into calmer water by pointing at another of the Spot Effects on the table. It was a small box, about the size of a clarinet case, painted in black and yellow stripes. There was a latch from which a padlock had been released.

Keith picked it up with a cynical grin. 'That is here because the bloody writer of this abortion can't think of a pay-off to the camping holiday scene. If you can't keep the audience laughing then at least keep them awake.' He flipped back the lid to reveal a very businesslike revolver.

'That looks distressingly real,' observed Charles.

'Oh, it is.' Keith picked the gun out of its padding and pointed it at him. 'It's the real thing all right.' Charles knew the young man was only fooling about, but there was an unpleasantly hard glint in his eye as he looked along the barrel.

'Presumably you only get blanks with it.'

'Oh yes, it's no fun. Just a bloody nuisance actually. You have to get it signed out of the safe in the Effects Library and you aren't meant to let it out of your sight while you've got it. Don't know why, the barrel's spiked, so even if you got a real bullet, it couldn't do much harm.'

'That's a relief. Otherwise you could have some nasty accidents.'

'Hmm.' Keith weighed the gun gently in his hand. Then, in a new, distracted voice, he said, 'I don't think there are any accidents really. I think everything's meant.'

The Paris had once been a cinema and its layout as a radio studio made no attempt to hide that origin. Set below street level, the main studio area contained about 350 seats facing a deep bare stage, with grey curtains at the back, where once the cinema screen had been. Behind the audience, beneath the former projection box, was the Control Cubicle. Through a glass window, from behind the long and sophisticated mixing desk, the producer and senior SM looked down towards the stage. The back row of seats was about two yards from the producer.

However, on that Monday lunchtime, the nearest member of the audience was a good fifteen yards away. Only three and a bit rows at the front were full, and those present sat with the resignation of a geriatric specialist's waiting room (where, judging from their appearance, they probably spent most of their time). The only advantage of their age was that they were well qualified to remember the days when 'This is Stockin knockin'' was on everyone's lips. (Charles, who had never heard the catch-phrase before, secretly wondered whether such days had ever existed, save in Dave Stockin's imagination.)

Tickets for radio recordings were free, and so the shows built up a repertory company of regulars. (No, actually it was not the shows that built up the following; it was the studios. The regulars turned up *whatever* was on.)

Because it was now mid-July, the regulars couldn't be accused of being there for their usual reason, which was to sit in the warm for an hour, but they still presented a somewhat motley appearance. One or two were just well-organised pensioners, taking advantage of free entertainment, but others manifested more positive eccentricity.

Charles was given a run-down of who to expect from the Drama Rep. actress. There was the Indian who wore a Union Jack waistcoat and socks and toted round a polythene carrier full of framed photographs of the Duke of Edinburgh. There was a beaming Spanish matron, who didn't understand a word of any of the shows, but applauded all the music links. There was a tall intense lady who sat in the front row eating bananas and who always tried to get every member of the cast and production staff to autograph her bank paying-in book.

And there was The Laugh. A lady in late middle age, who must have been destined at some point to win the Radio Personality of the Year Award, so great had her contribution been to the cause of radio Light Entertainment. Not a comedy show was broadcast without her trademark, a long trilling cackle, like a demented duck being goosed by a swan. Many comedians and personalities had suffered the diminishing effects of that laugh. Some had tried to defeat it ('All right, lady, you lay 'em, I'll sell 'em' or 'I'd call in the plumber to have a look at that, madam' or 'I think you got the wrong date – the bullfrogs' convention is on Tuesday'), but The Laugh could not be deflected and always triumphed. It became such a regular feature of radio comedy programmes that the listening public might have missed it if removed.

Needless to say, its effect was most devastating in a small audience. There was no hope that it might be swamped by sound from the handful assembled for *Dad's the Word*. And, with an uncanny instinct for immortality, The Laugh was always seated directly under one of the audience microphones.

Charles first heard The Laugh in action when Nick Monckton went on to do his warm-up. The poor young man looked even more nervous as he plunged through the curtains to face the senescent apathy of the audience and welcome them to the Paris Studio. But maybe the reaction to his first line would relax him. He said, 'Welcome to the Paris Studio' and he got a laugh, which should have been an encouraging start. Unfortunately, the laugh he got was The Laugh, and it seemed to fluster him more than ever.

When Charles heard it, he started to giggle. Childishly and uncontrollably. When Nick introduced him and he came on stage to a palsied rattle of applause, it seemed funnier still. The sight of three rows of Old Age Pensioners sunk in their seats and clapping like glove puppets soon had tears running down his cheeks. He sat on his chair and stared fixedly at the script; that should have been enough to stop anything from seeming funny. But for the next five minutes his eyes streamed, he let out spasmodic snorts and his chest ached from the effort of control.

Nick Monckton told the audience that it was a funny show and that they should laugh and, if they didn't understand a joke, they should still laugh and work it out on the way home, and, if someone raised both arms to them, it was a signal for them to clap and not to get up and leave. Then he introduced the 'star of our show, Dave Stockin' and went off 'to see how Max is getting on in the box.'

Dave Stockin walked up to the microphone and said, 'This is Stockin knockin'', which was greeted by a death rattle of applause. He then told the audience that it was a funny show and that they should laugh and, if they didn't understand a joke, they should still laugh and work it out on the way home, and, if someone raised both arms to them, it was a signal for them to clap and not to get up and leave. He then told three jokes, two slightly smutty and one extremely unwholesome. The audience laughed more warmly, in expectation of further filth (an expectation soon to be dashed once the cast started wading through the script, which was as clean as a whistle – and about as funny).

Dave Stockin then, to show what a warm, lovable personality he was, said, 'Finally, there's one more person who I got to introduce to you, a very important person, who's a great chum of all of us here. This is a BBC show and a BBC show can't start without a genuine BBC announcer and we're very lucky to have with us today a very fine announcer, one of the best, who's a terrific fellow and someone we've all known for years – ladies and gentlemen, will you put your hands together and welcome – Mr Roger Beckley!'

Dave Stockin gestured off towards the curtain and a young man in a tweed suit entered diffidently. Stockin threw an arm round his shoulders and led him to the microphone, where the young man said, 'Roger Ferguson is my name actually.'

The recording started. The bouncy signature tune, sounding like all the other bouncy signature tunes on the mood music LPs from which they have been selected from time immemorial, bounced out of the speakers, the announcer made his announcement with a little chuckle in his voice (because he had been told this was Light Entertainment) and the script trickled out.

The audience didn't find it any funnier than Charles had. But they were willing to laugh and react, if only someone told them where the laughs should be. They were fine on applause; every time someone raised their hands, they clapped long and vigorously, with the result that scenes which had gone through without a titter would be greeted at the end by a huge ovation. But laughs were more difficult to orchestrate. Dave Stockin worked very hard and found he could get some by sticking his tongue out or clutching his crotch on relevant lines. He was obviously quite capable of dropping his trousers if necessary.

It was a strange experience for Charles, something his acting career had not up until that point encompassed. Working from a script was one thing, and playing to an audience was another. It seemed odd to see actors standing at a microphone reading to a live (well, almost) audience.

Sharing the microphone with Dave Stockin was also a novel experience. In fact, sharing was not the appropriate word; it was a question of elbowing in and raising one's voice or being totally inaudible. Either because he was a complete egotist, or, more charitably, because he was used to doing stand-up routines in clubs, Dave Stockin worked directly in front of the microphone and very close. This meant that the rest of the cast were put at a considerable disadvantage. The microphone was live over a fairly limited arc, most of which the comedian hogged. The rest of the cast were increasingly pushed round to the flanks, on to the dead side of the mike, where their words made no impression.

The regular cast members coped well with the hazard. Everything is experience, and they had learnt to throw their lines in over Stockin's shoulders, bobbing in and out like small fish scavenging from a shark's teeth. Charles did his best to imitate the trick.

He gazed out over the audience. It was impossible not to see them all. Unnerving. Like his only experience of Theatre in the Round, *The Lady's Not For Burning* at Croydon ('Last night an audience with a hole in the middle was treated to a play with a hole in the middle'—*Croydon Advertiser*).

And then he saw a face he recognised. Sitting in the audience was Mark Lear.

It felt odd to have given a performance (however minimal) and be finished by lunchtime. He remembered the same emptiness after doing his one-man Thomas Hood show, on the Edinburgh Festival Fringe. And he remembered from then that the best way of resolving the mood was to have a drink.

The watering place for people working at the Paris is called The

Captain's Cabin. There Nick Monckton bought a huge round of drinks, terrified of missing out the most menial member of the cast or production staff. Dave Stockin then took him to one side and lectured him on why the show would be better if he had more lines and the rest of the cast had less.

Mark Lear had tagged along with everyone else. 'I met Nick in the Salad Bar the other day and he said you were going to be in this, so I thought I'd come along and give you support.'

'Thank you. We all needed it.'

'Yes.'

'Rather different from Further Education.'

Mark's brow furrowed. 'You know, I'm afraid I don't understand Light Entertainment.'

It was said very seriously and Charles realised that that was exactly what Mark meant. As a professional, he did not understand one particular thread of broadcasting. It wasn't that he had found *Dad's the Word* a bad example of it; all Light Entertainment was equally mystifying. Mark Lear had no sense of humour.

This realisation brought back other suspicions. The lack of sense of humour tied in with the obsessional note in the letter that Steve had discovered. Mark's self-dramatising was not flippant; he always meant what he said.

Charles knew he should start some investigation. Something inside him wanted an explanation of Andrea Gower's death.

And of Danny Klinger's. He felt sure Mark Lear held the key.

But subtly. He had to probe subtly or he'd arouse Mark's suspicions.

An opportunity arose easily in the course of conversation. Dave Stockin had finished his drink and left, causing some mutterings among the SMs. Unlike a lot of stars they worked with, he was a man with long pockets who, even at the end of a series, had never been seen to reach his hands into them to buy a round of drinks. Nick Monckton, relief relaxing him by the second, came over and joined them, offering more drinks. Mark said he'd get the round and while he was at the bar, the conversation turned to a programme from the previous night's television, which had been about human memory. One of the SMs raised the subject and Nick Monckton fell on it avidly, keen to talk about anything, so long as it wasn't *Dad's the Word*.

They discussed the imprecision of human recollection and how half a dozen witnesses of a crime could come up with half a dozen widely diverging descriptions of the same criminal. They moved on to the fallibility of their own memories and, when Mark returned laden from the bar, it was easy for Charles to bring him up to date on the conversation and ask casually, 'I mean, how much do you remember, Mark? Even of recent events. Say last week. What did you do last Tuesday?'

Mark was game to test himself. 'Let's see. Up about eight, office about ten – that bit never changes. Then I . . . let me see, was I in the studio? No, editing. Right, morning spent editing. In fact, editing your Swinburne epic, which I must say sounded very good. I'll fix a playback at some point if you'd like to hear it.'

'I'd love to. But go on, what did you do after your editing? See how your memory holds up.' Charles wasn't going to be deflected so easily from finding out Mark's whereabouts at the time of Danny Klinger's death.

'Okay.' Mark still played along. 'Right . . . lunchtime spent in the Salad Bar, too much wine consumed, in the knowledge that all I had on that afternoon was an ideas meeting with HFE(R). Had said ideas meeting – predictably sterile – my idea for a series of Comparative Marxism and accompanying expenses-paid trip round the world rejected for the millionth time. Then what? – let me think back. Right, a few drinks in the club and then . . .' He looked up, suddenly shrewd. Or was Charles being hypersensitive? 'Yes, of course, back home to Vinnie and the kids. Latter still up, which they shouldn't have been at seven-thirty, but which they always are. Dinner with wife, early bed. Typical domestic evening.'

'Not bad,' said Charles. 'Almost total recall after six days.'

The conversation moved on. One of the SMs started bemoaning how little sociology she remembered from three years at LSE.

It was only after the pub closed at three and Charles was gliding towards Piccadilly Circus tube that he remembered what Mark had said on the night of Andrea's death. That his wife and children were going to spend the next week with her mother.

He was aware, from previous experience, that it was risky impersonating police officers, even on the phone. On the other hand, people do tell things to the police. And from a coin box it wasn't such a risk.

For nostalgic reasons, he decided he'd be Detective-Sergeant McWhirter of Scotland Yard. The Glaswegian voice was one he had first used in a Thirty Minute Theatre ('Is competence the highest we can now hope for in a television play?'— *The Financial Times*).

'Is that Mrs Lear?'

'Yes.'

'Forgive me troubling you, Mrs Lear. This is Detective-Sergeant

70

McWhirter of Scotland Yard. I'm investigating a series of burglaries which took place in your area last week and I'm doing some routine checks. Just asking people if they saw anything suspicious during the week. You know, people hanging about, unfamiliar vehicles parked in the streets, that sort of thing.'

'I'm sorry, I don't think I can help you.' The voice had the bored languor of a girls' public-school education. 'I'm afraid I was away all last week, staying in Gloucestershire with my mother.'

'Oh.'

'My husband would have been here in the evenings. If you'd like me to give you his office number, I could –'

'Oh, no thank you. I needn't trouble him. Most of the break-ins seem to have occurred in the afternoons. We believe it may be schoolchildren playing truant.'

'As I say, I can't help you.'

'No. Well, if you could keep an eye open . . . I'm sure you don't want your house to be the next.'

'Our house is adequately burglar-proofed, thank you,' came the frosty reply. Perhaps not so surprising that Mark felt bound to look outside the frigidaire of his marriage bed.

'Right. So just to confirm, you were away all of last week. From the Monday right through to the weekend.'

'That's what I said.' The phone went dead. Mrs Lavinia Lear didn't suffer fools gladly.

He rang Steve Kennett straight away and, after the statutory wait on the BBC switchboard, got through to her. She was about to leave for a trip to Birmingham where she was producing one end of a current-affairs link-up discussion. The car was arriving in ten minutes at Broadcasting House Reception. He said he'd hurry up there and try to catch her for a quick word before she left. He had something new on Andrea's death.

It took longer than he had anticipated to weave through the crowds of Arabs in Regent Street and, when he finally arrived at the ocean-liner frontage of Broadcasting House, Steve was looking very agitated. A taxi waited on the kerb beside her with the back door open.

'What is it, Charles? I'm really in a terrible rush. Couldn't it wait?'

'It's about Andrea's death – well, not about hers, about Danny Klinger's death.'

'Danny Klinger's?'

Oh God. He realised he had never told Steve anything about the second apparent suicide. And this was hardly the moment for long

71

explanations. Someone inside the taxi called out, 'Come on, Steve. We'll miss the train. Don't just stand there nattering like a woman.'

The gibe stung her. It was presumably, like her bisexual nickname, part of a longstanding fight she had for her identity in a man's world. 'I've got to go, Charles. I'm back on Wednesday. Ring me then.'

'Basically,' he whispered urgently as she stepped into the taxi, 'Mark told me he spent last Tuesday evening, the evening Klinger died, at home with his wife and kids, and I've discovered that isn't true. His wife was away. So he was somewhere else.'

'Yes,' said Steve. 'He spent Tuesday night at my place.'

Charles tried to numb his feelings by a visit to the Montrose, a little drinking club behind the Haymarket, but when he got back to Hereford Road at half-past nine that evening, another shock awaited him.

A note had been pushed under his bedsitter door. Scrawled by one of the Swedes, it read, 'YORE MOTHERINLORE DIE. RING WIFE.'

CHAPTER SEVEN

CHARLES REALLY FELT unsophisticated when he saw how many children there were on the flight to New York. All these cosmopolitan tots were plugging in their in-flight entertainment earphones and summoning stewardesses as if they'd been doing it all their lives (which can't have been very long) and there was he, fifty-one years old, peering round at the unfamiliarity of a jumbo jet interior, locating the loos, reading his safety instructions, checking that he hadn't dropped his passport, and generally making it obvious that he had never crossed the Atlantic before.

And was childishly excited about it. In spite of the sadness of the reason for the trip, he felt a ridiculous glee at the prospect of finally going to America. All kinds of corny songs about Manhattan and Broadway and Fifth Avenue came unbidden into his head and he tried to stop himself from humming them. Apart from showing up his shameful inexperience of the world, it might also be an inappropriate invasion of Frances's mood.

Actually she seemed to be taking it pretty well. The second heart attack had hit her mother the night before she was due to be discharged from the hospital. It had been huge and final. Frances had been business-like and unsentimental when Charles rang through on his return from the Montrose. And she had maintained that practical exterior since then. No tears, just plans, organising the flight (she had done the trip many times before), sorting out things at school so that she could leave in the last week of the summer term. Very practical. Too practical. Charles, know-ing her, knew how much she was holding back. When she relaxed, when there were no longer any arrangements to make, that was when the tears would come.

He had wondered for a dark moment whether she had already broken down, succumbed to tears, but regarded him as now too distant from her to be privy to such weakness. But no, surely she wouldn't think of him as a stranger. In spite of everything, he felt very close to her and thought she sometimes shared the feeling.

He looked around the plane again. Of course all the sophisticated kids were with their parents. Happy families. To outsiders they must look the same. A happy family. The three of them, husband, wife and daughter. Charles, Frances and Juliet.

He took Frances's hand. She seemed to welcome the gesture. By instinct his finger moved to stroke the familiar kitchen-knife scar on her palm. At such moments it was inconceivable that they had ever split up. But he knew such moments were suspended of time, little capsules of experience, magic, but unrelated to daily life.

He looked across Frances to Juliet and the familiar numbness came over him. He knew he felt a lot for his daughter, but a lot of what? Not admiration, surely. She was a reasonably attractive housewife in her twenties, but he found her irredeemably boring. He knew, from observation and from conversations with Frances, that Juliet had deliberately restricted the horizons of her life in reaction against the lack of organisation in her father's, but he couldn't find that a justification for her total predictability.

And yet, although she bored him, she still affected him powerfully. He remembered her as a tiny child, how cuddly she had been, how giving. Then they had got on all right, then they had had a relationship. But not one that could survive growing-up. Presumably that was all he would ever feel for her now, a cumbersome bulk of undefined emotion.

Still, she seemed happy enough. Matched up with her husband Miles, who was apparently doing awfully well in insurance. Charles got on all right with Miles (or as all right as two men could, whose similarity was restricted to their number of arms and legs). The only two things he really objected to were that his son-in-law kept trying to sell him a private pension scheme and then compounded the felony by calling him 'Pop'.

It had been fun leaving Miles at the airport, though. He was in charge of his twin sons, at least until the weekend, when his mother, a strange lady interested in flower-arranging, was going to Pangbourne to help out. Miles, one of those boring young men who could always 'cope' and was 'sensible' about things, was clearly beginning to doubt his omni-competence as the moment came for the twins' mother to leave them. He was in complete control while he explained the intricacies of his camera (which he was lending to his wife at great personal cost), but less secure at the prospect of being alone with his sons.

Damian and Julian, in spite of their names, or perhaps in reaction to their names, seemed determined to show that the sleeping gas of bourgeois convention had not yet penetrated their systems. After the most casual of farewells to their mother, Damian had found a melted Mars Bar, which he proceeded to rub into his hair, and while Miles was attempting to clean that up, Julian, who was in the process of being potty-trained, gravely lowered his dungarees and started peeing against his father's Marks and Spencer's checked trousers.

For a long time Charles would treasure the expression he saw on Miles's face as they disappeared into the Departure Lounge.

He was impressed by how quickly the flight went. All the seasoned cosmopolitan tots seemed to find it boring and predictable, but to his inexperience, the natural breaks were well spaced. First fiddling with the headset, dipping into the in-flight entertainment, noticing how it's always the same names who seem to corner the market on that sort of show biz spin-off production; then having a couple of drinks; then lunch (which, contrary to the accepted wisdom of hardened travellers, he found quite tasty); and then the movie. This was an unexpected bonus. It was a long time since he had last flown at all, and he'd never been on such a long trip, so the idea of watching a film in the middle of the Atlantic was mildly glamorous. The fact that it was an awful movie didn't matter. It passed the time and felt (though it wasn't) like something for nothing.

It was only after the film had finished, while Frances, who hadn't slept for two nights, dozed beside him, that he could think about the two apparent suicides. Since the news of his mother-in-law's death, things had moved quickly and the case had been pushed to the back of his mind. And, he suspected, because of his feelings for Steve Kennett he had been content to leave it there. But now he made himself think about it.

Apart from any emotions it might raise in him, Steve's revelation also provided Mark with an alibi for the night of Klinger's death. Which was inconvenient, because Charles had been working on a theory that Mark had killed Andrea to prevent her from revealing their affair to his wife, and then, following the threat in his letter, had killed Klinger because of his involvement with Andrea.

Mind you, that still required the premise that Klinger had got involved with Andrea. Which was by no means certain. Since they had only been in New York at the same time for four days, they'd have had to work pretty fast. And, since there was no proof that they'd ever even met, and since Mark now had an alibi for the time of the second death, the whole theory began to look pretty tenuous.

Unless Steve and Mark were in league. Maybe the alibi she had supplied for the Tuesday night was a lie, maybe she was just covering up for him. But why? He found it difficult to cast Steve in the role of villain. He was fairly sensitive to real and false emotion and Steve's distress at her friend's death had been genuine.

Then there was Andrea's husband, Keith, the BBC malcontent. But again, why should he be involved in his wife's death? Charles didn't even know if he had been in Broadcasting House at the time. Though that could be checked.

No, probably the true solution was the obvious one. Andrea Gower had committed suicide for reasons of her own which outsiders could only guess at.

And yet . . . And yet . . . Why did he think it was murder? Only really from what Steve had said about her friend and from his own brief meeting with her. Through all the confusion, he couldn't believe that Andrea Gower had deliberately killed herself.

Various other unlikely combinations of circumstances circled through his mind. He must have dozed off. He was wakened by Frances nudging him to do up his seat belt as they approached Kennedy Airport.

The hotel had been described by the travel agent as 'budget', but Charles was still impressed by the presence of a colour television in their room. (Somehow, there had been no question of Frances not sharing a room with him. Equally, it had been with mutual, almost desperate, fervour that they had made love on the evening of their arrival.) The funeral was to be at twelve and they would get there in good time. In the morning he lazed happily in his dressing gown, channel-hopping with glee from the confessional mania of breakfast-time evangelists to patronising children's programmes and endless cartoons. Frances had to chide him into showering and getting dressed in his one suit (believed by archeologists to date from circa 1965 A.D.), reminding him of the seriousness of the occasion.

They met Juliet, pursing her lips with impatience, in the coffee shop downstairs. She said they'd be late for the bus out to New Jersey, from long experience blaming her father for the delay. Frances calmed her, pointing out that they had plenty of time to get to the Port Authority Bus Terminal by ten o'clock. (She retained her ability to understand and memorise the bus system of any town within minutes of arrival.) The funeral was to be at twelve and they would get there in good time. Rob was going to meet them at the bus terminal in Summit. He had offered to drive into Manhattan to pick them up, but Frances had vetoed the suggestion, knowing that he'd have plenty of other things to cope with.

The waiter in the coffee shop was a jolly Italian, who recognised them as English and, as he served pancakes and sausages to Charles, asked which sights they were going to see that day. 'You should try the World Trade Center. Get up to the top. Amazing view there. You'll really enjoy it.'

'Another time, maybe,' said Charles. 'Today we have to go to a funeral.'

'Oh, well, have a nice day.'

The funeral was decorously conducted in Summit. None of the excesses of which Charles had read in articles on American funerals were in evidence. There was no open coffin, nor was he treated to the sight of his mother-in-law made up and dressed in her favourite ball-gown.

But it all seemed unreal to him, like something out of a television series. He kept expecting the proceedings to be interrupted by commercials. Partly, it was the modern discretion of the surroundings, the reticence of muted lights, lush curtains, bright stained-glass and flowers. He missed the anachronism of English churches, like those where both his parents had had their farewells said. Death stirred in him an atavistic need for ancient ceremony.

The other false note was struck by the fact that the minister had an American accent. Charles knew he was being very naïve, that, if he rationalised it, he would realise that in America everyone had an American accent. But, like most British people, his main contact with the United States had been through the country's enormous exports of films and television series. These produced a reflex reaction that anyone with an American accent must be acting. So the minister, with his neatly-trimmed silver-grey hair and the deep sincerity of his voice, looked to Charles like one of those very skilled character actors who turn up in every other American television series. By the end of the ceremony, he could almost put a name to him.

Charles realised that a lifetime of hearing about the States and not being there had filled him with a lot of silly prejudices.

After the ceremony, all the mourners went back to Rob's house for a party. Perhaps a more dignified word should be used, like 'wake' or 'memorial reception', but in fact this one was a party.

It wasn't that they forgot the occasion that caused it. It was just that they had not met for some time and were all agreed that Frances's mother would have preferred to go quickly than return home to be constantly aware of her invalid status. Also, Rob was the only one for whom she had been a daily presence and even he had been weaned from

77

such dependence by her stay in hospital. So, while there was no lack of respect or love for the deceased, it was still possible for them all to have a good time.

Charles certainly did. He was already disembodied with jet lag and a couple of drinks put him into a state of euphoria, triumphantly excited at just being in America.

He also met some very nice people and quickly revised his opinion that all Americans are character actors from soap operas and police thrillers. He got on particularly well with the twenty-seven-year-old daughter of Rob's first marriage, who was called Pattie. There was no sexual attraction (which was just as well, because it would have been singularly inappropriate under the circumstances), they just had similar senses of humour. Everything Charles said seemed to amuse her. She kept giggling and saying, 'Hey, that's neat.'

Charles didn't know what she meant. But he didn't think she was talking about his suit.

The following day Frances had to go and see her mother's lawyer. Charles offered to accompany her, but his lack of enthusiasm was transparent and she willingly released him from the chore. In fact, she was relieved. She didn't like official occasions when she had to define the lack of definition about their marital status.

So she set off in a cab from the hotel after breakfast, looking very businesslike. The night before, as they were going to bed, she had finally broken down, undamming the flood of emotion she had contained for so long. Charles was glad he was there when it happened and she seemed glad of his presence. He knew he was good at comforting her and at such moments he felt useful, a tower of strength, in command of their relationship. It was really the only time – well, then and when they were making love. If marriage were all making love and comforting wives when they cried, he would have been very good at it. But that was only a small part; there was all the waking up in the morning and going shopping and washing up and paying the mortgage and replacing fuses in plugs and spending evenings when there was nothing on the television watching it. Those were the bits that killed.

With his wife recovered and bound for a smart address on the Upper East Side, Charles was left with his daughter. Juliet didn't want to do any sight-seeing yet, but was very keen to buy some children's clothes in Macy's and Bloomingdale's and some toys in F. A. O. Schwarz. Charles tagged along dutifully, giving what he thought to be a reasonable impression of a properly interested grandfather, but it was an audition he failed. Juliet grew increasingly exasperated with his obvious lack of interest in dungarees and Spiderman T-shirts and soon dismissed him, arranging to meet up at one o'clock in Bloomingdale's children's clothes department, where they already had a tryst with Frances.

So he was free. Free to see a sight, go up a tall building, do whatever took his fancy. He walked up Broadway, while he decided how to use this precious bonus of time.

Just walking up Broadway he found exhilarating, just being there. He ambled along, unashamedly tourist, head bent back, fascinated by the height and unexpected peaks of the buildings.

It wasn't how he had hoped to come to Broadway. As an actor and playwright, his ambitions had been starrier. And when his one successful play, *The Ratepayer*, had been running in the West End, there had been talk of a transfer to Broadway.

Talk. Always talk, never action. And always talk to other people, never to Charles. He sometimes felt that all his life he had been in some sort of ante-chamber, an annexe to the real room where real things happened. All he ever did was hear talk through the door. But he had never passed through it. Or perhaps he had never had the nerve to try the handle. So he just knew there was talk. And with *The Ratepayer*'s transfer as with so many other projects, the talk had gone on for a bit, and then they had all stopped talking about it.

But he didn't let the memory spoil his mood. The elusive quality of major success was now for him a fact of life, not a constant source of disappointment. And here he was in New York, with a million sights to see, some of the most amazing feats of architecture in the world, an unrivalled selection of galleries, museums and exhibitions, all there and ready for him. He had only to decide which of them he should go to and hail a cab.

He decided to have a drink and went into a bar.

His first choice proved somewhat uncomfortable. He had sat down and ordered a beer before he noticed the askance looks of the two other customers and the barman's fishnet tights. He downed his drink quickly and left.

It was very hot outside and bright. Nearly August, the sun had gained power during his brief dive indoors. Maybe another drink was a good idea. But how was he to know the proclivities of the many different bars? He had a guidebook. Frances had thrust one into his pocket, convinced that he'd get lost on his own. He fished it out and waited at an intersection, obedient to the 'Don't Walk' light.

Now where was he? Broadway and . . . ? He looked up at the yellow sign on the traffic-light post. West 44th Street. Now why did that ring a bell?

Of course, that was the address of Musimotive, the source of the odd man out among Andrea Gower's cassettes.

It seemed criminal to come so far, to be presented with the opportunity for a little investigation, and not to take it.

The building was extremely tall by British standards, but now dwarfed in a constantly aspiring New York. When it had been built it may well have been the last word in efficiency and sophistication, but sixty years had passed since then and its smartness, like its height, had yielded to newer buildings. It carried an apologetic air of neglect.

Charles pushed through the revolving door and went up to the security desk. The uniform behind it had, like the building, once been smart, but suffered from the same lack of maintenance. It gave the impression of having had many incumbents, but its current owner was Puerto Rican. He looked up at Charles with surly interrogation.

'Good morning, I've come to see someone in Musimotive.' Charles indicated the name on the board behind the security man's head.

'Not here now.' The Spanish intonation was so heavy, Charles half expected the man to add 'gringo'.

'What, you mean, the office has moved?'

'No. Gone, finished, busted.'

'Is that because of Mr Klinger's death?'

The doorman shrugged. He didn't know who Mr Klinger was. He hadn't been there long. It wasn't his business what the people in the building actually did.

'So there's no one in the office now?'

A shake of the head.

'And you have no contact with anyone else from the firm?'

Again the head moved decidedly from side to side.

'What about post?'

'Post?'

The man's bewilderment reminded Charles that he was in a foreign country and should speak the local language. 'I mean "mail". What about mail? Isn't there someone you redirect the letters to?'

The head started its movement, but stopped in mid-shake. 'Oh, mail. Fat Otto picks that up.' He said it as if it were self-evident, that everyone should know it was Fat Otto's job.

'Did he work for Musimotive?'

'Sure. Still does bits for other outfits in the building. Music publishers, you know.'

'Do you know where I can contact him?'

The doorman looked at his large gold watch. 'Most mornings Fat Otto's in Motti's Bar. Two blocks down on the left.'

Motti's was not a gay bar, but Charles still had the feeling he was trespassing. It wasn't a tourist bar and it didn't want to be; the customers all had reserved seats. Charles went up to the bar and ordered a beer.

The barman produced one sourly. He didn't want to extend his clientele.

Charles decided to speak while he still had a modicum of the man's attention. 'I'm looking for Fat Otto.'

The barman wasn't going to waste words on a newcomer. He nodded to a corner table and turned abruptly away. Charles decided not to say thank you; he didn't think he'd get a 'You're welcome' back.

He could have worked it out for himself. Fat Otto was fat. His belly and buttocks were so big that he couldn't sit in the normal upright position, but subsided like a sack against a wall. His legs, crossed beneath him, looked incongruously small, too weak to support their owner's bulk. He was dressed in a marquee of a tartan shirt which bowed out between the buttons to reveal pod-shapes of black sweatshirt. Sweat glistened on his brow. His dyed black hair seemed to grow only on the very top of his head, an optical illusion created by the opulence of his chins. Eyes, nose and mouth looked unnaturally close together, three dots in the big circle of a child's drawing.

Charles went across to the pile of flesh. 'Excuse me, are you . . .' He hesitated. Maybe the man wasn't aware of his nickname. '. . . Um . . . Otto?'

He needn't have worried. 'I don't know about Umotto; I'm certainly Fat Otto.'

'I wondered if I could talk to you about Musimotive?'

Tiny furrows of suspicion appeared in the smooth expanse of face. 'You a cop?'

'No, no, certainly not.'

Fat Otto looked at him for a second, then emitted a wheeze of laughter. 'No, you wouldn't be either.'

'What do you mean?'

'Look, I know cops choose some pretty crazy fronts, but none of them's going to put on an English accent.'

'Why not?'

'Hell, they don't want to be laughed at.' He chuckled with the wheezing regularity of a bicycle pump.

Charles wasn't yet sure how good-natured the insult was, but laughed along and offered Fat Otto another drink. He accepted a Budweiser.

When they were settled, the fat man said, 'I can't tell you much about Musimotive. Never knew much. I only worked there. Danny did all the business.'

'Danny Klinger?'

'That's right.'

'So what did you do?'

'Just the dispatch, packing up the tapes, sending them off, that sort of crap. Answer the phones when he's not there, you know . . .'

The present tense prompted Charles to ask whether Fat Otto knew that Klinger was dead.

'Sure. I heard. Good thing, I reckon. Without the business, he hadn't got anything. And he needed a lot of bread for his . . . you know, the drinking.'

'That was a problem?'

'Not for him it wasn't.' Fat Otto puffed out another laugh. 'Danny sure liked his oil.'

'And you say the business was finished before he died? It's not because he's dead that it folded?'

'Hell, no. He heard about it. Happened while he was in England. I had to call him all the way to England to tell him. I guess that's why he killed himself.' Fat Otto spoke without guilt, even with mild satisfaction. He was only the messenger of bad news; he wasn't responsible for the effect that it had on the recipient.

'When you say it happened while he was in England, what exactly happened?'

'The cops came and said the firm was under investigation. Stop trading. They wanted to talk to Danny. Don't know, maybe they wanted to arrest him, they didn't say.'

'Do you know why?'

The fat head moved resolutely from side to side, rippling its chins.

'You mean you don't know of any malpractices that were being committed in Musimotive?'

'If I understand your question, and I'm not too sure through all those long words, the answer's no. Hell, I only packed up the cassettes.'

Only obeying orders, it was a familiar defence. And yet Charles believed it. Fat Otto gave an impression of detachment. He'd get on with what he had to do and wouldn't ask questions. Just as he felt no connec-

82

tion with Klinger's death, although he had passed on the news that may have caused it, so he would feel no connection with Klinger's crimes, although he may have helped in their execution.

He continued, clarifying that this was indeed his view. 'Listen, I knew Danny Klinger a long time, really long time, and he was always good to me. Whenever he moved on to something new, there'd always be a job in it for me. He was a nice guy, he'd always buy me a drink, always got a friendly word, so, so far as I was concerned, he was okay.

'Now I know he did some bad things, I heard people talk about them, but I never asked no questions. I just didn't want to know. I guess that's why he went on giving me jobs – well, and I hope he kinda liked me a bit – but really I don't know what he was doing. So far as I know, he never made me do anything illegal and that was good enough for me. I told all this to the cops. They kept asking me about the business, I reckon they still think I'm holding out on them, but no way. I just don't know anything – except that he's dead and I'm out of a job.'

'Hmm. Have I got it right – Musimotive produced background music for bars and factories and waiting rooms and lobbies, like Muzak?'

'Yeah, same sort of idea.'

'Did you have anything to do with the music side, the sessions and –?'

'Like I said, I only packed the cassettes and sent them off.'

'So Danny dealt with all the music recording and that sort of stuff?'

'Must have done. There was only him and me.'

'And so far as you know the business was pretty healthy?'

'Seemed okay. I got my paycheck every week. Danny could afford a nice apartment on the Upper East Side, always seemed to have enough for a bottle of Scotch.'

The mention of Scotch prompted the offer of another drink. Fat Otto accepted. The barman had not gained any social graces since the previous order.

When Charles returned with the drinks, Fat Otto's mood had changed. He started on a series of maudlin reminiscences of his former boss. 'He was quite a guy. When I first met him, he worked in this radio station where I was janitor. He used to do the lot, bit of disc jockeying – hell, he was a terrible jock – compiling shows, sorting out quizzes, fixing music sessions, jawboning record companies, organising the bread – it was a public subscription station, kept running out of bread. He was always dashing around, fixing, all the time until . . . well, until he left.'

Charles was quick to pick up the hesitation. 'Was there some trouble?'

'There was always trouble where Danny was. All kinds of talk after

83

he'd gone. Payola from the record companies, selling off pre-release discs, even putting some of the dough they raised on the auctions into his own pocket, but –'

'Auctions?'

'Yeah, they used to have these crazy auctions. When the station ran out of bread, they'd have twenty-four-hour non-stop programmes auctioning off all kinds of trash – you know, pop star's shorts, guitar strings, locks of hair – and the kids'd ring in with bids and they'd make enough dough to keep the station running another couple of weeks.'

How different, Charles thought, from the home life of our own dear BBC. 'And Danny was pocketing that money?'

'Hell, I don't know. Some people said so. Certainly he left the station. Wasn't my business. I liked the guy, and when he called a couple of weeks later and offered me a job in a record-plugging outfit he was setting up, I said sure. And I followed him around since. He was a lot of fun to know. I tell you, he could bullshit his way out of anything.'

'But he never said to you whether he took the money or not?'

'Never mentioned it. Hell, why should he? I wasn't interested. All I know is, him and Mike left at the same time and everyone said it was because of the dough, that they'd had their hands in the till.'

'Mike?'

'Mike was his buddy. Another jock on the station. Another real bright guy. Hell, the things those two got up to. They used to send each other messages over the air. Real dirty talk sometimes, but none of the listeners would ever know, because they had this code. They'd send out dedications and they'd choose discs with some kind of message in them. Hell, they were real guys, those two.'

Charles wanted to press on with questions about Klinger's criminality rather than his lovability, but Fat Otto was not to be deflected from reminiscence. 'I remember a time when Danny was screwing the wife of the guy in charge of the station and they'd got this great thing going where Mike would send a message when the poor jerk of a husband was on his way home. He'd say something over the air and give Danny and the dame time to straighten out the sheets. Don't know how many times they did that. They had these code-words. Mike'd play the disc of *Danny Boy* as a warning, or another one – they'd send out a message to Mrs Joylene Carter of Ditmas Avenue, Flatbush, never forget that. That was the signal that a message was coming. Time for one last screw.' The bicycle-pump laugh started up again at the recollection. 'Hell, Danny was a horny bastard.'

'And was this guy Mike involved in Danny's other business ventures?'

84

'Nope. Don't know what happened to him. Maybe he stuck in the music business, went into some other branch – plugging, producing, agenting – I don't know. Maybe he moved out to Salt Lake City and start selling insurance.' Two more strokes of the bicycle pump.

'What was his second name, this guy Mike?'

'Fergus. Michael Fergus. Never forget, when he was doing the all-night shift, he'd start, "This is Mike Fergus roaming in the gloaming with you until the wee small hours."'

'And you think it's possible O'Grady may also have been involved in taking the money?'

'Listen, I said I don't know anything about money being taken. I don't know nothing from nothing.' For the first time Fat Otto sounded annoyed. Charles bought him another beer and changed the subject. 'You don't know if Danny met an English girl over here the week before his death?'

'Hell, I don't know what he did with his spare time. I didn't have no bug in his bedroom.'

'No, this girl may have come to the office. English, as I say, fairly tall, blonde hair.'

'Oh, her? Yes, I remember her all right.' The small eyes looked at Charles with suspicion. 'She asked a lot of questions, just like you. Had some kind of swanky name.'

'Andrea Gower.'

'That's right.' Fat Otto now talked a lot slower, his suspicions hardening. 'You connected with her then?'

'No, I just know her – knew her.'

'You sure you ain't a cop?'

'Yes. Why do you ask?'

'I figured maybe she was some kind of police.'

'Why?'

'Dunno. Just she came round and a couple of days later we have the cops there closing us up.'

'Did Danny think she was a cop?'

'He never met her. He'd left for England a couple of days before she turned up.'

'Oh, really?' Farewell, all theories based on an affair between Andrea and Danny Klinger.

Fat Otto's expression was now one of total distrust. 'Hell, why is it all you English people get so interested in Musimotive? Did you have dealings with Danny over in England?'

'No, I never met him.'

'But you know the girl?'

'I met her once just before she . . .' No, there was no point in getting Fat Otto involved in all that. 'Just the once.'

'And what about the other English guy, the one who came over in the Fall?'

'Other English guy?'

'Yes, his name was Kelly. That's what Danny called him, Kelly.'

'I don't think I know him. Did he ask a lot of questions too?'

'Not so many. I think he and Danny may have been setting up some deal. They talked a lot.' Fat Otto was going slower and slower, undecided whether to release more information.

'What was this guy Kelly like?'

The gate came down. Nothing else was forthcoming. 'Since you don't know him, I don't see how it matters to you. I gotta go. Doing some deliveries for one of the music publishers.'

Fat Otto, with surprising grace and balance, rose from his seat and walked out of Motti's bar.

It was ten past two when Charles met up with two very cross ladies in Bloomingdale's children's department.

CHAPTER EIGHT

THE SECOND FULL meeting of the Features Action Group had an air of retreat about it.

Held again in John Christie's office, it started at six rather than seven, showing a greater urgency on the part of the participants to get home. And, even with the earlier assembly time, it was considerably less well attended than the first meeting. John Christie read out a long list of apologies at the commencement of proceedings. People were in the studio, they were editing, they were on courses, they were on holiday (the BBC virtually closes down for July and August), some just weren't there.

John Christie welcomed the survivors with the impersonal enthusiasm of a diplomat and said how more certain he was than ever that the setting up of a Features Department was a really tremendous idea and just the thing to get radio out of the doldrums into which it had been drifting for the past few years. He hoped that the assembled company shared his conviction.

At this point Ronnie Barron, the Studio Managers' representative, was called upon to read the minutes of the last meeting, which he did with the pace and variety of a metronome. None of it sounded even mildly familiar to Charles, but he knew he hadn't paid much attention at the time. All he was aware of was that John Christie seemed to have said a lot, ever coming in with a judicious summing-up, ever moving the conversation on to some new tack. He recalled something his solicitor friend Gerald Venables had once said, that the art of meetings is not what you do or say at the time, but what you manage to get minuted. It seemed that John Christie had influenced Ronnie Barron's selective processes.

Charles didn't really care much. When asked, he was quite happy that the minutes should be 'signed as a true and accurate record of what took place at the previous meeting.' However, he seemed to be in a minority.

There were strong objections from the girl with Shredded Wheat hair, who felt that her points about the sexist bias of the composition of the group had not been properly represented, thus compounding the crime of sexist bias and giving a distorted male-oriented view of the proceedings.

Then the young man with the wild beard made a similar defence of his remarks about the lack of blacks on the committee, concluding that he couldn't condone 'the suppression of the workers' right to free speech by the traditional forces of the bourgeois oligarchy.'

Somebody else complained that, though he didn't care from his own point of view, because he wasn't into that kind of reward-seeking, he still found it odd that the minutes contained no reference to the gagging of his programme on Buddhism in the London suburbs.

And, finally, in a long, apologetic monologue, Harry Bassett from Leeds let them know that, in a sense, he was, not to put too fine a point on it and speaking with his regional hat on, not a little disappointed to hear that the minutes contained no reference to the regions.

All this took time to iron out and Charles began to wonder why he had come. The primary reason was that John Christie had rung and asked him and he couldn't think of a previous engagement in time. But also he knew he wanted to see Steve Kennett again, in spite of, or perhaps because of, the mortification which he had experienced at their last meeting.

And he still wanted to know more about Andrea Gower's death. Any contact with the BBC offered the prospect of illumination. He didn't know what he thought now about the case, mostly just confusion, but through it percolated a conviction that a crime had been committed. His strange, in retrospect almost surreal, interview with Fat Otto in New York only went to reinforce that conviction. Something odd was going on somewhere.

The case was only one of the elements of his life that was in a state of suspended animation. There was also his relationship with Frances. The New York trip, in spite of its circumstances, had been good for both of them. They had, in a way, rediscovered each other. The sex had been good, Frances revelling in a new, post-menopausal freedom. In fact they had grown increasingly amorous. The Italian waiter in the coffee shop, who had let the information about the funeral, like all information he received from his customers, slip in one ear and out the other, asked on their last morning if they were on a second honeymoon. And that had certainly been the feeling of the latter part of the trip.

But arrival at Heathrow and the tedious business of getting back into

Central London had dissipated the mood. It was all too mundane, too ordinary. They had caught the new Underground line from the airport and, though Charles had contemplated some kind of declaration and offer to accompany Frances back to Muswell Hill, when the parting of the ways came at Earl's Court, he had only given her a peck on the cheek and the eternal promise that he would ring her. As the doors closed, he had seen her sitting on the train, surrounded by luggage and new purchases, and, not for the first time in his life, felt a heel.

And somehow, in the forty-eight hours they'd been back, he hadn't phoned her. And here he was sitting all maudlin, because he was in the same room as Steve Kennett, whom he believed to be having an affair with another. And he had never even expressed any interest in her.

Once again, he felt confused by the male psyche. Confused by the whole system of marriage. Once again, he concluded that it was a generalised system, designed to suit everyone in general terms all of the time, and suiting no one in detail any of the time.

Helmut Winkler, the mad German, was talking, his fingers embroidering the air. 'How can ve expect to produce interesting features ven ve are zo hide-bound in our sinking about ze whole concept off radio? Now ve should not sink in narrow terms about radio, but in more general terms, of ze philosophy off sound. Radio is not just ze programmes zat are broadcast, it is ze whole mechanizmus off radio, discs, ze cassette players, even television. Each vun off zeese media is anuzzer facet off ze same diamond zat is sound. And any sinking ve do into sound must recognise zese different elements and ze effect zey have on ze philosophical attitudes off man in an audio-society. Radio is not just radio, it is man in radio – more zan zat, it is audio-man in audio-environment. And yet ve go on producing ze same kind off programmes uninformed by zis realisation.

'Vy, for instance, do ve always use ze best bit off tape, vy ze best take? Isn't it better zat ve should use all ze tape, ze bad bits and mistakes viz ze good? Vy shouldn't ve pick up all ze bits off tape zat are left after an editing session and edit zem together in random sequence to create an alternative audio experience? After all, ze creative process should be unpredictable. Vy are ve in radio so committed to outdated concepts of sense and intelligibility? Surely sometimes, and particularly in ze features area, it is necessary to lose the audience to gain truth.'

Charles was convinced that the guy was completely dotty, but he knew from Nick Monckton that such pronouncements had often appeared in *The Listener* under Winkler's name and been greeted with serious academic approbation. Winkler was a licensed BBC intellectual, a species of which management preserved a few in reservations, and who they wheeled out to baffle and sidetrack any committee that might be set up to investigate the future of broadcasting.

But his views were not allowed to pass completely unopposed. The lady from *Woman's Hour* objected, 'I disagree completely. To be intelligible is the first duty of any broadcaster. When we did our feature on hysterectomy, not only did we make a damn good feature, we also made one that every damn person in the listening audience could understand.'

Ronnie Barron of the SMs department had another objection. 'I'm no intellectual, Helmut, but it strikes me that what you suggest is going to be very wasteful of tape. Every year recording tape costs more and we seem to use more of it. In times of straitened financial circumstances, I feel it hardly appropriate that we should be finding new ways of using tape; we should be economising on it, particularly when we have just received a directive from MDR insisting that we do just that.'

Winkler's hands swept away Barron's arguments like shoulder-high reeds. 'I am not concerned viz economy; I am concerned viz ze philosophy off audio.'

'Well, we still have to pay for it. We've recently done a survey on the amount of tape we actually used in the last year and, let me tell you, the findings are pretty shocking. Pretty shocking. Just on normal usage. I mean, setting aside the amount that gets spoiled and the still distressing amount which gets stolen, we –'

Winkler came in again forcibly. 'Look, I'm not concerned zat your staff are a bunch off crooks who keep valking off viz reels of tape –'

'Now that's not true! There have been very few cases where SMs have been found to be guilty of –'

'Now, gentlemen, gentlemen,' John Christie came in, trimming as ever, 'don't let's lose sight of the main issues.'

'But zis is vun off ze main issues. How can ve produce excellent features ven ve are hampered by incompetent studio staff?'

'They are not incompetent! You won't find a more highly trained group of –'

'If they are so good, vy vas it zat my feature on *Ze Metaphor off Similitude* vas massacred in ze editing channel? Mein Gott, I could haf killed ze girl who did zat. Zat blonde girl, Andrea, I could haf killed her.'

Everyone else in the room went cold, but Winkler was unaware of the implications of what he had said, and continued with his diatribe. Charles did a quick mental check. Yes, Winkler had arrived late for the meeting on the evening of Andrea's death, so he could in theory have had time to murder her. Certainly he was mad enough to do anything to someone who didn't share his view of 'ze philosophy off audio' and who threatened his precious programmes. On the other hand, it did seem pretty unlikely that this loony would set up such an elaborately disguised crime. Still, it was all food for thought.

John Christie managed to defuse the argument between Winkler and Barron, but unfortunately surrendered the floor to Harry Bassett from Leeds. 'I think it may be that I have a, as it were, solution to what can only be defined as the problem which we are, in a sense, talking about. It's something that most of us – and I hope I'm not being ungallant to any of the weaker sex amongst us –'

'I don't know who you're talking about,' seethed the girl with Shredded Wheat hair.

'Pardon me, I'm sure.' Bassett wiped his moustache. 'As I say, it's something many of us grew up on and something that we, out in what I hope are not the backwoods of regional broadcasting, are still not averse to the practice of. I refer, as those of you who have anticipated me will realise, to Live Broadcasting. We didn't use so much tape back in the halcyon days when everything was, as it were, live. Just the broadcaster there was, with the old apple-and-biscuit microphone . . .'

He droned on. Charles stifled a yawn. Not over the jet lag yet. His mind wandered.

He came back to life when he heard his name mentioned. John Christie was looking at him. 'Do you think that's the sort of thing you'd be interested in doing, Charles?'

'Well . . .'

'Oh, I'm sure it'd really be your scene,' bubbled Nita Lawson enthusiastically. 'I mean, with your experience of writing features and a subject like Dave Sheridan, I think it could really be a knockout.'

'Er . . . yes.'

'And you think it should be pitched at Radio Three, Nita?'

'Yes, I do, John, quite definitely. I figure one of the big hassles in this media – and all the others – and one of the reasons why things like this whole features scene get so heavy is that there isn't any cross-fertilisation between the different arts. I mean, particularly in music. Like I'm not saying the LSO and ELO are exactly the same, but they are in the same bag. I think we all gotta get less uptight about the differences between the arts and really get it together on the similarities. Radios One and Two are very big in the national culture and are going to be even bigger when twenty-four-hour broadcasting really gets away. And I think that for Radio Three heads to get into what Radio Two or Radio One heads dig has gotta be good news, hasn't it? And I mean, Dave Sheridan is a really great guy. I mean, like the public have got this really wrong image of what disc jockeys are about. They seem to think they're just mindless jerks who talk nonsense all the time. I don't know why.'

'Maybe they've listened to them,' murmured Nick Monckton.

'So I think a feature like this could really get everyone into the same groove, a bit of an eye-opener all round.'

John Christie gave an Olympian smile. 'Well, that's terrific. Our first positive proposal for a feature, and I must say it sounds a most interesting one. The idea of a mix of cultures is exactly the sort of lateral thinking that a creative umbrella unit like the Features Action Committee should be coming up with. A programme about a Radio Two personality, written by someone with a background of writing poetry features and aimed at a Radio Three audience cannot fail to be a stimulating departure.'

Or a total disaster, thought Charles. He saw Steve Kennett was looking at him. She smiled. He looked away.

'Charles, Charles.' She caught up with him as he hurried along the Sixth Floor corridor.

'Hello.'

'Don't rush off like that, please. There's something I've got to explain to you.'

'Really?'

'Yes. It struck me, after I left you last time, you must have thought I meant that Mark had spent the night with me.'

'Well, that's what you said.'

'Yes, but what I meant was – yes, he did spend the night at my flat, but no, he didn't *spend the night with me*. Do I make myself clear?'

Charles felt the beginning of a warmth within him. 'Yes, you do.'

'I would just hate you to have got the wrong impression.'

It really seemed to concern her. The warmth grew. She continued, 'I'll explain. Do you fancy a drink?'

'What, in the club?'

'No, I'm sick of this place, been here all day. We can have one back at the flat. It's on your way. Okay?'

'Okay.' Charles positively glowed with warmth.

'He is such a sod. He claimed he just wanted to come round to talk about Andrea, but of course he was trying to get into bed with me. I was meant to be all sympathetic and fall for his vulnerability and boyish charm. Well, I'm afraid the magic didn't work.'

'So he left in the small hours?' Charles's mind was making quick calculations. If Mark had left even at three o'clock, he would still in theory have had time to drive down to Woodcote, meet up with Klinger and . . .

But that idea was soon quashed. 'No, he was here all night. Gave me some pathetic line about being afraid to go back to his empty house, where he would just lie awake, haunted by the memory of Andrea. God, he was so spineless. So I let him spend the night in here. I think in his devious little mind he thought I might soften and come rushing in, begging him to honour my bed with his presence. Mark is one of those awful men who was told by someone – probably his mother – at a very early age that he was irresistibly attractive to women, and no amount of evidence to the contrary can shift that conviction.' She added ruefully, 'That seems to be the only sort of men I meet.'

'Do I gather from your tone that there's another of them on the scene at the moment?'

'There was. A young man called Robin. Also convinced he's God's gift to the female race. Works in the Beeb, inevitably. News reporter – travels a lot. We were quite – what should I say? close? thick? – until a couple of months ago. But now I think I can finally say it is over. Yes, I am an unattached bachelor girl, footloose and fancy-free.' There was more irony than insouciance in her words.

'I see.' Charles stored the information and tried to sound businesslike. 'Anyway, it seems that Mark is ruled out of any connection with Klinger's death.'

'Seems so.'

'What about Andrea's, though? Did you find out any more about his movements on the evening *she* died?' he asked.

'You mean, when he left the meeting for the booze?' Charles nodded. 'Yes. He told me that he did talk to her.'

'You mean he went into the channel where she was working?'

'Yes.'

Charles sat up, nearly spilling his wine. 'Good God. That changes everything, doesn't it?'

Steve sighed. 'I don't know whether it does really. Certainly not if you are still thinking it may have been murder. I mean, if he'd killed her and kept his visit to the channel a secret all this time, surely he wouldn't tell me about it.'

'I suppose not. Mind you, he has got a streak of exhibitionism in him.'

93

'You can say that again.' Steve screwed up her face with dissatisfaction. 'On the other hand, his seeing Andrea that evening does give support to the suicide theory.'

'In what way?'

'We were looking for something that could have changed her mood from one of euphoria to self-destruction. I would imagine a visit from lover-boy, treading with his usual sensitivity, could have done the trick.'

'Yes.' Charles mused. 'Oh, incidentally, you know our theory about Andrea having had an affair with Danny Klinger? I'm afraid that's fallen apart too.' And he filled her in on his visit to New York and conversation with Fat Otto.

When he finished, there was a silence. Then Steve said, 'It's very odd. Everything now seems to point towards suicide in Andrea's case and I think I'd accept that, but for one thing.'

'What's that?'

'The cassette. That's the one piece that doesn't fit. For a start, that Andrea, with her love of classical music, should possess such a thing. God, to think of the things she used to say about those terrible Radio Two music sessions she had to do, and yet the music on the cassette seems, to my untutored ear, to be virtually indistinguishable. Then one couples that with the fact that apparently something is rotten in the state of Musimotive, something bad enough to cause the normally ebullient Mr Klinger to kill himself. And she had Klinger's name written on the cassette.'

'And, we know from Fat Otto, she did actually put in an appearance at Musimotive.'

'Yes.'

'But didn't meet Klinger.'

'No.'

'You don't suppose . . .' Charles said slowly, 'that she had found out what it was that was wrong at Musimotive. I'm thinking of all those strange things she said on the night of her death about investigative journalism, about the truth having to come out. Previously, I had only thought of that in relation to her telling Vinnie Lear about Mark's infidelity, but really it's much more likely that it referred to some major crime she had stumbled on. There seems strong evidence that something criminal was happening at Musimotive, and we know that she went there only a few days before her death. Isn't the most likely thing that she had found out the details of Klinger's dirty deeds and had to be silenced before she told anyone?'

Steve Kennett's huge eyes sparkled. 'Yes, now that does make sense. I mean, it's quite possible that she passed on whatever she knew to the New York cops and that is why the company was raided and closed down.'

'So the damage was done. In that case, why should anyone bother to silence her?'

'Klinger was so furious that he killed her out of revenge for ruining his operation . . . ?' She didn't sound very convinced.

'Hmm. And then a few days later killed himself? Out of remorse for having killed her?' Back to bloody remorse. 'I don't like cases where the murderer kills himself. They are unsatisfying. You can't prove anything.'

'No.'

'On the other hand, it is the most likely solution we've come up with so far. Andrea shops Klinger, he kills her, then kills himself out of guilt – or because his business has fallen apart. Open and shut case. Dull, though. I don't like it. Let's pretend we haven't thought of it. Let's concentrate on someone else. Back to Mark – how about that?' he suggested randomly. 'Mark at least saw her on the night of her death. Did he tell you what he said to her?'

'According to him, he just went into the channel because he was passing – though going down to the Fifth Floor is a strange route from John Christie's office to the club. Anyway, he says he just offered to get her a coffee. They got talking, he got the strong impression that she no longer wanted anything to do with him, and left.'

'Makes sense.'

'Mind you, that's a translation of what he actually said. It didn't come out in those words. I had to read between the lines of his ego. He presented the case as that of the poor misunderstood lover trying to explain himself to the woman who had so capriciously rejected him. And of course he was also angling everything so that I should take pity on him and offer half my bed. He has an extremely devious mind, your friend.'

'I don't know him that well,' Charles offered in conciliation. 'Tell me, did Andrea accept the offer of a cup of coffee from Mark?'

'Why do you ask?'

'There was a cup of coffee in the channel. It contained traces of Mogadon. An unscrupulous person, who wanted her too dopey to object to the idea of committing suicide – or at least appearing to commit suicide – could easily bring her the coffee with the Mogadon already crumbled into it.'

Steve nodded in admiration. 'Yes, I like that. But I'm afraid the answer's no. Andrea refused Mark's offer of coffee – at least according to him. She already had one.'

'Which someone else could have supplied.'

'Yes. Or which she could have got herself.'

'Where from?'

'At that time of night, either from the Eighth Floor canteen or one of the machines.'

'Coffee from machines doesn't come in those polystyrene cups, does it?'

'No, that's true. It comes in thin white plastic.'

'So the coffee came from the canteen.'

'Yes.'

'Would she have had time to get it herself before she started recording the football?'

'Depends when she left the club. I talked to some of the people she was with, actually, and they said she had to rush off to get to the channel in time.'

'And she wouldn't have gone to the canteen once the match had started?'

'Not Andrea. She was meant to be there monitoring the recording to see that nothing went wrong. She may have complained a lot about the job being boring, but she was very conscientious.'

Charles smiled. 'So it looks as if we may have found out something new. Someone did bring a cup of coffee to her in the channel.'

'And that person could have been the murderer.'

'Could have been. If it's a murderer we're after.'

'Klinger?'

'I suppose that's the most obvious solution, but it does mean Klinger must have done his homework very well. To know that that was where she would be, to know where to get coffee in Broadcasting House, even to get inside the building at that time of night . . . I don't know, it strains my credulity.'

Steve shrugged. 'He's the only one we know with a Musimotive connection.'

'Yes. I just wish there was someone else, someone inside the BBC – that'd make so much more sense. Is there nobody else in the Features Action lot who has any connection with New York?'

'Possibly. I've *been* there and I dare say a lot of the others have, but that's not what you'd call a connection.'

'No.' He grimaced. 'Why did Andrea go?'

'To New York? For a holiday . . . To get away from Mark . . . To assert herself.'

'What do you mean – assert herself?'

'Well, to show she could do things on her own, that she was independent. I think she went particularly because Keith had gone.'

'Her discontented husband?'

'Yes, he went over some time last year, and I think she wanted to prove she was quite as capable of doing it as he was. They were terribly competitive, even after they split up – I think in Andrea's case, especially after they split up. She wanted to prove not only that she wasn't dependent on him emotionally, but also that she could do just as well as he could in her career. I think that professional jealousy was as much a reason why they split up as his infidelities. It was okay when they were both on the same level as SMs, but when he got his attachment and became Kelly Nicholls the Producer, she really felt she had to do something to assert herself.'

'I thought his name was Keith.'

'Oh yes, when he was an SM. But he didn't think that sounded impressive enough for a producer. So he started to call himself Kelly.'

CHAPTER NINE

'KELLY?' CHARLES REPEATED the name, but did not explain what it meant to him. Previous cases had suggested that one could be too lavish with murder allegations.

'Yes,' said Steve. 'A lot of people get dissatisfied with their names when they know they are going to be broadcast at the end of programmes . . .'

'To the listening millions.'

'Oh, come on, this is radio. To the listening thousands. Yes, you find a lot of people sprouting middle initials and hyphens and second barrels. Or, like Keith, having complete name-transplants.'

'Hmm. One of the oldest forms of cosmetic surgery. Favoured by the immigrant, the social climber and the criminal.' Steve smiled and poured him some more wine as he continued, 'Tell me, what's Keith like? I've only met him once.'

She grimaced with the effort of encapsulating his character. 'Well . . . he seems to think the world owes him a living, that what he is doing is beneath him.'

'Is that true only of his current job or of whatever he's doing?'

'I don't know. I sometimes think it's everything. Even sex. I think he feels all the little girls he screws so avidly are beneath him in more senses than one.'

Charles grinned. 'Tell me, has Keith, or Kelly, ever been in any trouble?'

'Trouble? How do you mean?'

'I don't know. Financial trouble, trouble with the law, trouble with BBC Management . . .'

'Hmm. He hasn't always been universally popular within the Beeb. He can be very bloody-minded when he wants to be.'

'I can imagine it.'

'I think he's had the occasional ticking-off for that. Then a few years ago he was reprimanded for illicit tape-copying.'

'Translate that for the layman, please.'

'It's something that happens quite often – at least Andrea said it did. Particularly on music sessions. The MD or one of the other musicians wants a tape for his private collection or for demonstration purposes or something, and if he knows the SM, he slips him a quid to do an extra copy.'

'On BBC tape?'

'Usually, yes.'

'So that's the sort of thing Ronnie Barron was talking about – or rather that Helmut Winkler was talking about and Ronnie Barron was denying.'

'Yes. I don't know how much of it goes on now. Only very few people were ever involved and, since there's obviously been some kind of clamp-down and indeed nowadays everyone's got their own cassette players to record off the air, maybe it doesn't happen anymore.'

'But it did with Keith . . . ?' Charles prompted.

'Oh yes. Sorry, I'd forgotten where we started. Yes, a couple of years ago Keith was found to have been doing it on a fairly regular basis and was duly hauled over the coals for it. I shouldn't think he does it anymore, now he's reached the dizzy heights of producer. Mind you, he was always on the look-out for some scheme to make a fast buck. Used to keep trying to invent formats for panel games and things. He's got quite a good sort of crossword brain.'

'Hmm. Of course, the producer's thing was only an attachment. And it's over now. He might be hard up again.'

'You're more up to date on his movements than I am. I haven't seen him for months.' A thought struck her. 'Why, are you suspicious of Keith?'

Charles shrugged. 'I'm suspicious of everyone.'

'Even me?' For the first time in their relationship, there was something girlish, almost coquettish, in her demeanour.

It was an obvious cue for him to make some verbal advance, but he didn't take it. The change of manner was still ambiguous and he didn't want to risk their growing empathy by moving too quickly. He liked her rather too much for that and he hadn't forgotten her remarks about Mark and men who can't be shaken in their conviction of their own attractiveness.

So he just replied, 'Yes, even you,' and rose slowly to his feet.

She didn't demur and accompanied him to the door. 'So you're continuing the investigation?'

'Oh, very definitely. It's rather handy that I'm meant to be seeing Nita tomorrow. She'd know more about Keith's behaviour at work than most people. And I wonder . . . How are your contacts in the SMs' world?'

'Pretty good.'

'Would you be able to check out Keith's movements on the night Andrea died?'

'I should think I could manage that.'

'I'll say goodbye then.' He kissed her gently on the forehead, which was at an appropriate height for such a gesture. It seemed an appropriate gesture too. As he walked home, he felt as close to her as if they had slept together. Time, it only needed time.

The phone rang the next morning, just as he was about to leave for an appointment with Nita Lawson to talk about the Dave Sheridan feature. It was Frances.

'Sorry, Charles, I just had to ring someone and tell them. I've done something very rash.'

'What?'

'I'm still shell-shocked from it.'

'Come on, tell me what it was.'

'I've bought a car.'

'Great.'

'Brand new. I've never written a cheque for so much money. I'm trembling.'

'You shouldn't. It sounds a good idea. Get what you can out of it before all the oil wells dry up. You've got less than twenty years.'

'But, Charles, I do feel awful about it. Awful and excited.' Her voice was very young; it was the Frances whom he had married. He warmed to her.

'What is it?'

'Renault 5. And I'm having a radio put in. With cassette.'

'Good.'

'I do really need it. Bus is awfully unreliable for getting to school. And since term's just ended and I was feeling low after Mummy's death . . . And I know there'll be some money coming there, so I got out all my savings from the Building Society and . . .'

'Stop justifying yourself. I think it's a very good idea.'

'Oh, do you? Good.' She sounded pathetically relieved. It was at such moments that Charles felt worst about having left Frances, when she needed someone to discuss things with, someone to be a sounding-board for ideas. 'Trouble is,' she continued, 'I am terrified at the idea of driving it. It's so long since I've driven anything, and the thought of having something whose bodywork I actually care about . . .'

It was true. The cars they had had as a married couple had not been noted for their elegance.

'You'll soon get back into it.'

'Yes, I suppose so. What I'd better do is go for a couple of long drives with someone else in the car and then I'll feel all right.'

Frances never begged, she was too proud for that, but Charles could hear the appeal in her voice and volunteered to go for a drive with her. She was probably taking delivery of the car the next day, she would phone him when it arrived and they'd make arrangements.

He lingered by the phone after their conversation, confused again by his ability to feel such strong affection for Frances, while dreamily contemplating an affair with another woman. Quickly deciding that such speculation was without purpose, he set off for the BBC.

Nita Lawson's office was in Ariel House, a tall, modern building in Charlotte Street, which was the home of Radio Two. In the foyer, disc jockeys' photographs beamed and everything proclaimed the belief that 'Two's Company'. The furniture in the office was neat and modern, but with that recoil from the edge of luxury which characterised all BBC décor. Nita's status as Executive Producer of the *Dave Sheridan Late Night Show* did not quite qualify her for a two-part office with secretary in the ante-room, so, throughout their conversation a girl called Brenda, a trendily dressed blonde teenager of thirty-seven, reacted nasally to revelations from the other end of the telephone.

Nita smiled brightly. Behind a desk, she readily prompted the image that had been eluding Charles since he first saw her. A village post-mistress behind her counter. A pile of letters in front of her reinforced the impression and the unlikely colour of her long red hair did nothing to remove it.

She indicated the letters. 'That's just today's lot for Dave. He seems to get more popular by the minute. The public really dig him.'

'Ah,' said Charles. 'Good.'

'Yes, it's partly because more and more people are getting into his musical bag, but also of course it's Personality with a capital P.'

'I'm sure it is.'

'But don't you think the idea of doing a feature on Dave is just too much?'

Charles said he thought it probably was.

'Triff. I think we could really be on to a biggie. And it's gotta be put out on R3. Show 'em what popular culture really is. I don't think there should be this big divide between classical and pop..It's all music, so far as I'm concerned. I mean, some of the sounds that are being made on the heavy metal scene are just . . . wow, well, mind-blowing. Not of course that that's Dave's scene. But, I mean, take Country. Are you into Country?'

'Um . . .' Fortunately Nita continued before Charles could say that actually he lived in Bayswater.

'You see, I think Dave could be big anywhere along the cultural scene. He's so together. I think a feature on him for R3 could really turn on a whole new audience.'

Charles was rescued from further reaction by the arrival of their conversation's subject. Brenda looked up from her telephone conversation and said, 'Hi, Dave.'

'Hello, beautiful.' The tall disc jockey gave her a peck on the cheek. Nita rose, blushing, to be similarly rewarded.

'And this is Charles Paris.'

To his relief, Charles didn't get a kiss. Sheridan shook him firmly by the hand, 'Yes, of course, I saw you at the first Features Action Group Meeting.'

'Yes.'

'Sorry I couldn't make it last night, Nita love. Simon wanted to rehearse.'

'Is that going all right?' asked Nita anxiously.

'Yes, sure.' Sheridan sounded relaxed. 'You know, new producer, new ways of working. It'll level out. He'll start to trust me soon.' He grinned boyishly.

'Dave, do say if he's fussing you. Simon hasn't done your sort of show before and I know he's slow, so if you're not getting on . . .'

'We're getting on fine. It's just he doesn't know I've been disc jockeying for years all over the world and he wants to *produce* me. Natural enough, and indeed very good for me – makes me think about what I'm doing, which doesn't hurt.'

'So long as he's not bugging you . . . ?'

'No way. Nice lad. I'm very happy to listen to his ideas. Mind you,' he added, 'I've a feeling that it'll be my style that will win through.'

It was said without arrogance, but there was an underlying firmness. Charles got the feeling that the new producer, Simon, would have to change his style of working with Sheridan or suddenly find himself on another show. But he admired the skill and charm with which the disc jockey registered his complaint.

'I'll have a word with him,' said Nita, writing a note on her pad. 'Actually, Dave, you missed a knockout idea that came up at the meeting last night. I suggested we ought to do a feature on you, you know, about being a jock, the kind of cultural mix you're into. Not bad, eh?'

'Interesting idea, certainly.'

'Yeah. I mean, it won't be any hassle for you. That's why Charles is here, really. Thought he might be the man to get it together.'

'Sounds fine,' said Sheridan.

Charles detected a note of uncertainty in the voice and said, 'I'm not a great expert on pop music, but I'm always interested in something new.'

'Thought it might be groovy getting in someone out of a different scene,' interposed Nita.

'Terrific idea,' said Sheridan. He wasn't dismissive, but he didn't sound that interested. The feature would be a novelty and might be quite amusing, but it wasn't an advance in the mainstream of his career. Sheridan would cooperate out of goodwill, but it wasn't important to him.

'We must all three get together and talk about it soon,' suggested Nita.

'Yes, good idea,' Sheridan agreed. And then, sliding gracefully off the hook, 'I'd say now, but I just came in to collect the letters. I've got to dash over to Telly Centre. Meeting about the next series of *Owzat?*'

'We'll get it together another time then. Glad there's a new series coming.'

'Yes, last lot did quite well in the ratings.'

'I always knew you'd be a great chairman of a quiz. Do you know, Charles, when they were setting up the first series of *The Showbiz Quiz* here on radio and were looking for a chairman, I said you gotta use Dave. They didn't of course, then telly picks him up, and, wow, it's a monster!'

Sheridan smiled in self-depreciation. 'Better take the letters. What've we got today?'

'Usual mix. Daily adoration from Mrs Moxon – do you know, Charles, there's this woman who writes to Dave every day, she's quite besotted with him, records every single show off the air, sends him birthday presents . . .'

'Gets slightly embarrassing,' said Sheridan with his engaging grin. 'What else?'

'A lot asking about that Jack Buchanan number you played on Monday.'

'I thought that would get the nostalgia buffs going.'

'Oh, and one letter of complaint.'

'About what?'

'Some guy in Hemel Hempstead's very uptight. Says why do you keep playing the same music all the time. He says he thinks the *Londonderry Air* is very inappropriate when we've got all these hassles in Northern Ireland. He's some kind of crank, obviously.'

Sheridan was mystified. 'The *Londonderry Air*? I've never heard of it, let alone played it.'

'Oh, you have, Dave, except you probably don't know it by that name.'

'Well, what's its other name?'

'*Danny Boy*.'

Charles felt a little surge of excitement.

'Oh, *Danny Boy*,' said Sheridan. 'Yes, we did play it a couple of times recently. Producer's favourite, I think. As you know,' he put on a voice as if reciting, 'in the BBC, so as to avoid any charges that the disc jockeys have undue influence over the choice of music, the running orders are worked out by consultation between the producer and the jock. And, if the producer has a favourite song,' he shrugged, 'it's rather difficult for the disc jockey to disagree.'

'Oh, I see,' said Nita. 'Well, I'll have a word with Simon about it.'

'I think this was a few weeks ago,' said Sheridan. 'Before Simon took over.'

'Oh, while Kelly was producing?'

Nita had to leave for an early lunch date, but said that Brenda would sort out a pink visitor's security pass for Charles and answer any queries he might have about the organisation of the *Dave Sheridan Late Night Show*.

To Brenda's delight, he professed himself very interested in how all the paperwork of music programmes was organised, and she seized with both hands the opportunity of initiating him into the mysteries of the P as B. This was something she did quite often, but usually to trainee production secretaries on Staff Training courses in the Langham, rather than to fifty-one-year-old actors.

Basically, reading through the information about production numbers (and how much worse it had been since they introduced the computer), the circulation list and the details of music reporting, Charles understood that a P as B stood for 'Programme as Broadcast'. It contained all of the relevant information of the ingredients of the programme, lists of artists, writers and anyone else who might need paying. It was typed up by the production secretary as soon as possible after transmission and it was one of the most time-consuming parts of a secretary's job. (Charles found a sympathetic nod was appreciated at this point.) In the case of a music show, or *any show containing the use of gramophone records* (Brenda stressed this point fiercely, as if Charles was about to go off and type up a P as B of his own with improper music reporting), all details of titles, writers, publishers and durations must be put down, so that the various payments due through the Performing Rights Society and other bodies could be made.

Restraining his impatience, Charles listened meekly through this lecture and then asked, with the casualness learnt of a lifetime as an actor, if he might see an example of one. And, even more casually, since they had been talking about the letter from a man in Hemel Hempstead, why not one of the ones with *Danny Boy* in it?

This suited Brenda well, because it gave her the opportunity to demonstrate the efficiency of her filing system. 'Oh yes, I can show you that one easily,' she said, removing a large ring file from the shelf. 'I remember it because I had to do an amendment.'

'Oh really? Why was that?' asked Charles sympathetically.

'Because they changed one of the numbers.'

'I don't understand.'

'Well, you see . . .' Brenda warmed to her task. It was wonderful having such a meek listener to her wisdom. Some of those trainee production secretaries could get a bit pert. 'What I usually do, to save time, is I get on with the P as B of the previous night's show first thing in the morning, before Nita comes in. And I just work from the running order. Quite often, by the time the programme boxes come back from the studio, I've already finished the P as B.'

'Oh well done,' murmured Charles.

Brenda took it quite straight and positively preened herself. 'Then, when the script comes back from the studio, I just check through to see there haven't been any changes, and get my P as B down to Duplicating.'

'I see. But on this particular occasion there had been a change?'

'Yes, and I had to Snopake over the item and retype it. I don't like doing that. I know I'm the only one who sees it, because it's only on the original, but I don't like things to look messy.'

'No. I wish more girls today had that sort of pride in their work,' said Charles. It was a line he had once had in a radio play where he played the part of an office manager ('About as exciting as a cold cup of tea.'—*The Observer*).

Again it was the right thing to say. Brenda glowed. 'Here we are.' She held the file open. 'Look, it was the opening number they changed. You can see the Snopake. Yes, they changed it to *Danny Boy*.'

Charles looked at the date. It was the P as B for the programme which went out on the night of Andrea Gower's death. The producer's name was Kelly Nicholls. The same Kelly Nicholls who, according to Fat Otto, had 'talked a lot' with Danny Klinger. The Danny Klinger who used to receive messages over the air prefaced by the playing of *Danny Boy*.

'That's extremely interesting. I say, it wouldn't be possible for me to have a copy of this, would it? But no, I suppose you don't keep spare copies.'

The tone was absolutely right. Silently, even smugly, Brenda reached into a filing cabinet and produced a spare copy of the P as B. 'There's always someone who loses one. I keep some spares.'

'You're very efficient.' He winked.

She beamed.

Charles looked down the list of titles. After the opener, none of them had any special significance for him. His mind was searching for a musical code like that described by Fat Otto, but the P as B didn't immediately offer anything. 'Brenda, is the programme just records?'

'Well, records and tapes. And the telephone competition, *Ten for a Tune*. And the Dave Sheridan Bouquet.'

'What's that?'

'It's a listener's choice of ten records. They get sent a bouquet of roses if their lot's selected.'

'Ah. And that's all the programme's ingredients?'

'Well, that and Dave's chat. Dedications, and so on.'

'Dedications. Who chooses which dedications they do?'

'It's done by Dave and the producer together.'

'And who has the final say?'

'The producer, I suppose.'

'Hmm.' Thoughts were orbiting his mind at vast speed. 'The programme goes out live, doesn't it?'

'Yes.'

'So it's not recorded in the building?'

'I don't think so. I'm not sure. It may be monitored somewhere, in case of libel, that sort of thing. I know they record some, but I'm not sure where.'

If Brenda didn't know, then the information was probably not generally available. But even as that idea was knocked down, another rushed in to take its place. 'Do you know, Brenda, I've had a very good idea of where to start with this feature on Dave Sheridan.'

'Where?'

'I'll go and see his Number One fan.'

'What, you mean Mrs Moxon?'

'Yes. Do you have her address?'

The address was a surprise. The name and the whole idea of a woman who devoted her life to the worship of a disc jockey had suggested to Charles an impoverished and slightly loopy pensioner in one of the poorer suburbs. Certainly, it hadn't prepared him for the elegant basement flat in Holland Park, nor for the equally elegant lady who opened its door to him.

Obviously he'd come to the wrong place. 'I am sorry, I was looking for Mrs Moxon.'

'I am she.' The oddity of the expression, and the way the woman held back from the door struck some kind of warning note. A hint of mental instability, perhaps.

'Oh. Good afternoon. I've come to talk about Dave Sheridan . . .' He paused, uncertain how to proceed.

But what he had said was enough. 'Do come in.' Mrs Moxon withdrew further into the hall.

He entered and, at a gesture from her, closed the door behind him. She walked ahead into a sitting room, beckoning him to follow.

He was aware of enormous opulence. The carpet was thick and giving under his feet. Pictures in heavy gold frames lined the hall, above each a small light in an arched brass shade. Jade dogs snarled at him from the shelves of tall glass cases.

Seen in the full light of the sitting room, Mrs Moxon was equally opulent. She sat down in a high-backed silk-covered chair and arranged her skirts as if posing for a portrait. This room, like the hall, was full of priceless jade and porcelain, displayed on spotless glass shelves. Here, too, the paintings on the wall looked as if they were by people Charles ought to have heard of.

Mrs Moxon was older than she had first appeared in the shadows of the hall, though so much money had been lavished on her appearance that it was hard to say how old. Her figure was trim and erect, though a certain stiffness about it suggested the ministrations of a corsetier. Her hair was neatly set and golden, though again a lack of mobility implied artifice. She was heavily, but skilfully made-up, and her fingernails, long and red, were too perfect to be natural.

She could have been any age between forty and seventy; only the mottling on the backs of her ring-laden hands hinted that she might be nearer the second figure.

107

She graciously waved Charles into an armchair upholstered in the same silk as her own and said, 'I have often hoped that someone would visit me on behalf of Mr Sheridan.' Her voice was highly cultured, the product of the British upper classes, but with a slight exaggeration of the vowels that suggested a period spent abroad. Africa, maybe, India, husband something in the diplomatic service, Charles speculated.

He told her that he had not in fact come on Dave Sheridan's behalf, and tempered her disappointment by remembering his cover story, that he was compiling a feature programme on the disc jockey.

'That must be fascinating work. A privilege for you,' Mrs Moxon said with great intensity.

'Um, er, yes, of course.' He wasn't quite sure whether or not she was completely mad. Still, maybe she could supply him with the information he required. 'Have you been a fan of Dave's for long?'

'I'm sorry, I don't like the word "fan"; it has rather vulgar overtones. But, in reply to your question, yes, I have been an enthusiast of Mr Sheridan for some time. Since I first heard him on the wireless. That was over two years ago. My charwoman left the wireless on, believing me to be asleep – I was just recovering from . . . had been ill. I awoke to hear Mr Sheridan's voice.' She brushed an invisible speck from her knee. 'Such things are meant.'

'Yes. Of course.'

'I discovered subsequently that he had already been broadcasting for some months before that time. I wrote to the BBC, requesting that they send me tape-recordings of the earlier broadcasts, but was told that this was impossible. I took the matter up with the Director-General, but to no avail.' She sniffed with pained contempt. 'An organisation of strange priorities, the BBC.'

'Yes, well, they do have to keep a lot of people happy, don't they?' Charles observed platitudinously.

Mrs Moxon looked at him with disdain. 'I don't see what relevance that has.'

He had by now decided that she *was* completely mad, but saw that agreeing with her was most likely to get him what he required. He ignored the rebuff. 'Yes, I've had similar problems with the BBC. Amazing. In fact, mine were over exactly the same issue. Obviously, for this documentary, I need to hear as much of Dave's work as I can. Yet, when I start to look for examples, I discover that they've hardly recorded any of it.'

'But you do listen to him regularly? Don't you?' Mrs Moxon quizzed fiercely, a schoolmistress wanting to know who'd been writing on the blackboard.

'Oh, of course, whenever possible,' Charles lied, hoping that he wouldn't get questions on details.

But Mrs Moxon seemed satisfied for the moment. 'Yes. They wouldn't entrust a mission like yours to someone who was not well versed in Mr Sheridan's work.'

'No.' He didn't give her time for doubts and questions. 'But it's in the matter of these tapes that I've come to see you. I was told by the Dave Sheridan office that your archive is rather more complete than the BBC one.'

Mrs Moxon nodded, smiling, gratified by the compliment. 'I keep a recording of every broadcast he makes. Since he has started to perform on the television, I have bought a video-recording machine – what a very unattractive expression that is – and I record all of his television programmes.'

'That's very impressive.'

'It's the very least I can do.' Mrs Moxon spoke as if to a rather stupid child.

'I'm sorry. I don't understand. What do you mean?'

'Well, Mr Sheridan is Teddy, after all.' Her patience with Charles's incomprehension seemed to be running out.

'Teddy?'

'Yes, Teddy. Oh, for goodness' sake, you can't be preparing a documentary on Mr Sheridan if you don't know he's Teddy.'

'No,' said Charles cautiously. He wished he had listened to Dave Sheridan, if only once. Perhaps Teddy was some funny character he had invented for his listeners.

'Teddy McCleod!' Mrs Moxon sounded exasperated and cross. 'Teddy McCleod, whose father was the ambassador. Surely you knew McCleod.'

'I don't think I ever had the pleasure . . .' Charles offered tentatively.

'But everyone knew Teddy. Everyone in London. And in America. And you must have heard when we got engaged. It was the talk of the season.'

Charles was completely at sea now. But he continued humouring her. 'Maybe I did hear something about it.'

'Of course you did. We were to be married at St George's, Hanover Square during his next leave. And then we heard he had been killed at Verdun.'

'Verdun? What, you mean during the First World War?'

109

'Of course,' she snapped. Good God, if she was on the verge of marriage at the time of Verdun, that must make her nearer eighty than seventy.

'And . . .' Charles tried to piece together some logic, 'you say that Dave Sheridan is Teddy?'

'Yes. Teddy always said he'd come back to me, that he wouldn't leave me, whatever happened. "Remember, my Glad One," he said, "nothing's going to keep me from you." So I waited. I knew he would come back. Oh, I married General Moxon, but that was nothing. It was never a real marriage, not in the true sense. I was just waiting.' She gave a little smile. 'It's fortunate, really, that poor General Moxon died before Teddy came back.'

'And you're sure that Dave Sheridan is the one?'

'Of course I'm sure.' Her intonation made Charles feel he was being very tiresome. 'I would recognise that voice anywhere. The trace of Scots, and the American from the time his father was in Washington, while Teddy was growing up. Of course it's the same.'

'But you haven't told him that you recognise him?'

Mrs Moxon looked profoundly shocked. 'That would be most improper. He will speak when the time is right. In the meantime I will keep the recordings together, just as I kept all his letters from the Front.'

'I see.' Charles decided to get to the matter in hand before he got embroiled in deeper coils of lunacy. 'I wonder, about the recordings . . . would it be possible for me to borrow one? Just for a brief while. For the documentary.'

Mrs Moxon pondered. 'Obviously I have to keep my collection intact.' Then, making up her mind, 'I will record a copy for you.'

With surprising agility she rose from her chair and opened a large panelled cupboard, behind which was an impressive array of audio equipment, as well as shelf after shelf of cassettes. 'Were there any particular programmes you wished to hear?'

Charles gave the date of Andrea's death.

'Just the one?' Mrs Moxon was shocked by the shallowness of his research.

'For the moment, yes. There may be others. I hope you won't mind if I trouble you again.'

'No,' Mrs Moxon replied vaguely. Her concentration was waning. 'So long as it's for Teddy.'

With unexpected efficiency, she fiddled with the cassette decks in the cupboard and started copying the programme. They listened in silence, as if they had entered some shrine. Charles, while not a devotee of the religion in question, was prepared to obey its observances.

Anyway, it was useful for him to hear the programme. Though he couldn't work out any real sequence of clues, there were details in it that filled him with wild excitement. Now he knew he was on the right track.

Mrs Moxon listened with the concentration of an early Christian anchoress. Even when she had to turn over the cassettes, she acted as if in a trance.

After the programme's closing signature tune, she switched off the machine, gave him the cassette and escorted him to the front door.

'Thank you very much, Mrs Moxon, you have been most helpful.'

'Of course.'

He lingered for a moment. 'By the way, have you ever met Dave Sheridan?'

'No. That too would be most improper.'

'But I'm sure you could. If you wrote to him. You could go and meet him, see him doing the show at Broadcasting House.'

A frisson ran through her. 'What, you mean . . . go out?'

'Yes.'

'I never go out.' She slammed the door and shrank back into the recesses of her flat and her mind.

CHAPTER TEN

CHARLES WAS SURPRISED by the colour of Frances's new car. Yellow. Vivid daffodil yellow. Presumably that was what the image of a head-mistress required, buzzing into the school car park like an avenging slab of butter. Again he felt distant from her. She seemed to be growing away from the person he had known, in so many ways.

He had volunteered the day to sit beside her and help her feel at home in the new car, but he hadn't revealed his ulterior motive. He would introduce that tactfully, as they went along.

She sat in the driving seat, he beside her, both with their seat belts neatly done up. The interior of the new car smelt of plastic, character-less. 'Right, where are we going, Frances?' Make it sound random, then guide her gently the way he wanted to go.

'I don't mind. Up to you.' Playing into his hands.

'Okay, if you really don't mind, if this is really just going to be one of those aimless joy-rides which energy conservationists tell us we shouldn't be taking anymore . . . I do have an idea of where we could go. Let's drive through town and head South.'

'Drive through town?' Frances echoed pallidly.

'Yes. There's a theory I want to work out.'

'But I can't drive through town.'

'What do you mean?'

'Charles, I haven't driven for nearly ten years, just kept my licence up. And you may remember, even when I drove a lot, I'd never drive into town.'

'But driving through London is only the same as driving anywhere else. Easier. The traffic goes slower.'

'But there's more of it. Especially on a Monday.'

'That's why it goes slower. You can't have it both ways.'

'I'm sorry. I can't drive through the centre of London. Let's go out the other way. Towards Barnet or . . .'

112

No, no, this wouldn't do at all. They were in danger of getting into a marital row. Not only that, he was in danger of not working out his theory. 'Okay, Frances. Look, suppose I drive through town, then you start when we get to the other side.'

'All right.' She sounded unconvinced.

'Oh come on, you must have tried the car out locally. It's no different.'

'No, I haven't actually.'

'Haven't what?'

'Tried the car out.'

'Not at all? But you've had it all weekend.'

'Yes, well, I've sat in it.'

'So you know the seats work. That must be a relief.'

'And I've tried the radio. That works. And the cassette.'

'That is good news.'

He parked outside the Kensington Hilton on Holland Park Avenue. He had got over his irritation with Frances about driving in central London, remembering that that had always been one of the eccentricities in what was otherwise a very balanced and unneurotic personality. He had found the driving a little nerve-racking himself. It was a long time since he had driven anything, and he had never driven a new car. He felt as if he was in a cut-glass dodgem at a fairground.

On the way through the centre he had, if not fully explained the reasons for their trip, at least made clear what they were trying to do.

'So basically, Charles, we listen to the tape and go where it tells us?'

'Exactly. It should be a sort of guided Mystery Tour.'

'I take it this is part of another of your criminal investigations.'

'I suppose so.'

'I wish you'd take up golf. Hmm, maybe bowls now.'

'Thank you.'

The cassette he had got from Mrs Moxon was slotted into the machine. 'Do you want to drive yet, Frances?'

'No, wait till we get a bit further out of town.'

'It is your car. You've got to drive it on your own one day.'

'I know, but not yet.'

'Right.'

Music blared from the car's speakers. Charles listened intently. His first hearing of the programme had given some tantalising possibilities; now he wanted to see if his theory was going to work in detail. The signature tune dipped and continued behind, as the confident and distinctive voice began.

'Good evening, it's a few seconds after two minutes past ten and for the next two hours you're in the safe hands of yours truly, Dave Sheridan, with such delights as the Vintage Spot, the Ten for a Tune competition, the Dave Sheridan Bouquet, and, of course . . . Music!'

The signature tune was lost under his voice and on the cue a new musical introduction began at full volume. It was *Danny Boy*.

'Why don't you start the car?'

'There's no clue yet. This is just the introduction. This is just telling Danny that the message is for him.'

'I don't know what you're talking about.'

'Lovely relaxed sound to get our evening off to a s-mooth start. Andy Williams with "Danny Boy". From the LP of his Greatest Hits – Volume Two. Well, there's lots more good music on tonight's show and a lot of it is thanks to one particular lady, the lady who's chosen tonight's musical bouquet. Yes, she's sent us a list of her ten favourite records and we like her choice so much that we're going to feature them on tonight's show. And, by way of thank you, we're sending a great big bouquet of flowers winging their way to her. Yes, tonight's bouquet is for Mrs Joy Carter of Cockfosters . . .'

'Joylene Carter,' Charles murmured with satisfaction.

'And here's the first of Mrs Carter's bouquet – and it's also been requested by a family from Shepherd's Bush by the name of Smith – "If I Had a Hammer" – here's Trini Lopez!'

Charles started the engine.

'Is that a clue?'

'Certainly is.'

'What?'

'Make for Shepherd's Bush.'

'But we're virtually at Shepherd's Bush. Where do we go from there?'

'Hammer – Smith.'

'Oh God.'

They had circled the Hammersmith Broadway one-way system three times before Frances asked meekly, 'Run out of clues so soon?'

'No, no, just waiting for the next number from Mrs Joy Carter's Bouquet . . .'

'And now on with Mrs Carter's choice – and my, you've picked some beauties, Mrs C, maybe there's a job for you here in the Beeb as a music producer – it's a number by those furry funny folk who hate litter so much – yes, the Wombles with . . . "The Wombling Song"!'

114

'There's no clue in that, Charles.'

'Ssh, it may be in the lyric. There – *The Wombles of Wimbledon Common are we*. Come on, we take the road for Wimbledon.'

'And the next pick of the bunch in Mrs Carter's Bouquet – My, that sounds formal, Joy – I think I'll call you Joy from now on – lovely name, Joy – the next number's an oldie, not quite old enough for our Vintage Spot, but still a great favourite. Yes, "On Mother Kelly's Doorstep" by that great old man of the British Music Hall – Randolph Sutton.'

'On the road to Sutton we go.'

'This is rather fun, Charles. Like a treasure hunt.'

'If my theory's right, the treasure at the end of the trail is a meeting with murder.'

'And now it's time for another number from Joy's lovely selection. This one's a – oh, just a minute, my producer has just handed me a piece of paper from the BBC Motoring Unit. I'd better tell you all about this. Troubles, I'm afraid, for those of you travelling on the M23 motorway, where it meets the M26 at Merstham. There are roadworks on the spaghetti junction there where the two motorways come together, so drive with special care as you approach the area. Okay, got that, all you late-night drivers? Watch out on the M23 Motorway at Merstham – my, what a lot of Ms! That's the M23. Now on with the next bloom from Joy's fragrant bouquet – it's Ol' Blue Eyes himself, Frank Sinatra, from the film "The Joker is Wild" – "All the Way".'

'Hmm. I don't get much from that. Maybe it's in the lyric again.'

'Oh, Charles, really. It's perfectly obvious. We go on from Sutton till we get to the M23 and then we follow it "all the way".'

'You're rather good at this, Frances.'

'Well, that's the end of the motorway and Mrs Carter doesn't seem to have had any of her bouquet for some time.'

'No, what do you reckon we do, Charles?'

'Well, the road goes straight on.'

'Yes, maybe we drive on till the next instruction comes. If we've overshot anything, we can wind the tape back and go on.'

'Yes, we can, but the bloke for whom the trail was originally devised couldn't.'

'No.'

'*Mmm, nice. Some time since we've had one of Joy's excellent selection of numbers, but now we come back with another from the Bouquet, a change of mood and style. It's also an answer to all those people who keep writing to me saying I never play enough military-band music. It's the Regimental Band of the Grenadier Guards, with that rousing march by Sousa – "Hands Across the Sea".*'

'That doesn't give me much, I'm afraid.'

'Nor me, Charles.'

'Shall I spool it back and see if there's something we missed?'

'No, not for a minute. Let's just think . . .'

'Sea. Across the Sea? We aren't expected to cross the Channel, are we?'

'We're heading in the right direction. But no, that's impossible. The whole programme only lasts two hours and we've already had the tape running an hour and a quarter.'

They listened in silence to the Grenadier Guards. 'No lyrics to help us either,' observed Charles.

'No. Perhaps we should stop and –'

'Look! That signpost. "Handcross" – that must be it.'

'Handcross – Hands Across? I don't think much of that.'

'You got any better suggestions?'

'No.'

'I think this must be wrong, Charles.'

'I don't know. We won't know till we get the next bit of the bouquet.'

'*Stirring sounds there from the Grenadier Guards. Just one of the fine pieces of music chosen by Mrs Joy Carter of Cockfosters, whose Bouquet you are hearing tonight on the Dave Sheridan Late Night Show. And I'm sorry Joy, I forgot to say, but my producer's just pointed out to me that there was a dedication to go with that particular number. It was specially for Joy's brother, Reg Crabtree, who's a great lover of military bands. And Reg hails from Lower Beeding in Sussex. Hope you liked the music, Reg.*

'*Well, we'll be having more of Joy's Bouquet very shortly, but right now it's time to get the telephones busy with our Ten for a Tune Competition . . .*'

'Lower Beeding?'

'I've never heard of it. I don't know this part of Sussex very well.'

'Nor me. I suppose, this being such a new car, you aren't kitted out with such things as maps.'

'No, I am extremely efficient. I have the AA Great Britain Road Map. I was given it as a present when I got the car.'

'Who gave it to you?' Charles felt a sharp pang of jealousy. He tried never to think of the almost certain fact that there were other men in Frances's life, but occasionally he couldn't avoid it.

She smiled, perhaps flattered by his transparency. 'Someone from School.' An enigmatic pause. 'Molly Hughes – do you remember her?'

'Ah. No, I don't think so.'

Frances was already poring over the map, reverting automatically to the old marital role of navigator.

'I say, do you want to drive yet? That was meant to be the aim of the exercise.'

'No, no, I'm far too excited. I'll drive on the way back. Here it is! Lower Beeding. Very near Handcross.'

'On we go.'

'More now from Joy's selection of music – and my, what variety she's giving us tonight – and with this one I must complete Joy's message to her brother Reg Crabtree. Apparently it's Reg's birthday tomorrow, and what Joy says is – obviously some sort of family joke here – "Don't go past the pub, Reg." I'm sure you won't Reg, I'm sure you'll be in there tomorrow for a few beers to celebrate your birthday. Joy doesn't say how old you are, Reg – discreet lady – but she does say that the next piece of music she'd like to hear is a lovely number from Judy Collins' album "Recollections", and it's called "Turn, Turn, Turn".'

'Blimey, I've no idea what all that means.'

'Well, this is Lower Beeding. The sign said so.'

'Yes. There doesn't seem to be much to it. Some big estate by the looks of it up there.'

'Leonardslee it said on the gate.'

'Then a couple of houses, what's that? ah, a post office, a pub . . .'

'Stop, Charles.'

'What?'

'"Don't go past the pub, Reg."'

'Of course. We have gone past it. Sorry. I'll have to turn when these cars have gone.'

'And look, Charles. The pub's called "The Crabtree".'

'Wonderful.'

'So what do we do – go inside?'

'Yes, I could use a drink anyway. Oh no, just a minute, no we don't.'

'Why not?'

'*The Dave Sheridan Late Night Show* starts at ten at night. We're over an hour and a half into the tape. The pub would be shut when Danny Klinger got here – if he ever did.'

'Then what do we do? It said don't go past the pub.'

'No. There was a little lane leading off just before it.'

'So?'

'So, Frances, what we have to do is to turn down that little lane. Turn, turn, turn.'

The lane, which started off metalled and residential, narrowed, and the houses gave way to woods on one side and fields on the other. It narrowed again as it started a steep descent.

'I can't believe this leads anywhere, Charles.'

'Well, I reckon it must be right. We just go along it as far as we can. Or until we get another order.'

The tape was playing Johnny Mathis, but the introduction had not said it was part of the Bouquet. At the foot of its descent, the road came to a narrow bridge over a stream. The metalled surface gave way beyond it to a muddy farm track, rutted by the heavy wheels of tractors.

'I'm afraid that lot wouldn't do your beautiful yellow bodywork much good, Frances.'

'Oh, don't worry about that. We can't stop now.'

But the bodywork was saved by the ending of the Johnny Mathis record. Charles let the engine idle while they listened to the next link.

'*Hmm, Mr Mathis there. Ooh, that voice, always makes me think of black coffee and cream. Well, time's ticking past, the witching hour approaches, and we come to the last blossom in Mrs Joy Carter's Bouquet. And she's chosen us a lovely rousing pub song as her final contribution. Before we play it, I'd like to thank Joy for her beautiful bouquet and to assure her that soon winging its way towards her will be, courtesy of the Beeb, a huge bouquet of red roses. And if any of you out there would like to have your musical bouquet featured on the programme, just drop a line to me, Dave Sheridan at . . .*'

'Oh, for Christ's sake get on with it!'

'*. . . so we come to Joy's last piece of music. As I said, a great favourite, this, in the pubs and clubs, so sit back and enjoy Kim Cordell singing, from the LP aptly entitled "A Pub, A Pint and a Song" – "Nellie Dean"!*'

'Couldn't be clearer.' Charles pointed out of the window at a dilapidated and overgrown wooden shed which slumped by the side of the bridge. As he did so, he softly joined in the lyric:

'*There's an old mill by the stream, Nellie Dean . . .*'

'So what do we do now?'

'I think I get out and have a look inside the old mill by the stream.'

'Do be careful.' It was said as a reflex, a flash of concern to match his earlier flash of jealousy. There was still a lot left in their relationship.

'How do you undo these bloody seat belts?' Charles ruptured the mood.

Frances released them both and they got out of the car.

Maybe the building had once been a mill. Its position was right, projecting over the stream, where a pool formed at the foot of a waterfall. But if it had been a mill, it had lost many of its mill-like appendages. There was nothing connecting it to the water, no signs of an axle on which a millwheel could turn. It was just a rickety old shed, supported on wooden brackets out over the water. There was a drop of some twenty feet to a clay-beige pool below, from which the rusted hump of a fridge and the pointed frame of a dead bicycle poked.

By daylight it just looked decrepit and dingy. After dark, as Danny Klinger must have seen it, it would have had an air of menace.

But what had Danny Klinger seen when he got there? More important, *who* had he seen when he got there? Maybe it was Keith Nicholls. Maybe his murderer.

Or perhaps the rendezvous was never kept. If Keith had been at Broadcasting House, feeding clues to the unwitting Dave Sheridan, possibly even organising his wife's death, then he couldn't have got to the old mill before Klinger.

Charles decided to leave further conjecture until he had found out what the shed had to offer.

As he approached the door, which slouched from one hinge, he decided that it would probably have nothing to offer. Whatever confrontation had taken place there twenty-five days before, it was unlikely to have left any trace. Words of passion or confession, like all words, vanish as they are spoken. A forensic scientist might be able to prove the presence of individuals in a given place at a given time, but, without the premeditated fixing of recording apparatus, no one could know what they said there.

So Charles went into the shed expecting nothing. He felt hungry. That pub, the Crabtree, had looked rather nice. Maybe they could get some lunch there. A couple of pints, bread and cheese, a pie maybe.

The shed was damp and suddenly dark after the brightness of the sun. It was a minute or two before he could see anything. When he did, it was the usual detritus of such uninhabited places – unwholesome-looking scraps of paper, a couple of beer cans, a broken bottle, a shrivelled

119

condom . . . Ugh, to think that anyone would choose this damp, urine-scented hole to make love in.

Everything had been there a long time. There was nothing that looked out of place, no clue, nothing. Oh well, the treasure hunt had been fun. Deep down he had known that there wasn't going to be any treasure. Maybe there had been some on the night that Andrea Gower died, but by now someone else had come and claimed it.

'Are you all right in there?' Frances's voice sounded distant and still flatteringly tinged with anxiety.

'Yes, there's nothing here. Let's go and get some lunch at the pub. I'll just have one more look and . . .'

His eyes swept round cursorily. They snagged on something on a crossbeam by the window. He hadn't noticed it before, because the colour of its brown paper wrapping was so close to that of the woodwork.

A parcel. About twelve inches square. Wrapped in brown paper, neatly sellotaped.

That hadn't been there a long time. Only about twenty-five days, Charles reckoned.

Maybe Danny Klinger hadn't come to the old mill to meet someone. Maybe his role had just been that of a delivery boy.

Charles stepped forward across the wooden floor towards the window. He reached out to the parcel.

As he did so, he heard the creak and split of wood. At the same time the floor beneath him tipped crazily. The sound of the waterfall increased as if at the turn of a switch.

He saw the water, saw the timbers of the shed wall only inches from his face. He flung out his arms towards a crosspiece, but was too late to reach it as the weight of his body bore him down.

CHAPTER ELEVEN

FRANCES GOT HER driving practice; Charles was too shaken and, after four restorative pints in the Crabtree, too drunk, to be safely in charge of a car.

He had been lucky. The fall into the water had only jolted and bruised him. There was a slight scrape on one shin, where it had met the dead bicycle, but nothing worse. Frances thought he ought to go to hospital and get a tetanus jab, because the water in the stream had looked pretty noxious, but Charles said he'd be okay and promised to go to his doctor in town if he had any trouble from the wound. (He omitted to mention that he wasn't registered with a doctor in town or anywhere else; since he'd left Frances, he'd never got round to it; she had always dealt with that sort of domestic detail.)

Before adjourning to the Crabtree (where he had sat, soggy and clay-streaked, attracting conjecture but no comment from the phlegmatic regulars), he had had a good look round the shed. And, in spite of his discomfort, what he found there excited him.

For the first time, he had proof that his suspicions were justified. Here was definite evidence that the deaths of Andrea Gower and Danny Klinger were connected. Not quite enough to prove that Keith Nicholls was responsible for both of them, but at least a starting point, from which a case could be built.

Because closer examination of the shed made it quite clear that it had been booby-trapped. The wood of the floorboards was splitting and rotten, but would probably still have been strong enough to support a man's weight. What ensured that they didn't was the neat line of saw-marks through them at the point where they joined the far wall. New saw-marks, too. There were traces of sawdust and the sheared wood had not yet had time to discolour, still revealing a yellow core.

The booby-trap had been designed for Danny Klinger. As Charles's survival had proved, it wasn't an infallible murder method, but Charles had been lucky. He had been there in the daylight. In the darkness, that

121

sudden descent would have been infinitely more dangerous. Nor would Klinger have had Frances on hand to pull him up the steep bank of the stream. And in his customary state of inebriation, he would have been less capable of saving himself. At midnight in such a deserted spot, he would have had no chance of summoning help by shouting. No, it wasn't an infallible murder method, but Charles reckoned Klinger would have been lucky to survive it.

Or maybe Keith's plan was just to immobilise his quarry and then arrive in person later and finish him off.

Whatever had been intended, it was clear that it had failed. Klinger had either not reached the end of the treasure hunt or, once there, had become suspicious and not entered the shed. The fact that the brown paper parcel was still there suggested the former was more likely.

The parcel was the most baffling element in the whole set-up. Once he had recovered from the shock of his fall and confirmed the sabotage of the floorboards, Charles set about recovering it. Frances held him round the waist (with frequent admonitions that he should be careful), as he groped for the package with two sticks.

It was difficult. He didn't want to knock it off its perch and send it down to the soaking he had just received. He wanted the contents intact.

As he fished, he conjectured what those contents might be. It was now clear that his earlier hypothesis, that Klinger had been delivering, was incorrect; he had come to collect, and the saboteur had reckoned he would want the contents of the parcel sufficiently to abandon caution as he reached for them.

Obviously the contents were related to some sort of crime or there was no point in the whole elaborate charade of secrecy. But what crime? Transferring loot from a robbery seemed a possibility. But the fact that Klinger was American limited what that loot could be. He was going to have problems getting stolen jewellery or family silver through customs. Pictures might be easier, and the shape of the package fitted that conjecture. But most likely of all was drugs. That sorted well with Keith's Alternative Society image and the connection of both parties with the pop music business.

As Charles finally got a grip with his long chop-sticks and lifted the parcel, its lightness also supported that explanation. Gingerly, he lifted it over the void to safety.

They sat on the grass outside the shed to examine their treasure. Charles reached to slit the Sellotape.

'Of course,' Frances cautioned, 'that might be part of the booby-trap too.'

'What do you mean?'

'A bomb, maybe.'

He hesitated.

'To make assurance doubly sure,' Frances continued.

'Oh, come on. It's not heavy enough for a bomb. There can't be any metal parts in there.'

'Plastic explosives?' Frances murmured.

'Don't be ridiculous. If he was out to blow Klinger up, then why bother to saw through the floorboards? No, I'd stake my life that this isn't a bomb.'

'Apposite last words, Charles,' murmured Frances.

He slit the Sellotape carefully with his fingernail and opened the parcel.

Inside were about a dozen sheets of corrugated cardboard, each some twelve inches square.

They were silent as he inspected his find. Each sheet was identical. There was nothing written on any of them. Charles raised them in turn to the light and looked along their corrugations. 'See right through. There doesn't seem to be anything in there.'

'What were you expecting?'

'Drugs, maybe?'

'Might be stuck between the layers.'

'Might be.' He split one of the sheets. 'Looks just like glue to me.'

Inspection of the others was equally unrewarding.

'What do you make of it, Charles?'

'I can't be sure, Frances, but I think we could have unearthed an international cardboard-smuggling ring.'

Though it was sunny, Frances had put on the car heater in an attempt to dry Charles out a bit. Radio Four purred urbanely from the speakers, discussing new provisions being made for single-parent families.

'I'm sorry, love, I'm afraid I'm making rather a mess of your swish upholstery.'

'Oh, don't worry about that. It'll sponge off; it said so in the brochure. Are you very uncomfortable?'

'Not too bad. It's probably useful acclimatisation for the incontinence which will no doubt strike me in later life.'

'Charming.' A pause. 'Do you think a lot about getting old, Charles?'

'I am old.'

'I mean old old.'

'Yes, I think about it.'

'So do I.'

'Does it worry you?'

'Not really. It seems pretty logical. Menopause sorted out, it's the natural next step.'

'Yes.'

'The only thing that worries me about it is being alone, completely alone.'

'You won't be alone, Frances.' He could feel her waiting for him to elaborate. As always, he evaded the issue. 'You're not the sort of person to be alone.'

They were silent. Radio Four talked earnestly about the social problems of the handicapped.

Charles broke the silence. Inevitably with a change of subject. 'The only thing I can think, Frances, is that the parcel was a dummy.'

'What do you mean?'

'That the would-be murderer made up that bundle of cardboard to look like whatever it was Klinger was expecting. Shrewd idea. Klinger would reach for it and be caught in the trap, and if anyone else found it, it wouldn't be incriminating evidence. They'd be as puzzled by it as we are.'

'That sounds logical. Yes, I accept that.'

'Good. The thing I can't work out, though, is why Klinger never got there. He must have known the signals, and yet I'm sure he never arrived at that shed. If he had done, he would have either gone through the floor or taken the package.'

'Hmm. Maybe he got lost with the clues. Some of them were pretty obscure. *Hands Across the Sea*, I mean, really.'

'Yes, but it was a game he was used to playing. I'd have thought, if we could get it right first time . . .'

'He was in a foreign country.'

'True.'

'Charles, why did you put the parcel back?'

'It's evidence. I wanted to leave it all as far as possible as it was, so that if it ever gets to the point of bringing the police in –'

'Why don't you go to the police now?'

'I've nothing to offer them. And I have some experience of how they react to fanciful theories expounded by enthusiastic amateurs.'

'Yes, but you could have been killed by that booby-trap. I mean –'

'But I wasn't killed by it,' he said firmly.

'You mean you're going on investigating?'

'Oh yes.'

'Next time you might really be killed.'

'Save me from getting old and incontinent.'

Frances sighed with resignation. 'What do you do next?'

'Well, I've checked out the trail Danny Klinger should have taken the night he didn't die; I suppose the next thing is to check out his route the night he *did* die.'

'I suppose so.'

'I still wish I could sort out why it didn't work the first time. Where did he lose the trail?'

'We turn off at this junction, don't we, Charles?'

'Yes, we want the M23 towards Sutton.'

'Oh, I don't fancy doing that spaghetti junction bit.'

'You don't have to this way, only in the other direction. And, incidentally, Frances, you are allowed to go at above forty on motorways.'

'I'm driving, Charles. I choose thé speed.'

'Fine.'

She negotiated the South London suburbs well. Charles, full of beer, dozed. Radio Four earnestly discussed the difficulties of Senior Citizens in supermarkets.

He awoke with a start to hear Frances swearing.

'What's the matter?' He peered blearily round him. They were in slow-moving traffic under Hammersmith flyover.

'The bloody radio's packed in. I don't know, I've only had the thing three days and . . .'

Charles turned up the volume knob. Nothing. 'No, it seems completely gone.'

The car in front of Frances moved ahead and she jerked the Renault forward in annoyance. As she did so, the radio suddenly blared forth its concern with huge volume. Charles hastened to turn it down.

'Oh, thank God it's working.'

'Yes, Frances, not only that, you have also told me why Danny Klinger never got to the first rendezvous.'

'What do you mean?'

'The radio only stopped because the flyover cut out the signal. We weren't aware of that problem on the way down, because we were listening on cassette. But Klinger was listening to a live broadcast. So if he got held up under a bridge or something – like, say, under the spaghetti junction between the M23 and M25 because of road works – then he could easily have missed one of the clues. Couldn't he?'

'Who's a clever boy then?' said Frances.

Charles began to think that the Swedish girls' spelling was deliberately perverse. No one could abuse the English language so consistently without conscious effort. The latest offering, which was affixed to the telephone when he got back, read:

YOUR AJINT SKOLLIN RINK RINK HIM.

He deduced from this that his agent Maurice Skellern had rung and, though still in his damp clothes, could not resist the reflex to ring back straight away. The actor's motto rang through his head – 'It might be work'.

'Maurice Skellern Artistes,' said a bad impression of Noël Coward.

'Oh come on, Maurice. It's one thing pretending you have hundreds of people to answer your telephone, but claiming Noël Coward's one of them comes under the heading of false pretences.'

'Charles. Sorry you don't like it. Next time I answer the phone, I'll do my Jimmy Cagney.'

'I can't wait. What is it, Maurice? Work?'

'Yes, yes, all in good time . . . "you dirty rat". Recognise it? Cagney to the life, isn't it?'

'Sounds nothing like him.'

'Oh, come on. You can't see what I'm doing with my hands.'

'No, I can't.'

'Probably just as well, eh?' Maurice went into a spasm of his gasping laugh.

'Maurice, Maurice, what is it? I am standing here in wet clothes, I have incipient gangrene in my right leg and I want to have a bath. What is it?'

'All right, all right, don't lose your sense of humour. It's good news. It's a booking. My policy's paying off.'

'Policy?'

'You know, keeping your presence more in the vanguard of the public eye. This is another radio booking.'

'What, a return to *Dad's the Word* by popular demand?'

'No, no, this is a quiz programme. Same producer, though, Monckton? Thing called *The Showbiz Quiz*. I've never heard of it.'

Charles felt a little flutter of excitement. Was this the moment when he became recognised as Personality rather than just as an actor? Would he soon be invited to open supermarkets and describe his bathroom to the *TV Times*? 'You mean, they want me as a panellist?'

'No, no. They want you to be the Mystery Voice.'

'The Mystery Voice? What, you mean "And the next object is Queen Mary's Umbrella. Queen – Mary's – Umbrella." That sort of thing?'

'That sort of thing, yes.'

No, not the big breakthrough into personality broadcasting. Just another benefit of Nick Monckton's shyness and desperate habit of booking people he knew.

Nita Lawson wasn't in her office later on that afternoon, but the ever-efficient Brenda was more than happy to supply Charles with the information he required. To have found someone as interested in P as Bs as she was herself was more than she had dared hope from life. She became quite frisky, even coquettish. For a ghastly moment, Charles feared that she thought the motive of his visit to be ulterior. Oh well, there was nothing he could do about it. He remained resolutely charming, though the various aches of his body, particularly of his right shin, were beginning to nag.

With another deft demonstration of her filing efficiency, Brenda produced the P as B for the night of Klinger's death.

The first item was an immediate disappointment. *Island in the Sun* – Harry Belafonte.

'That can't be right,' said Charles involuntarily.

'Pdn?' Brenda had perfected a way of saying 'Pardon,' which completely eliminated vowels.

'Well, I just . . . I mean, it seems unlikely that that could have been the opening number.'

'But it's on the P as B,' she objected devoutly, as if he were questioning the authenticity of the Dead Sea Scrolls.

'Yes, but isn't it possible that they changed the number after the running order had been arranged?'

She shook her blonde head. 'But then I'd have done an amendment. Like I did on the last one you were talking about.'

'But mightn't they have changed it and then not told you?'

'Oh no, there'd have to be an amendment. The P as B has a very wide distribution list.' Again she chided his heresy.

Charles saw his rather finely constructed theories begin to topple. 'But did you actually hear the programme go out?'

'Oh no, I do go out some nights, you know. Not every night, though,' she added, simpering.

Oh dear, she did fancy him. Charles put on his most debonair smile. 'No, have to fight off the boyfriends sometimes and wash your hair, eh?' She simpered further. 'Tell me, who would be responsible for telling you if the number was changed?'

'Pdn?'

'Who would tell you about the change?'

'Look, there wasn't any change. If there were, there would be an amendment on the P as B and there is no amendment on the P as B.' She was now talking to him with impatient precision, as she did to the least intelligent trainee production secretaries.

'Yes, but in general terms – I mean, not in this specific instance – if a number were changed, who would give the information to you?'

'The producer.'

'Who on that date was . . . ?'

'Kelly Nicholls.'

Good. The one person who would not want to draw attention to the substitution. 'Tell me, is your filing system for listeners' letters as efficient as the one you have for the P as Bs?'

Brenda preened herself. 'Of course.'

'Do you remember, when I was last in here, Nita mentioned a letter from a man complaining about the constant use of the *Londonderry Air* on the programme?'

'Of course.' She reached down a file with studied efficiency and opened it with a flourish at the right page.

Charles read the letter and looked at the date. Exactly right. 12th July. The day after Klinger's death. In other words, the listener wrote it the day after hearing the music on the programme. Charles flicked through the P as Bs for the rest of that week. No, no sign of *Danny Boy*, unless he went right back to the night of Andrea's death. And surely no one would wait a whole week to register that kind of complaint. Anyway, the objection was to the 'continued' use of the tune.

Ah well, it could all be checked with Mrs Moxon's personal archive.

'Brenda, you've been wonderful. Full marks. Immediate nomination for Secretary of the Year.'

'Only too happy to have been of service. Call any time, day or night, if I can help again.'

Yes, he felt sure she meant it. He shrugged ingenuously. ' "Beggar that I am, I am even poor in thanks." '

'Pdn?'

Mrs Moxon did not appear surprised by his visit, but she seemed to him changed, vaguer. The grooming was still immaculate, but he was more aware of her real age. He felt perhaps she had not much longer to live, that soon she would leave the confusion of her hallucinations and go to join Teddy.

Neither did she seem surprised by his request to hear another specific

128

tape. She found it more slowly than she had the previous one and when she sat down after switching it on, looked abstracted and old.

The signature tune started and dipped in the prescribed place. '*Good evening, one and all. Good evening, ladies and gentlemen. This is Dave Sheridan welcoming you to my Late Night Show. I hope you'll stay with me for the next two hours, when you'll hear all kinds of good sounds and fun things. There's the Vintage Spot, there's our Ten for a Tune Competition on the telephone, there's a Bouquet of records from one of our listeners – and of course the very best of music. Like this from Mr – Harry – Belafonte!*'

'Oh dear,' said Charles.

But then the lyric started.

Oh, Danny Boy,
The pipes, the pipes are ca-alling . . .

Charles Paris smiled. Sacrilege though the idea would seem to Brenda, even P as Bs could lie.

CHAPTER TWELVE

'COULD I SPEAK to Mr Venables, please? This is Charles Paris.'

'Certainly, Mr Paris,' said Polly, the solicitor's secretary, and put him through.

'Charles. What a pleasure to hear from you.'

'Nice to hear you too. How's crime?'

'As I have told you many times before, Charles, I have very few dealings with the criminal side of the Law. Most of my work is in –'

'No, I just meant your own crime, the regular solicitor's crimes of procrastination, misrepresentation and extortion.'

'Mustn't grumble,' Gerald Venables replied smugly. 'But what about you? How's crime with you? Are you on to another case?'

'Yes, I think I may be.'

'Can I help? Gimme the low-down.' At the mention of a possible criminal investigation, Gerald regressed from solicitor to eager schoolboy.

'There is something you could do for me, if you've got a free day and a car.'

'Of course I've got a car, Charles. And a free day can be organised. Polly, what's in the diary for tomorrow? Oh well, cancel that, move Margolis to Thursday and tell Lady Harker I have to be in court. Yes, I'm free tomorrow.'

'Good. I was going to ask Frances, but she's off staying with some schoolfriend for a couple of days.'

'Are you and Frances back together again?'

'Occasionally. Not very often.'

'Oh really. I wish you'd get that sorted out. It's very difficult for Kate and me always having to send two Christmas cards.'

'Knock me off the list. I don't mind.'

'I might just do that. Well, are you going to fill me in on the action?'

'I'll tell you in the car tomorrow. Pick me up here, can you? We've got to start from the Kensington Hilton.'

'Kensington Hilton? What is all this about, Charles?'

'I'll tell you tomorrow. Actually, lucky I've remembered. I must go down to the Kensington Hilton now to check something out.'

'Oh, very well. Perhaps it's better if you don't tell me over the phone. I'll pick you up at – I say, do you still live in that awful hole in Bayswater?'

'Yup.'

'I'll pick you up there . . . what, about ten?'

'Fine. Have you still got the same car? The Mercedes?'

'Charles, that was three years ago. No,' he confided complacently, 'I've just taken delivery of a new one.'

'Has it got a cassette player?'

'Oh, really, Charles, what do you take me for? Of course it has.'

Not only did it have a cassette player, it also had a telephone, air conditioning and a fridge. It was in fact a brand new Rolls Royce, discreetly dark blue, which looked in Hereford Road like the Queen going walkabout in the slums.

'Why on earth did you get this?' asked Charles, as he sank into the upholstery.

'Oh, there are certain tax reasons,' replied Gerald vaguely. 'And of course it's an investment.'

'So soliciting really is doing well, is it?'

'Charles, soliciting is what loose women do in small rooms, extorting money from and denying satisfaction to the ignorant and the innocent. Whereas what I do . . .'

'Yes?'

'Where are we going?' Gerald asked abruptly.

'Kensington Hilton, for a start.'

'And then?'

'If my hunch is right, out along the M4 towards Wallingford.'

'Oh excellent.'

'Why?'

'A client of mine, Sir Arnold Fleishman, lives near Henley. That means I can put the day in my books as a visit to him.'

'Does it also mean we actually have to go and see him?'

'Oh Charles, don't be childish. Of course not.'

They started from the Kensington Hilton and the clues did lead to the M4. Having followed the previous tape, Charles found the directions much easier to recognise this time. He explained the system with glee, indicating how *Sitting on the Dock of the Bay* by Otis Redding must

131

inevitably lead them to Reading, and so on. In the gaps between the clues he filled in the background to the case.

Gerald got boyishly excited about it all and that, coupled with his transparent pride in his new car, made him a very giggly and good companion.

It was only when the final musical clue, *A Walk in the Black Forest*, led them into the dark little wood off Greenmoor Hill near Woodcote that their mood of adolescent euphoria was dampened. There is always something desolate about the scene of a murder.

Gerald parked on the roadside; he wouldn't drive into the wood for fear of spotting his car's immaculate paintwork. ('You've no idea how many coats of paint they put on,' he kept saying.) They got out of the car in silence, their change of mood reflected by the tall trees' sudden switching off of the sunlight.

'We don't really even need to get out,' said Charles. 'The fact that the clues brought us here is sufficient proof of my thesis.'

'Yes, but we might find something, some evidence or . . . I mean, look, those tracks could well have been made by the car he was driving.' Gerald pulled up the perfect creases of his cream linen trousers as he crouched to point.

'They could, but even if they were, so what? The police will have been over this whole area with a fine-tooth comb. I think we're pretty unlikely to find anything they missed.' Charles shivered slightly. 'Strange, how cold and damp it is in here. I suppose the sunlight never penetrates through the trees. Must take a long time to dry out.'

'Yes.' Gerald spoke briskly to halt the descent into morbidity. 'So what do you reckon happened here three weeks ago? Klinger followed the instructions and arrived . . . what, just before midnight?'

'That'd be about it. The last clue was in the closing number of the programme.'

'And found Keith Nicholls here waiting for him?'

'Oh, how convenient that would be if it were so . . . . But no, it can't be. Keith Nicholls was producing Dave Sheridan. That means he was in Broadcasting House until midnight. If he leapt straight into a car and drove like a maniac down the M4, there is still no way he could have been here before one.'

'So what does that mean? He had an accomplice?'

'Yes, or Klinger just waited for him.'

'Does that seem likely? Surely, if the set-up in the shed is anything to go by, all Klinger was expecting at the end of his treasure hunt was a parcel full of cardboard.'

'Let's say "cardboard or substances unknown", shall we?'

'Okay.'

'But no, Gerald, I think Klinger did wait. I mean, as soon as he got here it would be apparent that there was no obvious place to hide a package – unless he was expected to look behind every tree in the wood. So he may have anticipated a personal approach. Or he may have had some message telling him to expect someone. Anyway, he had ways of whiling away time.'

'What do you mean?'

'Booze, Gerald. It works very well. I know. I sometimes seem to have whiled away most of my life with a glass in my hand. Certainly the police post mortem on Klinger showed that he had got a lot of the stuff inside him. As Fat Otto said, "Danny sure liked his oil."'

'So you reckon he just waited here in the car, drinking.'

'Yes, and was pretty well insensible by the time Keith Nicholls arrived. Certainly too fuddled to do much about it when Keith fixed up the tube and started feeding carbon monoxide into the car. He was probably asleep by then. A pretty painless death really.'

Gerald look sceptical. 'It's all conjecture.'

'A bit more than conjecture.'

'How so?'

'I went down to the Kensington Hilton last night and had a word with a friend of mine down there. Amazing what a fiver will do, even in these inflationary days. I only wish I could afford to get information that way more often. Anyway, I found out that on the evening of his death, a present arrived for Mr Klinger. A bottle of whisky.'

'Who from?'

'No card. And, according to the guy on Reception, there wasn't one inside, because Klinger opened it there and then.'

'I see. So it was all set up.'

'Yes. Whoever sent it knew Klinger's tastes well enough to ensure that if he had to wait around in a dark wood for an hour, at least he would have something there with him for comfort. A bottle of whisky with two Mogadon crushed up in it.'

'But why didn't the police find that suspicious? They must have checked the bottle.'

'Yes, but presumably they came to the conclusion Klinger had put the pills in himself to make his passing easier. After all, they had no reason to think it was anything other than suicide. Klinger had a motive, with his failing business. It's only because I saw his name on Andrea's cassette that I started making connections and thinking of murder.'

133

'Very good. It's all coming together nicely, isn't it?'

'Yes. Except that it's all theory. I don't have a single piece of hard evidence, nothing that ties it directly to Keith Nicholls.'

'No, but at least you know what you're looking for. I'm sure it's easier to find evidence once you know who your culprit is.'

'I hope you're right.'

Gerald mused. 'Death in Broadcasting House . . . You know, I once read a rather good thriller with that title. Set in the Thirties, when radio really was top medium. Written by Val Gielgud, as I recall. The dénouement is a dramatic chase across the roof of Broadcasting House.'

'Hmm. Maybe there'll be one in this case too. If there is, it'll be a longer chase. They've built an extension to Broadcasting House since the Thirties.' Then, with a swoop into gloom, 'Mind you, I'm afraid this case is unlikely ever to reach a dénouement.'

'Come on, cheer up. Let's get back into the Rolls and go and have an extraordinarily good lunch as homage to Sir Arnold Fleishman.'

'You've talked me into it.'

Once back in the galleon, Gerald said, 'What in-flight entertainment can I offer you? You don't want to listen to the programme again for more clues?'

'No, thanks. What have you got?'

'Vivaldi, Mozart, Brahms. Bach, Telemann, Haydn . . . the list goes on for ever – excluding Wagner, of course. What do you fancy?'

'Well, I – just a minute, no. I've got something for you to listen to. Perhaps I do have one piece of hard evidence in this case.'

After the Musimotive tape had been running for a couple of minutes, Charles looked across at Gerald. 'Does it tell you anything?'

'Not a thing. Except that I don't like it. It's just light music, isn't it? The sort of stuff the au pair has playing in the house all day long. While Kate and I are not there, I hasten to add. As soon as we get in, the dial goes very firmly back to Radio Three.'

'Hmm. I wonder if there's anything in the titles . . . if this tape is a kind of treasure hunt like the others.'

Gerald listened for a minute. 'Does this sort of music have titles?'

'All music has titles. If only to its composers.'

'Does this sort of music have composers?'

'Now stop being a snob, Gerald. It might be worth finding out what the titles are. It might lead us somewhere.'

'Since you don't know the titles and I don't know the titles, there's no point in torturing ourselves by playing any more of it. You must know someone who could advise you about that sort of thing.'

'Yes, I think I do. The lovely Brenda.'

'Is this another of your paramours, Charles?'

'Please God, no.' And then quickly, to avert further censure of his ill-defined relationship with Frances, 'Where are we going to lunch, Gerald?'

'I took the precaution of booking at a rather nice place called The Waterside Inn at Bray. Good Food Guide distinction and all that.'

'Sounds expensive.'

'My accountant can stand it.'

'God, look at that place.' Gerald pointed to a huge roadhouse which appeared to have undergone recent refurbishing and additions. Tiers of garish neon signs proclaimed BRASSIE'S – 3 BARS – RESTAURANT – DISCOTHEQUE.

'This country's getting more like America daily.'

'I didn't know you'd ever been to America.'

'Oh really, Gerald. Of course I have.'

The roadhouse was on a roundabout and they had to slow down as they went past. Charles glanced idly out of the window at its new fascia, a monument to an architectural style possibly known as Tudor Swiss Chalet. On the fence which skirted the car park were rows of posters for forthcoming and past excitements at the Discotheque. Suddenly his eye was caught by a name on a poster.

'Gerald, stop the car!'

'What is it?'

'Reverse into the car park.'

'What for?' asked Gerald testily, as he obeyed the instructions.

'Park just there, in front of that poster.'

The galleon halted with a scrunch of gravel, its gleaming prow inches from the fence. The poster was crude, large black letters printed on luminous orange paper. It was torn and faded. An obscene word had been aerosoled on to it. But what remained was easy to read.

. . . SIE'S OPENING NITE ALL-NITE DISCO PARTY
ENTRANCE – £1.50 UNACCOMPANIED GIRLS FREE TILL MIDNITE
NON-STOP BOP WITH CAPITAL RADIO'S BUCK REDDY
DISCO DANCE COMPETITION, JUDGED BY TIGGI KNUCKLE
OF T.V.'S 'NAUGHTY BITS' DANCE TROUPE.
AND, AT ONE O'CLOCK, A TWO-HOUR SESSION WITH RADIO TWO'S
. . . DAVE SHERIDAN.

'Coincidence, wouldn't you call that?' said Charles. 'Only ten minutes from where Klinger was murdered.'

'Maybe. It depends when the Opening Nite All-Nite Disco Party was.'

'I'm sure we can find that out from somebody in one of the 3 bars. Come on, let's go in.'

'All right,' Gerald grudged. His detective enthusiasm was succumbing to the imperative of hunger. 'But not for long. The table's booked for one. I tell you, they do a duck in green Chartreuse which is out of this world.'

Getting a simple piece of information, like when Brassie's had opened, proved more difficult than expected. Only one of the three bars, the Balmoral, was open, and the morose youth reading the *Sun* behind the counter had only started work that Monday. From his tone of voice he gave the impression that he would be unlikely still to be working there the following Monday. No, he didn't think there was anyone around who would be able to help. Most of the staff were either new or didn't speak English. The manager wouldn't be in till about half-past one. Yes, somebody in the restaurant might know, but the restaurant didn't open until one.

When finally asked for two pints of beer, the barman looked up from his paper with an accusing sigh and pumped fizzy fluid into glasses. Charles thought fondly back to New York, where a concept of service still existed.

They sat down on a prickly tartan bench beneath a plastic spray of dirks and claymores behind a buckler, and put their glasses down on a Formica 'Monarch of the Glen' table-top.

'This is ridiculous, Charles. It's quarter to one now. We're never going to make it to the Waterside in time.'

'Ring through and cancel if it worries you.'

'I suppose they might be able to hold the table for half an hour.'

'Look, Gerald, I'm sorry, but the aim of today's expedition was investigation of a murder, not just gluttony.'

'Hmm. I'll ring through and see. Just so long as we don't have to eat here, that's all. Anything but that.'

The waitress had obviously been issued with a uniform, but had decided she preferred her own clothes. The uniform was represented by a tiny frilly apron over her black dustbin-liner trousers, a frilly mob cap pinned to the top of her purple-dyed hair and, pinned to her silver lamé T-shirt, a plastic badge meant to look like brass, which bore the legend, BRASSIE'S – JUDE IS HERE TO SERVE YOU.

'Do you have a menu?' asked Charles. Gerald was still too pained by the thought of the lunch he was missing to speak.

'Well, we do,' said Jude in a young Cockney voice, whose softness was in surprising contrast to her punk appearance, 'but most of it's off today, so I better just tell you. Starters we got prawn cocktail, avocado prawn or fruit juice.'

'With prawn?' murmured Charles.

'And then afters there's steak or chicken in the basket.'

'And that's it?'

'Well, with chips – that is, French fries.'

'I'll have prawn cocktail and steak. Rare.'

'Sorry?'

'Rare.'

'Oh.' Jude nodded to give the illusion that she knew what he meant. 'And the other gentleman?'

'Gerald?'

The solicitor groaned. 'Oh, the same. No, I'll start with the avocado. And can I have it without the prawns?'

'I'm not sure about that. I'll have to ask chef.'

'Oh, for God's –'

Charles cut across the outburst. 'Tell me, have you been here since this place opened?'

'Oh no, I only started last week. Anything to drink?'

'What have you got?'

'Beer . . . wine.' She didn't sound very sure.

'What sort of wine?'

'I know we got red.'

'We'll have some of that then.'

'Here you are – one prawn cocktail and one avocado with prawns.'

'Without prawns,' insisted Gerald.

'No, with prawns. Those are prawns, those pink things.'

Gerald groaned.

Charles tried again. 'Is the manager in yet?'

'No, no, he probably won't be in till this evening now. He says he reckons the place runs itself lunchtimes.'

'Evidently,' said Gerald blackly.

'That's very inconvenient. There was something I wanted to find out from him. Look, is there anyone else who would know? I'm just trying to find out when this place opened.'

Jude looked blank.

'You know, when the Opening Nite All-Nite Disco was.'

Her face cleared. 'Oh, I come to that. It was dead good. That's why I thought I might like to work here. Mind you, working here's a bit different from being in a disco, know what I mean? But it was good that night. I went in for the Disco Dancing. Nearly won and all.'

'But when –'

'They had Dave Sheridan and all. You know, from the Beeb. He was dead good. I was dead surprised. Thought, you know, Radio Two, going to be a bit old, middle of the road, you know, all rubbish music. But he done some good stuff. Fifties and that. I don't mind Fifties. I mean, I'm really into Rats and Squeeze, but Fifties is great. He done a lovely long Smooch Session, too. I thought he was good. Course, I've seen him on the telly. That helps. But no, I enjoyed it.'

She paused for breath and Charles managed to get his question in again. 'And when exactly was this?'

'Oh, it was a Tuesday. I remember that, 'cause me Mum done her perm. About three weeks back. The 11th July it'd be.'

The night that Danny Klinger had died.

Steve Kennett rang through to Hereford Road that evening. 'I've checked out Keith's movements for the night Andrea died.'

'What, with the other SMs on the *Dave Sheridan Late Night Show*?'

'Yes. Well, with the guy on panel. Bloke called Bill Hewlett. And it rather throws our theories.'

'Oh.'

'He said Keith was in the studio all evening. Except for a meal break. And they ate together in the canteen.'

'And you think he's telling the truth?'

'Can't see why he shouldn't. I suppose if Keith hadn't been there, Bill might cover up for him – honour among SMs and all that – but I should think it's more likely to be the truth.'

'Hmm. How many work on the show?'

'Three. One on panel, one tape and grams and one to route the telephone calls. Usually a secretary'd do the telephoning but because it's so late, one of the SMs does it.'

'Quite a big operation.'

'Yes. That's because of the telephones. Without them the show could be done from one of the self-operating studios in Continuity. As it is, it's done from B15 in the Basement.'

'Well, thank you for finding that out.'

'You don't sound very upset about it.'

'Why should I?'

'For goodness sake!' Steve sounded exasperated. 'If Keith was in the studio all evening, then he couldn't have sneaked out and killed Andrea.'

'No.'

'And our whole theory depends on that.'

'Did.'

'What do you mean?'

'Steve, do you know the old expression: When one door closes, another door opens?'

CHAPTER THIRTEEN

CHARLES WAS SOMETIMES mildly depressed by how fickle his logic could be. He had had the same experience in the theatre. He would see a production of a play with a central performance of such power that he thought it must be definitive. Then, years later, with another actor in the role, he would see the play again and find the new interpretation, though totally different, equally compelling. And, as a strong central performance sometimes can, he would find that it often changed all the performances around it, changed the shape of the whole play, so that he left the theatre feeling he had seen a completely different work.

So it was when he recast the script of Andrea Gower's and Danny Klinger's deaths. With Keith Nicholls bowing out and having his part taken by Dave Sheridan, a new play emerged. And all the supporting roles of evidence and logic shifted and changed their emphasis to accommodate the new character.

It clarified many things. Some bits made a lot more sense. The whole elaborate procedure of sending musical clues over the air became much more acceptable if the person who wanted to send them actually did the speaking; from the start he had felt uneasy about the opportunities for error with Keith feeding the clues to an unwitting Sheridan.

What the new play did not offer was any clear motivation. It presented Sheridan with opportunities to do both murders. (He had left the Features Action Group meeting twice on the night of Andrea's death and his presence ten minutes from the scene of Klinger's murder on the relevant night had to be more than a coincidence.) But so far Charles had no link between the disc jockey and his two victims. He knew that Sheridan had known Andrea, but had no idea of the nature of their relationship. And he had no proof that Sheridan and Klinger had ever spoken to each other.

Still, such things were investigable, and who was better placed to investigate Dave Sheridan without causing suspicion than someone who was compiling a radio feature on him?

140

Charles rang Brenda, who again regrettably misinterpreted his call, and got the number of Dave Sheridan's agent.

While the phone was ringing to Creative Artists Ltd, Charles tried to visualise the agent. He knew he had seen him in the bar after the Swinburne recording. But all he could bring to mind was a shiny chestnut-coloured toupee. Of what was underneath it he had no recollection.

He also tried to decide whether he should use his own persona for the call or assume another identity. He rather fancied using the accent he'd perfected for a revival of *The Second Mrs Tanqueray* ('Effete and degenerate capitalist rubbish'—*Time Out*). Or maybe the Welsh he'd done in *See How They Run* in Darlington ('Presumably a comedy'—*Yorkshire Post*).

But by the time he had been put through, he had opted for caution and told Mr Michael Oakley that he was Charles Paris, he was working on a feature for Radio Three about Dave Sheridan and he wondered if he could ask a few questions.

'Well, okay, but make it quick. I'm a busy man.' Oakley's accent was firmly American, making him sound like every agent in every Hollywood movie.

'I really just want to know about the sort of work schedule Dave keeps up. He seems to me to put in a daunting number of hours.'

'Sure, he's a hard worker.'

'I mean, with the radio show and the television as well. It must be very tiring.' Charles decided that naïve ignorance was going to be his most fruitful approach.

'That's only the half of it. There's also all the personal appearance stuff, his weekly column in *Teen Dreams*, guesting on quiz shows, even got a pantomime coming up for Christmas, talk of hosting a telly chat show, if Thames can get themselves together. I tell you, that boy is very big and about to get a lot bigger.'

Strange how all the show business agents Charles encountered said their clients were about to become very big. He wondered if Maurice Skellern had ever said that of him. It somehow didn't seem likely.

'Yes. But, Mr Oakley, his work doesn't seem to stop at the end of the radio show. I mean, that's over at midnight, but I gather he still goes on and does personal appearances after that.'

'Sure, if the money's right. That's my business, to sort out how much he does. Dave's a professional, anyway. Been in this business all over the world, one way and another, for years.'

'I mean, I was driving in the country the other day, long way out, towards Wallingford, and I saw that Dave was opening some big disco out there *at one in the morning*.' Charles hoped he wasn't overdoing the wide-eyed innocent bit.

It seemed not. Oakley took it without suspicion. 'Sure, does a few of those. Did two hours, the money made it worth doing.'

'But he must have leapt into a car the minute he came off the air.'

'Exactly what he did do. I know. I went with him.'

'Do you usually go along to that sort of thing?'

'Well, not all the time, of course. Just a few here and there. See how it's going. I'm his personal manager, you know, not just an agent.'

Oh, I see, thought Charles – twenty per cent rather than ten.

'So you leapt into the car and went straight down there . . . what, and then you had a little break before he went on?'

'Nope. He arrived on the dot of one and went straight on stage. I tell you, he's a professional.'

'But then he had a break in the middle of his session, did he?' Charles's whole new script depended on Sheridan having half an hour in which to leave Brassie's, meet up with Klinger, kill him and get back to the disco without anyone noticing his absence.

The script was quickly rejected. 'Nope. He didn't get a break. He got there at one, did the gig, finished on the dot of three, I got the money from the manager – you can never trust these new outfits, better to get it straight away – then we were back in the car by five past three and all in bed by four.'

'Dave didn't stay down there for anything, for –'

'Hell, no. The guy's got to sleep sometime.'

'Yes . . .' Charles felt dejected. It had been a nice new script and he had begun to envisage dramatic success for it. Now he was nowhere.

But not for long. Unwittingly Michael Oakley threw him a lifeline. 'Look, Mr Paris, I'd love to chat to you all day, but there's no percentage in it for me, do you see? I do have other things to do. Look, if you really want to know about Dave's working methods, why not follow him round for a day? I could arrange that for you.'

'Oh, I'd be very grateful,' murmured Charles, still dejected.

'And if you want to know more about that Brassie's gig, ask Dave's producer. He went down with us that night.'

'His producer?'

'Yeah, producer of the *Late Night Show* at the Beeb. I don't think he's still doing it, but the guy's name is Kelly Nicholls.'

'Kelly Nicholls?' Some instinct told Charles to probe a little further.

'Oh yes, I think I met him once. The same evening I met you in fact.'

'I didn't know we'd met.' Oakley didn't sound suspicious, just uninterested.

'In the BBC bar. Nita Lawson introduced us. It was the night that girl committed suicide, I don't know if you remember.' It was worth the risk. Oakley must get introduced to a lot of people; he'd be unlikely to remember a passing introduction in a bar.

So it proved. 'Oh yes, I remember vaguely.'

'I think I met Kelly that night. He was producing the show. You must have seen him. I remember you were showing a young lady the studio in action.'

'Oh, it comes back to me, yeah.'

'I dropped into the studio during transmission and saw Kelly then,' Charles lied.

Oakley disagreed. 'No, must have been another night. Kelly wasn't in the studio that night.'

'What?'

'All the other SMs were, but not Kelly. Dave does that show on his own, anyway. Just needs some jerk to play in the tapes and route the phone calls. An experienced jock doesn't need a producer; it's just one of those quaint old things the Beeb insists on.'

'So Kelly wasn't around all that evening?'

'Certainly not when I was there, no.'

Which, if it was true, meant he was somewhere else. Organising his wife's murder, perhaps?

He rang Steve at work and found out how to contact Bill Hewlett, the custodian of Keith's alibi. She had to consult some schedule and find an extension number for him.

Though she couldn't really discuss the case in the office, she was obviously hurt that Charles didn't tell her more about the progress of his suspicions. But he felt an inclination to secrecy, until he had something more positive to offer. Once he had a proven case, then he would present it to her as a rich gift. And maybe claim some sort of reward.

He decided to get Detective-Sergeant McWhirter out of mothballs again for Bill Hewlett's benefit. The extension number he had been given was for a studio control cubicle. When the phone was answered, the first thing he heard was treacly, undistinguished music like that on the Musimotive tape. Radio Two. He asked if Bill Hewlett could have a quick word and was told, yes, they were only rehearsing at the moment.

'Mr Hewlett, this is Detective-Sergeant McWhirter of Scotland Yard.'

He had a moment's doubt; should he say 'New Scotland Yard' these days?

But Bill Hewlett was not in a mood to notice irregularities. He sounded frightened as he asked in what way he could help. Illegal it might be, but impersonating a police officer brought results.

'This is just a routine enquiry, Mr Hewlett. You may remember an unfortunate incident some weeks ago when a young lady called Andrea Gower committed suicide.' Better stick to talk of suicide; no need to raise even more suspicions.

'Yes.' Bill Hewlett sounded properly awed.

'Well, please understand that there are no grounds for suspicion in the lady's death, but I'm afraid I do have to check out the movements of various people connected with her. Now I've been investigating her estranged husband, Keith Nicholls.'

'Ah.' Bill Hewlett didn't sound at all happy.

'So far I've checked with one or two people and received conflicting reports. Some say he was in the studio all of the evening in question working on the . . . *Dave Sheridan Late Night Show*, have I got that right?'

'Yes,' said Bill Hewlett miserably.

'Now I believe you were working on that show that evening?'

'Yes,' said Bill Hewlett even more miserably.

'I wonder if you could confirm that you were with him all evening. Well, the time I'm really concerned about is the hour between nine and ten when the show started.'

'Mmm.'

'I'm sorry? Was he there?'

'No, he wasn't.'

Charles Paris kept the elation out of Detective-Sergeant McWhirter's voice. 'Oh, really?'

'No. You must understand, one or two other people have asked me that, you know, people inside the BBC, and I've said Keith was there. I just thought, you know, that he had enough problems at the moment, without getting into trouble at work for not being where he should have been.'

As Steve had suggested, honour among SMs. 'Very loyal,' said Detective-Sergeant McWhirter laconically.

'I'm sorry, it just seemed –'

Charles took pity. 'No, I think you did right. There's no need to make extra troubles for him, as you say. In fact, if anyone else – anyone else unofficial, that is – asks you again, I'd stick to your story.'

'Oh, thank you.' Bill Hewlett sounded pathetically relieved.

'And, by the same token,' the detective said cunningly, 'I wouldn't mention my call to anyone either.'

'Oh no, no, I won't. If that's it, I'd better go. We're about to record.'

Charles Paris put the phone down with some satisfaction. He had got his old script back, but with two excellent rewrites.

Brenda flushed when he walked into Nita Lawson's office, confirming his worst fears. And when he stated the purpose of his visit, he felt he was only adding fuel to her fire. Its importance to him was very real, but he knew it didn't sound convincing when he said, 'I've got a tape of music here, and I wondered if you'd be able to name some of the titles of the numbers.'

'Oh, *Ten for a Tune*, is it?' asked Brenda with – horror of horrors – a wink.

He laughed uneasily, realising that that probably made him sound like the eager lover, confused at first sight of the desired object. Under the circumstances, he feared that absolutely anything he did was liable to similar misinterpretation. Still, he had to press on. Brenda worked with light music all the time and, if there was some code hidden in the sequence of tunes, she would certainly be able to provide the key to it.

'Well, all right, I'll see what I can do,' she went on. 'But I'll have to get on with my work at the same time. Most of us restrict playing games to outside office hours.' Lest the ambiguity of the final sentence should be lost, it was reinforced by another wink.

'Oh certainly, thank you.' Charles went across to the office music centre. 'Shall I put it in?'

'Yes.' Brenda picked up two square black boxes from the floor, put them on her desk and started to empty out records.

'I don't seem to be getting any sound from the tape.'

'Ah, that's because you've got it switched round to Line.'

Charles nodded, mystified.

'Look.' Brenda clicked round a switch on the wall until the now-familiar sound of the Musimotive tape filled the office. Then she assumed her talking-to-trainee-production-secretaries voice. 'You see, the points on the wall correspond to Radios One, Two, Three and Four, Radio London, even Capital' – she giggled naughtily – 'and the Playback Lines. It was switched to Playback.'

Charles nodded sagely, Moses receiving the tables of testimony on Mount Sinai.

145

'And,' Brenda continued, 'the first tune's *On A Clear Day*. How many points do I get for that?'

'Oh, lots,' replied Charles waggishly, and wrote it down.

While unpacking the discs and filing them according to some obscure system known only to herself, Brenda identified from the tape *Gingerbread Man*, *The Rhythm of Life*, *Send in the Clowns*, *Here, There and Everywhere* and *Love Is Blue*. Charles could discern no pattern or meaning in the sequence. He felt as he did on those hangover mornings when *The Times* crossword was just a patchwork of accusing blanks and might as well have been in Finnish for all the sense it made to him.

But his attention was abruptly shifted from the puzzle by Brenda's action. She had finished putting the LPs away and was now opening a new box, from which she drew another package of records. They all had green sleeves and they were packed in a sandwich of cardboard squares, tied with coarse string.

'What are those?'

She looked up with surprise at the intensity of his question. 'Archive Discs. We had them out for one of the competitions.'

'May I have a look?'

She handed him one of the green-sleeved records.

'No, at the cardboard.'

For the first time an expression of doubt replaced the simper which she had been training on him all afternoon. But she handed over the cardboard.

It was identical to the squares which he had found in 'the old mill by the stream'.

'What are these used for, Brenda?'

She looked bewildered. 'Well, packing. Like this.'

'Always packing discs?'

'Discs or tapes.'

'Tapes are this size too?'

'Bit smaller. Ten inches, but we use the same packing. They're like that.' She pointed to a thin square blue and white box.

Before Charles could complete the deduction running through his head, he heard a voice behind him. 'Why are you playing this?'

It was Nita Lawson. Brenda blushed, as if she and Charles had been caught *in flagrante delicto*, then said, 'Charles just wanted to know what some of the titles were.'

'I thought you were having a playback. Gave me a turn, I thought it might be something I'd forgotten.'

'Oh no.'

146

'That's all right then. Hello, Charles.'

'Hello.' She sat down at her desk. 'I'm sorry, Nita, did I understand you correctly? You recognise this tape?'

A new number had just started. Nita conducted the intro. 'Seventy-Six Trombones in the Big Parade . . . Yes, it's Sounds Sympathetic.'

'Sorry?'

'That's the name of the group.'

'Oh. And you recognise this actual tape?'

'I should do. The recording's from six months ago. I produced the session.'

'And now I know what the crime was,' Charles announced to Steve with triumph. 'I don't mean the murders, but the crime that precipitated the murders, the crime that the murders were meant to cover up.'

'Amaze me, Sherlock,' said Steve with a grin, and poured him some more of the Frascati. It seemed very natural to sit in her flat drinking Frascati. The sort of thing that could very easily become a habit. Perhaps was already becoming a habit.

She was wearing a skirt for once, which made her look less of a child. More of a woman. She seemed more relaxed. Maybe it was just that the shock of Andrea's death was receding. Whatever the reasons, the welcome in those huge eyes was genuine and warming.

And Charles felt pleased with himself, ready to show off a little as he presented his conclusions. 'It all fits in, you see, fits in with things you said, fits in with things Fat Otto said in New York, things Ronnie Barron said here – it just ties up the whole package.'

'You'll have to spell it out for me, I'm afraid. I'm not there yet.'

'No.' He paused with satisfaction. It was like playing one of those terrible party guessing games, once you know the solution, you greet the continuing ignorance of everyone else with smug condescension. But he didn't want to be cruel, least of all to Steve. 'I should have worked it out from what you said about Keith once getting into trouble for illicit tape-copying. That's what he continued to do, take copies of sessions recorded for Radio Two. But he wasn't just doing it for a surreptitious quid from the MD, he was into a bigger league.'

'When he went over to the States and met Danny Klinger, they worked out the deal. I would imagine Danny suggested it – the whole set-up, with the clues and everything, bears his stamp. What they agreed was that Keith would keep up a regular supply of BBC Radio Two session tapes, and they would become the Musimotive repertoire.'

'From Klinger's point of view it was very attractive, because, if he didn't have to make the major outlay of setting up music sessions and paying musicians, the only expenses of his business were tape-copying, advertisement and despatch. He would make trips over to this country to pick the stuff up and, to avoid direct contact and because he liked that sort of game, he and Keith would never speak, but arrange the pick-ups by the old code system Klinger had devised all those years before with Mike Fergus. Dave Sheridan, unwittingly, was their messenger boy.

'I've checked through with the files of the programme, and the dates which Andrea wrote on the Musimotive cassette were all times when Klinger must have been over here, because during each span, there was a *Dave Sheridan Late Night Show* which began with *Danny Boy*.

'So they'd got a nice little system going. Klinger would come over here every now and then to pick up tapes that would cost him thousands of dollars to make properly, and Keith was presumably getting some sort of pay-off for setting the thing up. Keith ran the risks of copying the tapes and leaving them in these obscure hideouts, but since he never made direct contact with Klinger, he wasn't in much danger of being found out.'

'Then why did this workable little system have to break up?' asked Steve.

'I'm not absolutely sure, but I would imagine it was because of the investigation into the company. I talked to Nita a bit about musical copyright and what have you, and it seems both sides of the Atlantic there's been a clamp-down on what they call bootlegging or pirating music. It may have been just that Musimotive came under the scrutiny of some general enquiry which discovered there was something fishy about its sources of music.'

'Like . . . that no studios or musicians were ever booked to produce the stuff?'

'Exactly. As I say, it may just have been a random check. However, I think it more likely that your friend Andrea had something to do with it.'

'Really?'

'Yes. Think of all the things she said about investigative journalism and being on to something big and the truth coming out. You see, I found out from Nita that Andrea actually worked on the Sounds Sympathetic music session which appeared on the Musimotive tape. She recorded it. So what I reckon happened – and this can only be a conjectural reconstruction, unless she actually spoke to anyone about it – was that she heard the tape playing somewhere – could have been anywhere – in a hotel lobby, in a lift, in a restaurant, in a store – and, with her fine musical ear, she recognised it as the session she had recorded. That's what led her to Musimotive to try and investigate further.

'I assume Fat Otto was as ignorant for her as he was for me, but she did manage to get from him a copy of the tape as evidence and also the dates of Klinger's most recent trips to this country. Armed with that, she returned here to investigate the BBC end of the business, possibly alerting a lawyer or someone in New York to the situation and suggesting that Musimotive might bear investigation.'

'So then you reckon she came home and confronted her ex-husband with her findings and he –?'

'No, I wouldn't have thought so. She had no reason to make any connection with Keith. I would think she just saw him on the night of her death and told him about her investigations. You said they were very competitive and she went to the States partly to show she could do anything he could.'

'Yes.'

'Wouldn't it then be in character for her to crow to him about her achievements over there?'

Steve shook her head sadly. 'Yes, I'm rather afraid it would.'

'So, as soon as she told him of the connection she was making, Keith realised he had to keep her quiet or it was only a matter of time before the investigation got to him.'

'But just a minute,' Steve objected, 'there's something that doesn't work in all this.'

'What?' said Charles, slightly aggrieved to find any obstacle in the course along which he was bowling so happily.

'You say that the first *Danny Boy* message was in the programme which went out on the night Andrea died?'

'Yes.'

'Well, that must have taken quite a bit of preparation on Keith's part. If he only heard about the investigation into Musimotive from Andrea, who got back into the country that day, then surely . . .'

'I agree. That worried me for a bit. And I confess I haven't got a complete answer to it. I can only assume that Keith heard about the investigation from somebody else, maybe Klinger himself.'

'I suppose he must have done.'

'I admit there are quite a few details which haven't slotted into position yet, but I'm pretty certain that the outline's right.'

'It sounds very convincing. Congratulations.' Charles glowed under her smile. 'So what do you do next?'

'I think I talk to Keith.'

'Is that wise?'

'I think it'll be all right, if I do it in the right place. Anyway, I have no choice, really. Though I'm convinced I know what happened, I haven't a shred of evidence that would stand up to serious scrutiny.'

'No, I suppose not. What about the booby trap in that shed?'

'I don't think that'd be enough on its own.'

'No.' She mused. 'One thing about that . . . why was the package full of cardboard?'

'I think Keith did that to obscure the evidence. He didn't want to leave real tapes there, only to leave something that looked sufficiently like a package of tapes for Klinger to reach forward and get it. Then if Klinger's body was found the next morning, the package of cardboard would mean as little to the police as it did to me.'

She nodded, smiled and stretched like a little cat. 'Well, don't do anything silly when you talk to Keith. I don't like the idea of him killing two of my friends.'

'No.' Charles rose, warmed by the avowal of friendship. He looked at his watch and hesitated. 'I must go. It's late.'

'Yes.' She rose too.

He went towards her and put his arms round her. It was very natural. He met no resistance.

She was tiny without her shoes on. She laid her head against his chest and purred, 'That's nice.' Echoing his thought.

He felt very gentle and paternal. 'How are you?' he asked fatuously.

'Not at all bad,' she replied. 'In fact, pretty good. I'm surviving very well.'

'Surviving what?'

'I mentioned a young man called Robin.'

'Yes.'

'He's been away for a month or so. He's now been back in this country ten days. And he hasn't phoned me.'

'And that's good news?'

'That is wonderful news. You've no idea how good that news is.' She looked up at him. Close to, she was all eyes. Big, brown eyes. 'Soon,' she said softly, 'very soon I think I'll be leading a normal life again.'

'Good,' he murmured. He understood her completely. She was saying, no, not now, not yet, just give me a little more time to flush Robin out of my mind. And then . . . there seemed to be a promise in her words too.

He kissed her gently on the lips. They were soft and giving. They did

150

not draw away from him, but he had understood her message, and kept it as just a gentle kiss.

'I must go,' he said. And went.

CHAPTER FOURTEEN

'Hello, Charles, it's Gerald.'

'Ah, hello.'

'What gives?'

'Gives?'

'I last saw you on Wednesday, after the worst meal ever perpetrated on a human being, and you were about to charge some disc jockey with murder. Have you done so yet?'

'No, Gerald. Things have moved on a bit since then. But I have the feeling they are coming to a head. A confrontation will take place this afternoon. After that, I think everything will be a lot clearer.'

'Can I do anything to help? Or can we meet so that you can fill me in on the details?'

'Meet, certainly.'

'What, a drink this evening?'

'I think I'll need a good few, yes. If I'm still in one piece.'

'Well, would you like to come to the Garrick and . . . ?'

'Yes, fine. Oh shit, no.'

'What's the matter?'

'I've suddenly remembered, I'm booked to do some radio recording this evening. A six-to-nine booking for something called *The Showbiz Quiz*. I'm the Mystery Voice.'

'Oh, I often wondered who it was. Well, look, why don't I come along to the recording? You know how keenly I like to follow your career.'

'Ha ha. Okay, if you can stand it, come along. It's at the Paris Studio in Lower Regent Street. I'll leave a ticket in your name at Reception.'

'Okay. And by then you'll have solved both the murders?'

'Yes. Or I'll be the victim of the third.'

Charles was beginning to know his way around Broadcasting House very well; soon, he reflected, he'd be calling it BH like a native. The security man on the door seemed happy with the pink pass that Brenda had given him, so he got into the art deco lift and pressed the button for the fifth floor. Steve had been able to consult the SMs' schedules and give him Keith Nicholls's bookings for the day.

They were not without irony. From two-thirty to six he was scheduled to do music editing in the very channel where his wife had died. And from nine till midnight he was booked to route the telephone calls for the *Dave Sheridan Late Night Show.* Charles received confirmation of the feeling that he had confided to Gerald, that things were coming to a head.

He felt strangely calm. Although he was about to confront a double murderer, he did not feel afraid. Somehow it'd work out.

As he walked along the corridor from the old part of Broadcasting House to the Extension, he saw a familiar figure coming towards him. If he hadn't recognised the face, he would have recognised the unnatural gloss on the toupée.

'Michael Oakley, isn't it?'

'Yes,' came the mystified reply. The American accent seemed even stronger in the flesh.

'Charles Paris. We talked on the phone yesterday.'

'Oh yes, I've just been having a meeting with Dave and his Executive Producer.'

'Ah. I'd really like to take you up on that offer of following Dave around for a day.' Difficult as it was to think beyond the next hour, Charles supposed at some point he was going to have to get together his Radio Three feature.

'Sure. Whenever you like. Today he's . . . well, he's just gone off to the *Teen Dreams* office to check this week's column, but of course he's doing the show tonight. I'll be along, because I'm bringing a friend who wants to take a look at the programme going out, so come then if you'd like. Studio B15. Or any time. Give me a buzz.'

'I'll do that. Thank you.'

Nothing in the editing channel had changed since the night of Andrea's death, except that four new carpet tiles made an accusingly aseptic square on the floor.

Keith was on his own. A script was open on a lectern beside him and he was cutting tape with a razor blade. He looked up as Charles came in, with his customary scowl.

'Hello. Charles Paris. We met on that sit. com. I was doing the other week.'

153

Keith nodded. He remembered the incident, but didn't see its relevance.

'I wanted to have a talk.'

'What about?'

'Are you busy?'

Keith shrugged. 'Just making cuts in these programmes for a shortened repeat. It's not frantic.' Then he added with resentment, 'Notice the bloody producer doesn't even turn up. Arrived at nearly three with the tapes and marked scripts, asking me to "use my judgment" about the edits. Huh, SMs aren't paid enough to use their judgment. When I see wankers like that who've got producer's jobs . . .' He grimaced. What he thought about the subject was too deep for words.

'I want to talk to you about copying tapes,' Charles said bluntly. It would have been more effective if he'd said 'I want to talk to you about your wife's murder', but he hadn't quite got the confidence for such a frontal attack. Build up to it slowly.

The effect of his remark was good enough, anyway. Keith froze for a moment, his razor blade poised in space, and then bent back to his work, saying, with an effort at casualness, 'Oh yeah.'

'Copying tapes of BBC music sessions and then selling them.'

'Look, who are you? Have you been planted in this place as some sort of copper's nark?'

'No, I'll explain my involvement in a minute. Let's just talk about this tape-copying for a start. You've been warned for it before. Do you deny that you've been doing it recently?'

Keith looked at him defiantly, but maybe with a hint of relief. Perhaps for a moment he had feared a more serious accusation. 'Okay. So I've copied a few tapes. It doesn't do anyone any harm. Good God, on the money they pay us, it's hardly surprising I try to make a few bob on the side.'

'I'm not talking about a few bob on the side, I'm talking about a highly organised business.'

Keith looked at him blankly, so Charles gave a nudge. 'I'm talking about Musimotive.'

Keith gave a good impression of bewilderment.

'Are you saying you've never heard of Musimotive?'

'No, sure I've heard of it. I went to their offices when I was over in New York last autumn.'

'Yes. And may I ask why?'

'I'm interested in the music business. I wanted to find out how it all worked in the States. So I got names of contacts from everyone I knew and just looked around. Musimotive was pretty useless from my point of view. Just some kind of muzak outfit. I'm more interested in creative pop.'

'And of course you met Danny Klinger over there.'

'Yes, I think that was the guy's name. Yes.'

'Oh come on, Keith, I'm not bluffed that easily. You may not have met Danny Klinger too often face to face, but you've had rather a lot of indirect contact with him.'

'I don't know what you're talking about.' Keith Nicholls turned back to the green tape-recorder on which the razor blade that had killed his wife had been fixed. He pressed a button to spool back a reel of tape.

Charles spoke firmly. 'I'm talking about the deal which you set up to supply Klinger with music tapes, the sweet profitable little deal that by chance your wife Andrea found out about. Which was why you had to kill her and why you had to kill Danny Klinger.'

Keith turned, his face red with fury. 'What the hell are you –'

But he got no further. His words were cut off by a cry of pain. The top of one of the fast spinning ten-inch spools on the tape machine had come loose and shot off towards him, a fatal frisbee with an edge as sharp as the razor blade in his hand. With an involuntary, but life-saving, reflex, he raised his right arm to shield his face. The spinning disc sliced through the flesh on his forearm like a circular saw, was deflected by the bone and continued its career towards Charles. He just had time to duck and heard the whirring metal graze his hair before slicing through the sound-proofing fabric on the wall and falling to the ground with a diminishing clatter.

Keith looked with horror at the gash on his arm. Its clean line was soon distorted with welling blood, which dripped from his fingers on to the new carpet tiles. 'Good God,' he said. 'If I hadn't had my arm there, it would have taken my head off.'

Charles rushed an inadequate handkerchief to the wound. 'Is there a doctor in this place?'

'Surgery. First Floor,' Keith replied dully, his face white with shock.

'Can you walk?'

He nodded.

They walked along the corridor, a small cortège, dripping blood, attracting looks of amazement. As they waited for the lift, Keith asked, still without intonation, 'What was all that about me killing Andrea?'

Shock had stripped off all the layers of cynicism, contempt and anger; his question was simple, childlike.

Charles pressed his accusation, gently, but firmly.

'I know you did, Keith. You had to. Because she had found out about your deal with Klinger. I also know that you weren't in the studio that night for the hour before the Dave Sheridan Show.'

Keith looked at him and the colourless lips smiled. 'No, I wasn't. I was moonlighting.'

'What?'

'Producing an album session at a studio in Berwick Street, group called Scrap Metal.'

'What?'

'Session was from nine to one in the morning. 8, Berwick Street. Check if you like. There are six witnesses in the group and one engineer. The police have already checked it.'

'What?'

'I told them when they asked. But they agreed to keep it quiet here. Don't want to get me into trouble. Nice of them.'

The lift arrived and they got in. They were the only passengers. 'Anyway,' Keith continued softly, 'I wouldn't have killed Andrea. I . . . I don't know, I always hoped, in a few years, we'd get back together again.'

'Tell me,' asked Charles abruptly, 'have you ever known a spool to come apart like that before?'

'No. I've heard of it happening in the old days. But now they're firmly screwed down.'

'Perhaps you got a faulty one.'

'Unlikely. I'd been spooling it back and forth all afternoon and nothing happened.'

'So what does that mean?'

'I don't know.' Keith looked very faint, unwilling to pursue thoughts to their logical conclusions.

'That someone unscrewed it?' Charles suggested softly. Keith did not reply. The lift stopped. Keith staggered as he stepped out and Charles put an arm round him for support. As they walked along the corridor to the surgery he asked, 'Did anyone have a chance to tamper with it in the course of the afternoon?'

Keith answered as if in a trance. Each word had equal emphasis. 'I went out to get a coffee. When I came back, there was someone in the channel I knew. He said he was looking for Dave Sheridan.'

'Who was it?' asked Charles, but he knew the answer. There was one other person who had been in Broadcasting House on the night of Andrea's death, who had been down at Brassie's for the Opening Nite

All-Nite Disco Party, whom Charles had even met leaving the scene of his latest crime.

Keith's trembling answer confirmed it. 'Dave's agent, Mike Oakley.'

The new casting had such a powerful effect on his script that Charles virtually reckoned he had a new play. But it was one with a much better chance of West End success than all his previous out-of-town try-outs.

The more he thought about Michael Oakley in the leading role, the better he seemed to fit it. He had definitely been on hand to commit both murders, and probably on hand with far less calls on his time than any of the other suspects.

And it was not hard to sketch in his motivation. Throughout the case Charles had been looking for someone with an American connection to explain the link with Klinger. Oakley was American by nationality. It was much more likely that he had known Klinger a long time before than that Keith should have set up their elaborate criminal connection in the course of one very brief meeting.

Desperately Charles thought back over his conversation with Fat Otto, and, as he did so, a breathtakingly exciting new possibility suggested itself.

Fat Otto had talked about Danny Klinger's companion in crime back in the days when they worked in the New York radio station. Mike Fergus had been the name.

Mike Fergus – Michael Oakley. Just a change of surname. Sufficient if you wanted to take on a new identity in a new country, though. If you wanted to hide your past.

And what was the past that needed to be hidden? Fat Otto had spoken of some financial scandal which had led to the disappearance of both Klinger and Fergus from their radio station. Nothing was proved, but they were both reckoned to have had their hands in the till. So they were joined by crime.

Charles's mind raced on. Suppose the two had parted after that, lost touch . . . then remet in London, where Klinger found Fergus doing very nicely thank you in his new identity. Successful agent in one of London's biggest agencies. What would be more in character than for Klinger to apply a little pressure, to work out an ingenious system of payment for his silence about past misdemeanours? Oakley, with his contacts in the BBC, could provide tapes of music sessions in exchange for Klinger's silence. That at last would explain the elaborate system of clues and hiding of the tapes. They needed the secrecy and reverted to the code they had used in their radio-station days.

157

And the relationship could have stayed balanced like that indefinitely . . . if Andrea Gower hadn't had such a trained musical ear. She started the investigation which was to put paid to the Musimotive operation. Klinger heard about the arrival of the police from Fat Otto while he was in London, contacted Oakley and maybe suggested that the blackmail payments should be made some other way. His demands were too high, so Oakley decided he was too much of a threat and would have to be eliminated.

Then he heard of another danger. His client Dave Sheridan mentioned a story which Andrea Gower had told him during a music session on the afternoon of her return from New York. It was about an elaborate musical fraud and, as Sheridan unfolded it, Oakley realised that Klinger was not the only threat to his safety. The girl had to go too.

He had tried to mop up both threats on the same night, Andrea directly and Klinger indirectly. He would have done it too, if Klinger's radio hadn't cut out when his car got delayed under a road bridge on the M23. So he had to try again. The second time he succeeded.

Charles tried to slow his brain down. It was all too fast, too manic.

And yet he couldn't help being excited by it. If Klinger's contact in England were his old friend Mike Fergus under a new identity, the whole case made sense in a way it hadn't begun to previously.

And he was going to see Michael Oakley that evening in the *Dave Sheridan Late Night Show* studio.

CHAPTER FIFTEEN

THE SHOWBIZ QUIZ was just what its name implied, a quiz about showbiz. (There was a fad at that time in the Light Entertainment Department for descriptive rather than wacky titles.) A jovial personality chairman posed questions about famous showbiz personalities to a panel of famous showbiz personalities (or less famous showbiz personalities or whoever happened to be available and didn't think the fee for recording two shows in three hours too derisory).

The questions were devised by a senior Light Entertainment producer, who made a tidy packet from payments called Staff Contributions for this work. At one stage there had been grumblings that he was doing rather too well out of this little racket, so the Head of Light Entertainment had clamped down and controlled him by putting another producer in charge of the show. Since the other producer was the young, nervous and amiable Nick Monckton, the older producer was even better placed. He still got paid as much for devising the questions, he still had artistic control (because Nick was too deferential to his experience to argue), and he was relieved of the tedious responsibility of actually producing the show.

Most of the questions were merely pegs for anecdotes. ('Tell me, Arthur, do you recognise this voice?' 'Why, yes, it's Robb Wilton.' AUDIENCE APPLAUSE. 'Tell me, did you ever work with Robb Wilton?' 'Well, as a matter of fact I did. I remember a show we did for the Forces in . . .' INTO LONG, TEDIOUS ANECDOTE ENDING IN MORE AUDIENCE APPLAUSE, AND ON TO THE NEXT RIGGED QUESTION.) However, there were some rounds where the answers required actual knowledge, and it was for these that Charles had been booked as Mystery Voice. His presence was the one innovation which Nick Monckton had managed to graft on to the established show. The young producer felt that these rounds would gain extra piquancy if the audience knew the correct answers while the panellists groped towards them. The older producer did not see any way in which this departure could affect the amount he was paid for devising the questions and so raised no objection.

Nick Monckton appeared more relaxed on this programme than he had on *Dad's the Word*, perhaps because *The Showbiz Quiz* had been going for so long that it ran itself. And also because the team were semi-regulars whom he knew and wasn't afraid of.

Rehearsal was simply a matter of arranging the order of the cued anecdotes and working out some ad libs, before adjourning to the pub for a good few drinks to ensure that they sounded spontaneous. All Charles had to do was to say a few words into his microphone so that the Studio Manager could adjust his level. Being a Mystery Voice, he did not appear on the stage in front of the audience. He was tucked away in the Narrator's Cubicle, where the first read-through of *Dad's the Word* had been held. This had distinct advantages. First, he could think without the distraction of listening to comedians trying to be funny, and, second, there was a telephone there.

His mind was still racing. New details fell into place.

Oakley's keen interest in his client's work, so rare in an agent, was suddenly explained. He needed always to be hanging round the BBC, getting to know the personnel, so that he could maintain the supply of pirate tapes. And he needed to hang around Sheridan to influence his programme's running orders when necessary.

Keith must have been the source of the tapes. Charles thought back to their conversation of the afternoon, when the SM had virtually admitted to illicit copying. If Keith could be persuaded to admit his part in the crime, then Charles thought Oakley could be nailed. An arrest for pirating tapes would lead to an investigation, which would reveal the greater depths of his villainy. Charles wished he had had longer to talk to Keith. The flurry of concern which their arrival in the Surgery had prompted had made further conversation impossible.

Still, it might be possible to make contact. It was quarter to seven. He rang through to Steve to get Keith's home number.

She sounded glad to hear from him, which in itself was flattering, and even disappointed when she heard his request. Maybe she had hoped that he was going to suggest a meeting. He almost did, but held back. Get the case solved first. Anyway, he wouldn't lose anything by delay. Don't push it, let it happen naturally. To him who waits . . .

There was no reply from Keith's number. Perhaps his injury had landed him in hospital. Oh well, try again later. In the meantime, round to The Captain's Cabin with the facetious panellists of *The Showbiz Quiz* for a few preparatory drinks . . .

160

They were into the recording for the second show before Charles got through to Keith. He had been ringing the number at five-minute intervals since their return from the pub, every now and then breaking off on the orders of a green cue-light to intone some new revelation from the Mystery Voice.

It was a good time when he did finally get through. He had just given some answers and had a long break while the panellists went through their tired saga of Noël Coward anecdotes. His next cue was to give the answers in a 'What are the Names by which These People are Better Known?' round, which wasn't going to tax his intellect too much.

Keith sounded weak, but there was a more positive note in his voice than Charles had ever heard. The petulant scorn had been replaced by determination. After answering Charles's enquiries about his well-being, number of stitches, etc., he said, 'I've been thinking a lot, putting two and two together. I'm glad you called, because you can explain a few things to me. From what you were saying, I gather you think Oakley sabotaged that spool.'

'Seems most likely.'

'And also killed Andrea?'

'I think so.'

'The bastard.' Keith's voice was low and intense. 'You've no idea what I've felt like since she died. Okay, it hadn't worked out with us, but there was still a lot there. And I've been blaming myself for her death, as if it was my fault. God, the bastard.'

'Would you be prepared to help me get him convicted?'

'I'd do anything.'

'Even if it meant admitting your illicit tape-copying and moonlighting in studios in Berwick Street?'

'Anything. Okay, I might get sacked, but I've been thinking of getting out into commercial recording anyway.'

'Good. Well, listen, there are a few details you can help me out on and then we must decide how to proceed.'

'Okay. Ask away.'

'Right, first, a few things about that night down at Brassie's. Oakley says you all left Broadcasting House straight after the show finished and came back as soon as Dave's two-hour stint was over.'

'Right.'

'So did you see Oakley there all the time? Or did he go out at any point?'

'Oh, he was out most of the time. I assumed he'd picked up some totty and was having it away with her in the car. He has rather a taste for young girls.'

'Excellent. That gave him plenty of time to get to Klinger's car and sort him out.'

'He killed Danny Klinger too, did he?'

'I think so.'

'The bastard,' Keith hissed again. 'God, I'd like to get my hands on him. Yes, I'll admit anything I've done just to nail that swine. When are you going to see him?'

'Tonight. He's going to be along at the Dave Sheridan show and I said I might pop in.'

'I'll come too,' said Keith quickly.

'But you can't. Your arm . . .'

'Sod that. It's all right. Bandaged up, but I can manage. I was scheduled to do the show anyway. Alick's been called in on stand-by, but I'll give him a buzz and say I'm okay.'

'Are you sure?'

'You bet. I want to see that bastard Oakley squirm. He nearly killed me. I should have realised he was up to something that night down at Brassie's. He arrived back in the disco in the middle of the Non-Stop Smooch Session, looking as guilty as a dog that's just shat on the carpet. I assumed he'd just been doing something disgusting to a little girl in the car park. Never thought he'd been committing a murder.'

Charles was intrigued by the expression 'Non-Stop Smooch Session'. He had wondered what it meant when he'd first heard it from Jude, the punk waitress down at Brassie's. He asked Keith.

'Oh, it's rather a good idea. Dave always does it when he's doing a late disco. Towards the end, when most of the kids have formed couples, he just does a long sequence of slow, sexy numbers, so they can dance real close, you know.'

'And he chats away to them in his sexy voice?'

'No, straight *segue*.'

'What's a *segue*?'

'Record to record, no chat.'

'So he just puts the discs on?'

'Used to. But then he didn't see the point in that, so he got me to make up a tape of a really good Smooch Session, which he uses all the time. Works a treat. And, what's more, it gives him half an hour's break in the middle of the session.'

'Half an hour?'

'Yes.'

162

But Charles did not have time to evaluate the implications of this new information. The green light in the cubicle was flashing frenetically. Oh, shit, he thought, and quickly put on the headphones which gave him a feed of studio output.

The chairman's jovial voice came over, slightly less jovial than usual. *'No, not yet, my friends, not yet. We appear to have something wrong with our Mystery Voice. Don't know what, it's a complete Mystery.* AUDIENCE LAUGHTER. *Still, I'll try the question again. By what name is Reg Dwight better known? That's Reg Dwight?'*

'Elton John,' Charles read from his script sepulchrally. 'Elton – John.'

'Margaret Thatcher?' suggested one of the panellists waggishly. Other, equally fatuous suggestions were put forward until, at a prearranged moment, someone got the right answer.

'Right, the next one – by what name is Marion Morrison better known?'

'John Wayne,' read Charles. 'John – Wayne.'

'Raquel Welch,' said one of the panellists and got the prescribed laugh.

The panel squabbled round the answer in simulated confusion. Charles turned the page of his script and looked at the next question. For a moment he could hardly breathe.

'Funny name for a feller, isn't it – Marion? On to the next one. Be surprised if you get this one, though it's someone you all know. He's even been a guest on this programme. Right, by what name is Mike Fergus better known? That's Mike Fergus.'

'Dave Sheridan,' gasped the Mystery Voice. 'Dave – Sheridan.'

CHAPTER SIXTEEN

DAVE SHERIDAN HAD quite an audience for his *Late Night Show* in the Basement Studio B15 that evening. Apart from the BBC personnel, his new producer Simon, his former producer Keith Nicholls (now relegated to Studio Manager), and two other SMs, his agent, Michael Oakley was there with a new vacuous dolly-bird. Also present were the actor Charles Paris (researching a feature on the disc jockey for Radio Three) with a solicitor friend, Gerald Venables.

Dave Sheridan was unaffected by their presence. Long experience, stretching back to working for a small New York radio station in the Sixties, had made him into a deeply professional performer. He manipulated the disc jockey's hardware of turntables and cartridge players with grace and skill, keeping up between the items continuous talk of great charm and warmth. It was small wonder that his career was doing so well, that he was increasingly in demand for personal appearances and that the television companies were beginning to realise his potential as a quiz-programme host.

Apart from the larger gallery of watchers, the regular observer of the scene would have noticed nothing unusual about that evening. True, one of the Studio Managers looked pale and his right arm was bound round with a crepe bandage. The actor, Charles Paris, also looked rather strained. But these were details, there was nothing to suggest that this was not just one more programme in a successful sequence, and that there were many more such to come.

Charles had talked further to Keith after the revelation of Sheridan's earlier identity on *The Showbiz Quiz*. Not only had they been able to confirm certain details of how the three crimes had been perpetrated, but they had also worked out a plan of campaign to expose their perpetrator. Keith was determined to make his revelations about copying tapes at Sheridan's request as soon as the time was right, but they thought their first approach should be a shock tactic, which might well precipitate a confession or crisis of some other sort.

The ingredients in the *Dave Sheridan Late Night Show*, apart from the geniality of its host, were single and LP records, tapes, jingles on cartridge and occasional phone calls from listeners. These last focused particularly on a competition called *Ten for a Tune*, in which members of the public stood the chance of winning ten pounds if they could identify the title and the singer of a snatch of music which had been distorted and speeded up. The phone calls were routed into the studio by one of the Studio Managers.

Charles stood in the adjacent editing channel. The glass between that and the studio was masked by a venetian blind, but through the slit he could see Dave Sheridan smiling into the microphone, wooing it, seducing it.

For a moment he had a clear vision of Mrs Moxon sitting at home in her demented dignity, listening to the voice of her long-dead lover.

Yes, it was a fine voice. As an actor, he should have analysed it before, broken it down into its components of Scots and American, should have realised that its owner must have spent a lot of time in the States and understood the clue. But he had been too intricately involved in details of half-truths and timetables to see the obvious. And the answer was in the voice all the time.

'Well, right after the next piece of music, we'll be playing our music game, "Ten for a Tune", and tonight's contestant, the card in front of me tells me, is a Mr Kevin Piggott from Birmingham. Hang on just a few more moments, Mr Piggott, and we'll see if we can win you ten pounds for identifying our mystery tune. But first, Bobbie Gentry says, rather disappointingly for us chaps, "I'll Never Fall In Love Again". Aah . . .'

The voice-over was perfectly timed and the vocal came in just after his 'Aah . . .' Dave Sheridan sat back and relaxed.

The telephone beside Charles Paris rang, just as Keith had told him it would. He picked it up and said, 'Hello,' in the voice he had used for a production of *The Caretaker* in Cardiff ('Take care to miss this.'— *South Wales Argus*).

'Ah, hello. Mr Piggott?' asked Keith's voice.

'Yes.'

'I'm calling from the BBC. *The Dave Sheridan Late Night Show*.'

'Oh,' said Mr Piggott, properly impressed.

'I believe one of our production secretaries rang you earlier in the day to ask if you'd like to take part in our *Ten for a Tune* competition.'

165

'Oh, that's right. I sent in a card a few weeks back.'

'Well, Mr Piggott, you'll be talking to Dave Sheridan in about two minutes, just when this piece of music's finished.'

'Oh yes.'

'If you've got your radio on, can I ask you to keep the volume down and keep it away from the telephone? Otherwise we can get technical problems.'

'Oh, that's all right. My wife's listening in the next room.'

'Good. Right, if you'd like to hang on for a minute, the next person you speak to will be Dave Sheridan.'

'Fine.'

Mr Piggott waited. The receiver in his hand was damp with sweat. Anyone looking at him would have thought that the prospect of winning ten pounds for identifying a piece of music meant a great deal to him.

'Mmm, I love that one from Bobbie Gentry. Very sexy voice, I always think. Right, now it's competition time. Yes, it's . . .'

TEN FOR A TUNE JINGLE.

' . . . and we should have Mr Piggott from Birmingham on the line. Are you there, Mr Piggott?'

'Yes, I am, Dave.'

'Good, good, the boffins in the backroom have got the phones working. Tell me, Mr Piggott – or can I call you Kevin?'

'Please do, Dave.'

'Fine. Tell me, Kevin, what sort of a night is it in Birmingham?'

'Oh, very nice, thank you, Dave.'

'Good. And let's hope your lucky star's out tonight as you play . . . "Ten for a Tune".'

'Let's hope so, Dave.'

'Right, to have ten pounds winging their way to you tomorrow, all you have to do is to tell me what this piece of music is and who's singing it.'

TAPE OF SCRAMBLED MUSIC.

'Well, there it was, Kevin. A fairly difficult one, but tell me – do you have any idea what it might be?'

'Yes, Dave, I think I know exactly.'

'There's confidence for you. Right, what do you think it is?'

'I think it's *There's an Old Mill by the Stream* and I think it's sung by Danny Klinger.'

The impact was immediate. Sheridan looked as if he'd been kicked in the solar plexus. Hard. He mouthed, incapable of speech.

'Is that right?' asked Charles inexorably, watching his victim through the slit in the blind.

'No. No,' Sheridan managed to croak.

'Oh, what a pity. Well, never mind. I'd like a dedication, please. It's for Andrea Gower and all at Musimotive and the number we'd all like to hear is *Confessin'*.'

'Well . . . you . . . can't have it.' Sheridan's shaking hands reached forward to the turntable, banged against the pick-up and knocked it jolting into the middle of the disc. Music started with an ugly rasp. He rose to his feet and rushed into the control cubicle as Charles hurried out from his hiding-place.

'Who – did – that?' Dave Sheridan mouthed incoherently.

'Is everything okay?' asked his new producer with concern.

'What's up, Dave?' asked his agent with equal concern.

'Who did it?' asked Dave Sheridan more firmly.

Keith Nicholls rose from the control panel just as Charles entered the suite. 'We did it, Dave,' he said softly. 'Now perhaps you know what it feels like to be really frightened, maybe you know what Andrea felt like when you pulled her wrist across the blade, what Klinger felt like when he smelt the exhaust fumes, what I felt like this afternoon when I saw that spool coming towards me.'

'You've no proof,' said Sheridan.

'Oh yes, we have,' Charles lied firmly.

'Look, what is all this?' asked Michael Oakley.

'The record's coming up in thirty seconds,' said the new producer feebly.

Dave Sheridan suddenly turned round to his case on the table. When he turned back, he was holding a small automatic pistol. 'Out of my way, all of you.'

'You won't get away,' said Charles.

'Yes, I will. I got away from the last bit of trouble I had, with Danny in the States. And I'll get away with this. Let me pass.'

The gun was held in a very purposeful manner and Charles felt discretion was the better part of valour. He drew back to make a gangway for Sheridan to leave the studio.

But Keith Nicholls was not going to let that happen. 'No. You're not going to get away with it. Not after what you did to Andrea.' And he launched himself at the disc jockey.

There was a sharp report from the gun. Keith was frozen for a minute in mid-air, then slumped to the ground. By the time the moment of shock was over, Dave Sheridan had left the studio.

'Good God, what shall I do?' the new producer asked. 'The record's finished. There'll be silence on the air. Oh my God – silence.' He stopped, appalled at the thought.

'Ring the duty office,' Keith's voice came weakly from the floor. 'Tell them there's been a shooting. Tell them to stop Dave Sheridan, not to let anyone leave the building.'

The new producer still hesitated.

'Come on, surely even you are capable of doing that,' hissed Keith, and passed out.

The producer got on the phone. Charles knelt down beside Keith. The bullet appeared to have hit his stomach. There was a lot of blood. 'And get a doctor too,' Charles said harshly. 'Quickly!'

He stood up. Gerald Venables, Michael Oakley and the dolly-bird looked at him in astonishment. 'Come on Gerald, let's get to the front of the building. There may be explanations necessary.'

Gerald nodded and they started to leave the studio.

'This is a tragedy,' said Michael Oakley. 'That guy was going to be very big.'

They met the Duty Officer, the Head of Security and a lot of other security men in the main Reception. The police had been called. Unwilling as the BBC always was to make its troubles public, on this occasion the Duty Officer reckoned there was no way of excluding the police.

And no, Dave Sheridan hadn't gone past them. No, there was no other way he could have got out. All the other exits were firmly locked.

'Couldn't he have broken a window or a door?'

'We've been round and checked on the ground floor and first floor. There's no sign of anything.'

'So you reckon he's still in the building?'

The Head of Security nodded. 'As soon as the police come we're going to have a thorough search.'

'Has the doctor arrived?'

'Yes, he's just gone up to the studio. Look, we'll want to talk to you later. I suggest you go up to the canteen and have a coffee or something. We'll find you there.'

'Okay.' Charles and Gerald got into the lift and pressed the button for the eighth floor.'

'Charles,' asked Gerald, 'had you really got proof to pin the murders on him?'

'No, it was complete bluff.'

168

'It worked.'

'Yes, and now there's no question about his having committed a crime. In front of seven witnesses. I just hope to God it's not another murder.'

'Yes.' The lift slowed down. 'I wonder where he's gone.' The lift doors opened. 'Ah, here we are at the top.'

They stepped out. Charles stopped suddenly. 'Gerald, that book you talked about . . . *Death in Broadcasting House* was it called?'

'That's right.'

'How did you say it ended?'

'In a chase across the roof of the building.'

'I wonder . . .'

Opposite them was a notice at the foot of a small staircase:

> UNAUTHORISED STAFF
> ARE NOT ALLOWED ON
> THIS STAIRCASE OR ON
> THE ROOF WHICH IS
> STRICTLY OUT OF BOUNDS

'What was that?'

Both froze.

'It sounded like a door. Along the corridor.' Charles whispered. 'It must be him. There can't be many people about at this time. I should think he is trying to get to the roof. Must be looking for the staircase.'

They started back along the old corridor towards the canteen.

They turned a corner. Both gasped. Dave Sheridan stood in front of them, holding his gun.

A shot sounded, appallingly loud, as they threw themselves back. They heard the bang of a door out of sight.

'Are you all right, Gerald?'

'I think so. I felt the wind of it, but I don't think it hit me.'

Charles peered round the corner cautiously. 'No sign.'

'Where do you reckon he's gone?'

'That way leads to the canteen. I wouldn't have thought he's gone there. Or . . .' Charles pointed to a stout pair of double doors.

'What's in there?'

'It's a studio. 8A. I've worked there.'

'What do you reckon?'

'I reckon we go in and try to find him.'

Gerald took a deep breath. 'Okay, buddy boy.'

They pushed the studio door open. It made no noise. It had been

169

muffled to prevent its sound from interfering with recording. Inside it was dark and deathly quiet. All sound was muffled. The two of them stood there, trying to accustom their eyes to the darkness, trying to prise its heavy drapes apart. But it was unyielding. They could see nothing.

Charles moved forward. His footstep sounded heavily on wood. Of course, damn it, this was the live end of the studio. The other end, behind a curtain, was carpeted for dead acoustics. This end the bare boards were meant to ring out with steps and voices.

Well, hell, if he was going to be audible whatever he did, there was no point in pussyfooting. Go the whole hog. He jumped forward, landing with a resounding thud on the boards and shouted, 'All right, Sheridan, you may as well give yourself up. Even if you get up to the roof, you won't get away.'

Fortunately he had taken the precaution of landing in a crouch. The bullet that zinged over his head would have found his heart had he been upright.

'Aagh,' he said liquidly, as he had in *Richard III* at Guildford ('Mr Paris perhaps a trifle overparted'—*Surrey Comet*) and fell to the floor with a thud. Then rolled, he hoped quietly, to one side.

Quietly enough. Another bullet dug into the wooden floor where he would have been if he hadn't moved.

Dave Sheridan's voice came coolly from where the gun had flashed. 'Right, if the other one of you wants the same, you just try and stop me getting up on the roof.'

Ah, thought Charles comfortingly, he thinks I'm dead.

Gerald, with the discretion which had made him such a success in the legal profession and contributed to the purchase of his Rolls-Royce, kept very quiet.

'Right. Goodbye,' said Sheridan's voice. Then there was a sound of footsteps running up stone stairs. They reached a level and stopped. Then there was a rattle and clang of at least six different bolts as he fought to open the door. Finally the last one gave, and he leapt forward to the freedom of the roof of Broadcasting House.

At that moment all the lights in the studio came on. Charles, from his vantage point on the floor, looked up to where the sound of the door had come from.

He saw Dave Sheridan clutching at his nose. The door with which he had struggled had opened on to a blank wall. It was a Sound Effects door and all its bolts and latches were only there for the illusions of *Saturday Night Theatre*.

And the stairs up which he had dashed were Sound Effects stairs. He had run up the stone side. Had he gone up the other side, he would have made the sound of running up wooden stairs.

Dave Sheridan had dropped his gun when he ran into the brick wall. Blood from his nose trickled through his fingers as he turned to face the police.

CHAPTER SEVENTEEN

THE THIRD AND, as it turned out, final full meeting of the Features Action Group was a somewhat muted affair.

A flamboyant touch was provided by the girl with Shredded Wheat hair, who appeared dressed in a man's pin-striped suit, shirt and tie 'as a protest against the sexist bias of the assembly'.

The young man with wild teeth and hair registered his protest against the lack of blacks in the group by not appearing at all, and rather a lot of members, for one reason or another, followed his example.

The most notable absence was that of John Christie, the scheme's instigator. Following his brief appointment as Coordinator, Drama Department (CDD), he had been elevated to a position in Secretariat so important that it didn't even have any initials. He was now involved in liaison with yet another government-sponsored committee which had been appointed to investigate the state of broadcasting.

So he continued his urbane climb up the Management ladder, forgetting none of the people with whom he had made contact during the brief but stimulating experience of the Features Action Group meetings. Oh no, they would all come in useful, their opinions would be quoted at Management meetings, their Christian names would be invoked to demonstrate his common touch, their ideas would be presented as his own. Nothing would be wasted in what he saw as his inexorable climb to Director-General.

He sent a fulsome note of apology, but felt confident that the project was very much alive and that he left the group under the more than able chairmanship of Ronnie Barron.

Ronnie Barron took his new responsibilities seriously, expressing this gravity by talking at half his normal speed. He read out John Christie's note and the apologies of all the other absentees who had bothered to send any. He then got Harry Bassett from Leeds to read out the minutes (now that he was chairman of the group he was above such menial tasks), and asked if he could sign them as a true and accurate record of what took place at the last full meeting.

This suggestion prompted considerable debate, not least from the reader of the minutes. Harry Bassett, with his group member hat on, could not help noticing that, not to put too fine a point on it, not only had his objection at the previous meeting to the lack of minutes of his references to regional broadcasting at the first meeting not been minuted, there was also no mention in the current minutes of certain telling points he made about the vitality of feature ideas in the main regional areas. As it were.

Others were equally incensed by what was described as the expurgation of the minutes. There was dark talk of censorship, threats to free speech and gagging the voice of the individual on a scale unequalled even in Nazi Germany.

Charles Paris found it difficult to get that excited. All he noticed about the minutes was that once again John Christie moved through them like a cross between Napoleon and Florence Nightingale, redressing a grievance here, giving a masterly summing-up there, expressing always superb judgment and supreme intellect.

Charles was only really there to maintain contact with the BBC, to find out if there were any more details known about the Dave Sheridan scandal, to check on Keith Nicholls's progress. . . and to see Steve Kennett.

It was with huge disappointment that he saw she wasn't at the meeting.

A sub-committee was appointed to check through the minutes and produce an impartial version of events at the previous meeting. Then the business of the current meeting started.

Harry Bassett again took the floor. His problem concerned the very nature of the assembly. It was an unofficial body, as it were, and so, in a sense, secret. Until its deliberations had taken what you might call concrete form, it had, if his recollection served, been agreed that the group's existence should be kept from the powers that be, as it were. This, however, placed him on the horns of a dilemma. Coming, as he did, from the regional centre of Leeds, he was involved in what could only be described as considerable capital outlay in fares and overnight accommodation, which he regarded as legitimate expenses on BBC business. His Head of Department, however, had refused to authorise his expense claims, unless he were informed, as it were, of the nature of the business on which Harry had travelled to London. Which, not to put too fine a point on it, put him in a bit of a jam.

Helmut Winkler, looking more like a mad professor than ever, was appalled by this. 'Vot hope haff ve got off producing anysing of artistic merit in zis country vile zat sort off petty-minded mercenary attitude obtainz? Vun must suffer for art. Vot does a few poundz matter compared to ze creation off a true vork off art?'

'Well now, that's all very well, Helmut,' reasoned Harry Bassett, 'but I do have a mortgage and a family and, in a sense, considerable responsibilities of a, as it were, financial nature. And while I sympathise with your, er, sense of priorities, I do feel –'

'Ass long ass zis attitude exiztz in ze BBC . . .' Helmut Winkler (who was a bachelor and whose income was well subsidised by the incomprehensible articles he wrote for *The Listener* and various higher-paying American periodicals) shrugged in despair. 'Novun seemz to be sinking about ze philosophy off audio anymore. Ven vill people learn zat radio iz not just a matter of communication? Not efen a matter of communication. Radio has nuzzing to do viz communication.'

'Bloody nonsense,' said the woman from *Woman's Hour*. 'Radio is communication, talking directly to the audience. That's what worked so well in our feature on hysterectomy.'

They were in the bar within half an hour. The discussion had not progressed and Ronnie Barron had closed the meeting with the intention of reassembling sometime very soon, when everyone had had a bit more time to work out their own views on the direction in which the group should be going. Everyone had agreed to this idea, but none had got out their diaries. Ronnie Barron had said that his secretary would ring round in a few days to fix a date and a venue.

It was about half-past seven on a Friday night. The crowd in the Ariel Bar was thinning. There were a few people Charles recognised. The Drama Rep. actress from the *Dad's the Word* recording perched on a tall stool in the middle of other Drama Rep. members. In a corner Mark Lear was talking intensely to a pretty young girl. And standing on her own in the middle of the room was Steve Kennett.

He went across to her. She looked better than ever. Her huge eyes sparkled animatedly. 'Hello, Charles, how are you?'

'Fine. Didn't see you at the meeting.'

'No. I didn't think it was going anywhere.'

'It didn't go anywhere.'

'Surprise, surprise.'

'Have you heard any news of Keith?'

'Yes, making good progress. Out of hospital next week, if all goes well. Apparently the bullet went straight through and didn't hit any vital organs.'

'Good.'

'And another thing's happened to Keith actually. A producer's job has come up in Radio Two, and, because he did so well on his attachment, he's been appointed to it without a board.'

'That's terrific. So no recrimination about the illicit tape-copying?'

'The BBC is unwilling to admit it ever took place. They made a mistake over Dave Sheridan, but this is the only crime they will recognise.'

'That sounds in character. I bet Keith's pleased.'

'Yes.' She smiled. 'It's funny, the Beeb can sometimes be very humane. Just now and then, you know, the right gesture at the right time.'

'Yes. The benevolent Auntie.'

'Exactly.'

'Look, you haven't got a drink. Let me –'

'I'm getting one got.'

At that moment a tall young man in a denim jacket came across to them carrying two glasses of white wine. 'This is Robin Davey. Robin – Charles Paris.'

'Oh, hi.' Robin didn't really take in the middle-aged actor. 'We'd better gulp these, Steve. I booked the table for eight-fifteen.'

'Sure.'

'I'll . . . see you,' said Charles, and started for the bar.

Steve caught his arm. He looked back and got the full benefit of the huge brown eyes. 'He rang after all,' she whispered helplessly.

His route to the bar led him past Mark Lear. The producer was saying, 'Sometimes I get the feeling there's no one out there, that we just make programmes for our own amusement and nobody hears them. It's a kind of masturbation, really.'

The girl nodded intently.

'I feel we're on the dead side of the mike and real life is going on somewhere out there without our knowledge.'

'Hello,' said Charles.

'Oh, hi. This is Charles Paris, an actor friend of mine. Charles – Lyn Frewer. She's just joined as a trainee SM.'

'Just going to the bar. Can I get you . . .'

'No thanks, we're fine.'

'Okay. See you soon.'

Charles moved on towards the bar. As he did, he heard Mark saying,

175

'Of course I'm not going to stay with the BBC. I'm just marking time really at the moment. But I won't stay . . .'

Charles eventually managed to get a barman's attention and ordered two large Bell's. He drained one, and with the other in his hand, started towards the knot of Drama Rep. He waved to the actress he knew vaguely. She waved fulsomely back. There's always someone to drink with in the BBC Club.

W24   A 9/1/00
LC 4/29/24   TC 6

12-4-80

F   Brett, Simon
        The dead side of the mike   Sc